Secrets & Deceptions

A Three-Generation Mystery

By Helene F. Uhlfelder

Purple Zebra Productions, LLC books are available for order through Ingram Press Catalogues.

This book is a work of fiction. Names, characters, places, and incidents either are products of the author's imagination or are used fictitiously. Any resemblance to actual persons, living or dead, events, or locales is entirely coincidental.

Helene F. Uhlfelder

Contact me: helenefuhlfelder@gmail.com

Visit my website at www.helenefuhlfelder.com

Follow me on Facebook: HeleneFUhlfelder

Printed in the United States of America
First Printing: 2015
Published by Purple Zebra Productions, LLC

ISBN: 978-1-62747-094-0
eBook ISBN: 978-1-62747-095-7

Dedication

This book is dedicated to:

My loving and supportive husband, Asa Shield, without whom this book would not be possible;

The memory of our wonderful golden retriever, Vinnie, who passed away while I wrote this book; and

The memory of a most remarkable friend, Michele McNichols. There is not a day that goes by that I don't think of her and wonder, "What would Michele do?" I will miss her until the universe puts us together again.

Note to Readers

It is said that one's first novel is always biographical, but I don't agree. *Secrets & Deceptions* is a work of fiction although some of the historical information is factual.

Also, it is true that my ancestors came to the United States from Germany. The rest of the book is a product of my imagination.

Enjoy!

The People

Horowitz

Mr. and Mrs. Horowitz
    (Hannah's parents)
Hannah
Agnes (Hannah's sister)
Karl (Agnes' husband)
Sarah (Hannah's sister)
Isaac (Sara's husband)
Myer (Hannah's brother)
Joseph (Hannah's brother)
Molly (Joseph's ex-wife)

Straus

Mrs. Straus (Saul's mother)
Saul
Sophie (Hannah and Saul's daughter)

Werner

Heinrich (Hannah's friend in Germany)
Brigitte (Heinrich's wife)

Right

Marie (Hannah's friend in New Jersey)

Rosenstein

Otto (Leopold's father)
Golda (Leopold's mother)
Leopold
Ester (Leopold's sister)
Simon (Leopold's brother)

Waxman

Alfred (Leo's cousins in New Jersey)
Bianca (Alfred's wife)

Leo's Cousins in Atlanta

Jack Bernstein
Carol Kohen (Jack's sister)

Rosen

Leo
Sophie
Adam (Leo and Sophie's son)
Joey (Leo and Sophie's son)
Madeleine (Leo and Sophie's daughter)
Jeffrey (Leo and Sophie's son)

Blum

Edwin (Hannah's cousin)
Martha (Edwin's wife)
Ellen (Oldest daughter)
Two sisters

Sophie's Friends

Richard Roth
Ruby Roth (Fox)
Dotty
Connie Finegold

Levine

Barry (Madeleine's husband)
Jane (Barry's mother)
Morris (Barry's father)

Prologue

2005

Jeff's phone rang at 6:00 A.M. His bedroom was dark except for a sliver of early morning light peeping around the corners of the window blinds. There was no traffic noise from the street behind his house. His wife of thirty years lay asleep beside him.

Jeff grabbed the phone and picked up the receiver, hoping the shrill sound didn't wake his wife.

"Get the paper now! Read the front page. I think Adam has done something awful!" Madeleine, his sister, screamed at him. Adam, their oldest brother, was often in the paper. He was a former senator so Madeleine and Jeff were used to reading articles about their brother.

Jeff yawned and looked at the clock. He didn't need to get up for another hour. "What is so bad that you had to call me this early? Couldn't it wait?"

"No! When you read the paper, you'll know why," Madeleine told him.

Taking his cell phone with him, Jeff went downstairs and opened the front door. He grabbed the newspaper off the bottom step. The flimsy plastic bag was damp with the morning dew. "Oh, my God, do you really think he did this?" he said to Madeleine after he read the headline and the first few lines of the article. "Why would you think that? He never believed us. Did something happen?"

"Yes. He called me yesterday and sounded depressed as usual. He said he changed his mind and hired a private investigator to find her." Madeleine paused to take a sip of coffee. "He was already so fragile. This may have been the last straw. Maybe he finally cracked."

Lead Story: *Palm Beach Post*
September 18, 2005
LOCAL WIDOW FOUND DEAD IN HER HOME

Ellen F. Berger, 70, was found dead yesterday morning in her winter home in Boca Village. Burglary was ruled out. There were no signs of forced entry and nothing was taken. Police are puzzled because Boca Village is a gated community with a security guard at the only entrance. The guard, Sergeant Ralph Thomas, could not remember any strange cars entering or leaving that night.

Unfortunately, the video camera at the entrance was not working. The police did not find any fingerprints other than those of the victim, her family, and her maid. The police are stymied. They have no motive and no evidence.

Ms. Berger's daughter, Allison Berger, said she had just seen her mother the previous night for dinner.

"How could someone do this to such a wonderful person? My mother was the kindest person anyone knows. My sisters and I are devastated. We haven't told the grandchildren yet that they lost their 'Bubbe.'"

Police are asking anybody who knows anything related to this case to please call 561-HELPS-US.

Funeral services and visiting hours will be announced later today.

Part I

The First Generation

Germany and America

1892 - 1938

"...Give me your tired, your poor,
Your huddled masses yearning to breathe free,
The wretched refuse of your teeming shore,
Send these, the homeless, tempest-tossed to me..."

Emma Lazarus, The Statue of Liberty,
from "The New Colossus"

Chapter One

1921

"I will not marry him," Hannah said as she stamped her foot on the living room floor. "I don't care what you have promised. I will not marry him. How dare you make arrangements for my wedding? To someone I have never met. To someone almost fifty years old and who lives in America. What were you thinking?" she hissed at her parents.

Now she understood why the house had been awash with frantic activity --- drapes pulled down and dusted, rugs taken outside and beaten, and the wood floors polished to a shine. Mama had yelled at Clarisse, the maid, to make sure the upstairs rooms were swept twice.

"You'll meet him, and you'll marry him," Hannah's mother said, loudly, which was unlike her. "Your papa and I are tired of answering questions about why you aren't married yet. People say something is wrong with you." She paced the room, moving objects from place to place. "I don't want people to think that you can't get a husband. Think that you are no longer a virgin. Your sisters and brothers are married --- it's past time for you." She paused, took a deep breath, and announced, "It's arranged, so there's no way to get out of it."

Hannah still lived with her parents. That was what proper, unmarried women did until they found a husband and raised a family. Instead, she worked as a seamstress, highly skilled knitter, and a hat and glove designer. She made enough money to live a comfortable life and to travel occasionally with her sisters or friends. That is if she remained with her parents and didn't have to pay rent. She'd accepted the fact that a husband was probably not part of her life and was content without one.

"Papa, please listen." Hannah turned to her father. "You already have eight grandchildren, so you don't need more. What's the hurry?" She paused and looked at her father's face to gauge his reaction. "You know I'm a virtuous woman and that I try to be the way you want me to be. But please, not him, not now. He's so old. At least find me a younger man, one who lives here." Hannah knew she was losing this battle. Papa's face was the color of a ripe tomato. His eyes were as dark as night.

"Hannah, do what your mother says. I'll hear no more of this," he said and turned to his wife for support.

Mrs. Horowitz, who felt empowered to force her opinion on her daughter, instructed, "Go put on the new dress you made, the one with the intricate lace pattern and the tiny pleats. Wear the white shawl with the seed pearls that you crocheted. I want him to see your talents, so he knows he's getting a wife who can make such lovely garments."

Hannah's mother, having asserted her authority over her daughter, lowered her voice and sat down on the gold brocade sofa. She fluffed the needlepoint pillow and continued in a softer voice. "We're also going to tell him that you cooked part of the dinner and made the desserts. We want him and his mother to see what a fine, accomplished woman you are."

Hannah knew not to talk back to her mother. She stormed out of the living room and went upstairs to her room to dress. Her room was her refuge from her parents. It was filled with books, her craft supplies, and photographs of her nieces and nephews.

"Please, God," she prayed. "Make him not too bad. Not too old and ugly. If I have to get married, at least give me a handsome man." She supposed he had to have a flaw or two if he was fifty and willing to marry a twenty-nine-year-old woman.

Hannah took off the beige frock that she wore when she was knitting. Yarn fragments of various colors fell to the floor. She had been making a baby blanket for her sister's newborn baby. As she took the dress her mother wanted her to wear out of the bedroom's small wardrobe, she decided to steel herself for the upcoming meeting. She brushed her hair and repeated quietly, "I will continue to be myself even if I marry. I will continue to be myself even if I marry." By the time she went downstairs, she felt ready to face her situation and make the best of it.

Chapter Two

Saul Straus left Germany in 1892, when it became evident he wasn't going to achieve his dream of starting a business in his small hometown in Bavaria. His mother, a short, unsmiling woman, who had been a widow for twenty years, stifled him and tried to control his every move. His father, a kind and silent man, died of a heart attack when Saul was in his twenties. Saul yearned to be rich, travel the world, and buy a nice home near New York City. After he achieved his dream, he would be ready to have a family. His mother had ideas of her own. She believed Saul should have moved back home to Germany many years ago, married, and started a family.

When Saul first went to America, he promised his mother he would be back in five years. He had to promise her something so she'd let him go without feigning a heart attack. What he hadn't told her was that he planned to stay in America and only come back to Germany to visit. His mother was a rigid woman who tried to run all of her children's lives, so he was not surprised when six months ago he received a letter with a picture of a woman enclosed.

My dear Saul,

I miss you terribly. I really wish you'd come back soon. My hips are getting worse. The doctor says I must stay off my feet. I need you to be here to help me. Your brothers and sisters have their hands full with their children and grandchildren. They don't have time for me.

("Had she developed any friends or interests since his father died, she wouldn't be so lonely," Saul thought as he continued reading.)

> *Enclosed is a picture of Hannah Horowitz. I know her family from synagogue. They are quite wealthy. She is a lovely, accomplished lady. I have arranged for you to meet her and her family when you get back home. Her father has promised her to you to be your wife as long as you approve of her, of course. Please book passage as soon as possible. Let me know when you think you'll arrive. Please don't wait too long.*
>
> *Much love,*
> *Your mother*

Chapter Three

Saul stood with his mother on the doorstep of a three-story, red brick townhouse wondering what kind of a marriage prospect he was. He knew he wasn't a great catch for a woman, even if she was almost thirty years old (practically a spinster.) He was only 5'5" tall in his shoes. He was at least twenty pounds overweight and bald. What woman would want him?

Mrs. Horowitz, who usually didn't answer the door but required one of the servants to do it, opened the door after the first knock. She was dressed in one of her fancier outfits, all shades of blues and grays, wanting to make the right impression on the Strauses. "Please come in and give me your coats. It's still a bit chilly at this time of year, isn't it? We have the fire going in the living room," she said as she called for the maid. "Clarisse, come here. Take the coats and be very careful with Mrs. Straus's fur. It's very expensive." Mrs. Horowitz couldn't help but run her fingers over the luxurious fur as she handed the coat to Clarisse.

Saul and his mother entered the tastefully decorated living room. The recently reupholstered chairs and sofa were arranged around a large cocktail table covered with hors d'oeuvres.

"Welcome to our home," Mr. Horowitz said as he firmly grasped Saul's hand, and then turned to Saul's mother. "Mrs. Straus, please sit down. Would you like some wine? Whisky? Water?" He walked over to a credenza in the corner of the spacious room where fine crystal glasses, a wide assortment of alcoholic beverages, and a pitcher of water were arranged. "We are so glad you could make it tonight. We look forward to your meeting our daughter. She's quite talented, you know. Yes, she knits, sews, designs dresses and hats, and is an excellent cook." He turned to his guests with glasses filled with each person's requested drink. "You'll see how well she cooks.

Our Hannah made most of tonight's dinner and the desserts. Wait until you taste them."

"Please excuse our daughter. She's not usually late. I'm sure she is taking extra care so she'll look good for you," Mrs. Horowitz added her voice quivering with anxiety and anger that her daughter was running so late. "She knows the importance of timeliness, especially when she has promised a client her dress will be ready." She sat back in her chair and folded her hands on her lap to keep them from fidgeting.

"You have a lovely home. It's in a very convenient location," Saul said as he glanced around the tastefully furnished room. "These three-story townhouses near the center of town are popular again. I've been trying to get my mother to move closer to town now that her children are all gone. But she's stubborn. She loves her home and doesn't want to move." He stood with his back to the large stone fireplace watching the door to the hall and waiting to get a glimpse of his prospective wife.

Mr. Horowitz, growing concerned about the impression Hannah's lateness would make, began, "I do apologize for Hannah. Women can be so fussy about how they look." He tapped his cigarette into the crystal ashtray with sterling silver trim. "All my girls were this way until they got married and moved out of the house." He chuckled and added, "I guess they get it from my wife. Don't they, dear?" He smiled at his wife. He walked to the massive stone fireplace to stand next to Saul as they waited for Hannah to make her entrance.

"You know they don't get it from me," Mrs. Horowitz corrected him. "I believe it comes from your side of the family." *Why must he always blame me for our children's faults in front of company?* She thought as she too worried about Saul and his mother's reaction to Hannah's behavior.

Ten minutes later Hannah entered the room. Her fashionable dress was pale yellow brocade with small pleats at the bodice. She wore a shiny silk sash tied at the waist, showing off her best features --- a small waist and large breasts. The skirt hit the middle of her shin, showing her lower legs and ankles. Her long brown hair, which she usually wore long and down her back, was pinned up in a chignon just as her mother vehemently suggested. Hannah had a strong, straight nose and a serious-looking face that brightened when she smiled.

As she walked across the room, her eyes were on Mrs. Straus. "So nice to see you again," she said politely.

"Hmm, you're Hannah? It has been a long time since I've seen you." Mrs. Straus surveyed every article of Hannah's outfit. "I think the last time I saw you was when you were in high school. It was your sister Agnes' wedding," she said. She turned to Saul. "This is my oldest son, Saul. He's been living in America too long, if you ask me. I don't think you've met him before."

Saul walked from the fireplace to where Hannah stood next to the sofa where his mother sat. He reached out his right hand to hold or shake hers. He wasn't sure what she would do.

Hannah slowly lifted her dark eyes and gave him her hand to shake. Her insides felt as if she had swallowed a sour drink; it was difficult for her to breathe. She didn't want to stare at him. It wasn't ladylike. As her eyes met his, she realized he was not much taller than her, and she was only 5'2". Her mother warned her not to wear heels, so she wore pale yellow flats. Hannah was glad she'd obeyed her mother this time. She didn't want to tower over her prospective husband.

She saw a solid, stocky man of fifty. He wore a light brown wool suit, a white, high-collared shirt, and a dark chocolate brown tie. His graying hair was thinning on top. His teeth looked healthy. He smiled at her and firmly shook her gloved hand.

"Hello, Hannah. I'm pleased to meet you. You are even prettier than the picture your father sent me," Saul said as he discreetly examined her face, her outfit, and her stature.

"Oh, I hadn't realized they sent you a picture of me." Hannah glared at her parents, who stood anxiously behind Saul. They looked terrified of what Hannah might say next.

"Yes, they sent it a few months ago for me to see if I wanted to meet you and consider you for my wife. I am sorry you didn't get a picture of me too. I hope my looks do not offend you." He smiled, hiding his fear that Hannah would find him unattractive.

Saul fidgeted with the change in his pocket and looked all around the room to avoid Hannah's gaze. They were in an awkward situation, promised to each other like adolescent children.

The tall heirloom clock in the hallway chimed eight times. "Let's go in to dinner," Hannah's mother announced, motioning for her husband to escort Mrs. Straus to the dinner table.

Saul offered his arm to Hannah, and they preceded Hannah's father into the richly decorated dining room.

The table was set with the family's Rosenthal bone china and cut crystal glasses. The good sterling silver that had been passed down from the Horowitzes' side of the family sparkled in the candlelight.

Polite, impersonal conversation dominated the dinner. When dessert was served Saul cleared his throat, and said, "Mr. Horowitz, as you know, we came here tonight to discuss your giving permission for Hannah to marry me." All eyes were on Saul as he continued. "I promise you I will be a good husband and take care of Hannah and our children. God willing, we have some."

Hannah's face reddened. *Oh my God!* She thought. *Why is he doing this in front of everyone? Why must he make this so public? I wish I wasn't in the room.*

"I would like to marry her as soon as possible so we can return to New Jersey. My job demands it." He paused and took a sip of wine. "I know I am probably older than most men who marry for the first time, but I am settled down and established. Will you give me your permission, please, Mr. Horowitz?"

Mr. Horowitz, who had practiced all day for what he would say, forgot his speech, and replied very quickly, "Yes. Of course you can marry Hannah," he hesitated remembering how headstrong Hannah could be about abiding by decisions other people made for her. "I'd like her to have a say in the matter." He turned to his daughter, who was politely wiping her mouth and said, "Hannah, is this arrangement satisfactory for you?"

Hannah nodded her head slowly. What choice did she have? It would be Saul or another man her parents brought home. She might as well say "yes" to the man sitting next to her.

By the end of the evening, all was arranged. Saul and Hannah would marry in late July so that they could book passage to America before winter arrived. The voyage to America would be their honeymoon. The families agreed that they would pay for an upgrade to a first-class cabin as their wedding gift to the newlyweds.

Chapter Four

Days later, Hannah fretted about what would be expected of her as a married woman on her wedding night. In many ways Hannah was naïve, especially about sex. Hannah asked her oldest sister, Sarah, about what happens on wedding nights. Her sister thought this was too personal to discuss with anyone and refused to answer.

Hannah pleaded with her other sister, Agnes, "Please tell me what will happen. What should I expect? I'm afraid I won't know what to do."

"Oh, Hannah, it's very difficult to describe such things." Agnes blushed as she spoke. "He'll kiss you for a few minutes." She gulped air and continued. "And maybe rub your breast." Her face darkened with embarrassment, but she continued. "He'll take your clothes off, or let you do that. I think Alfred asked me to undress while he was in the bathroom. You should put on your new white nightgown." Agnes paused, trying to think of the right words. "Then, you get in bed while he undresses. Sometimes men wear nightshirts, and sometimes they don't. He'll probably kiss you more and touch you in places you haven't been touched by anyone, not even the doctor."

The two sisters, who could talk about anything with each other, were now embarrassed to even look at each other. Agnes stalled for a few seconds trying to decide how to describe what happened next. "Don't be afraid when his penis grows very large. That's normal. He'll put it in the place where your monthlies come out."

Hannah's face blanched. "How does his penis grow? I've seen my nephew's small weenie, but is a man's much larger?" Hannah waited for an answer, but none came. So she asked, "Do you enjoy sex with your husband?"

"Yes, Hannah, I do. Enough of this talk. Saul will know what to do so just follow his lead." Agnes made it clear the discussion was over.

Chapter Five

The wedding was small, only family members, and was held at the local synagogue. After the service, the families went to the Horowitzes' house to eat. The plan was for the newlyweds to be at their ship at 7:00 P.M. so the wedding was at 3:00 P.M., and supper at exactly 5:00 P.M. Because the newlyweds had to be at the boat, there was no music and dancing as there usually was at a wedding. There was a small, white wedding cake that Hannah's mother baked and frosted the night before the wedding.

Once the cake was eaten and everyone hugged the couple, Saul and Hannah grabbed their packed suitcases that were hidden in the front hall closet. They didn't want to be late to check in at the dock for the ship to take them to America.

Later that evening, after Hannah and Saul settled into their cabin, Saul surprised Hannah with a bottle of fine French champagne. Still dressed in their going-away clothes, they sat stiffly on the small floral sofa in their cabin, sipping their drinks. Hannah was glad they had a few minutes to talk and for her to get slightly tipsy before they got into bed. She wasn't afraid of Saul, just anxious about the next step in their marriage.

After drinking his champagne as slowly as possible, Saul said, "Hannah, um, well, see, it is customary for me to let you have some privacy when you prepare for bed. I'll go into the bathroom so you can undress and change into your nightgown. I'll change in the bathroom and join you in bed."

Hannah poured a second glass of champagne before she got into bed. She drank it in two gulps and hoped it would settle her nerves. Saul came out of the bathroom in a long nightshirt. He pulled back the covers and joined her in bed.

"Are you frightened, Hannah, my wife?" Saul asked her while gently moving her long hair out of her face and caressing her neck. Hannah had undone her hair and let it fall naturally down her back.

"Yes," she answered. "A little. Will it hurt?"

"I have been told it does hurt at first, if you are a virgin, which I understand you are. I will try to be fast so it won't hurt long." He had little experience himself with sex, just a few occasions with a widow he knew through his work and a woman from his synagogue who he dated on and off for several years.

Saul kissed Hannah several times, the last time putting his tongue in her mouth and moving it around as if he was searching for a hidden morsel of food left over from their wedding dinner.

Hannah didn't pull back. He withdrew his tongue from her mouth and kissed her behind her ear. After repeating this procedure two more times, he thought she might be ready for him. He lifted her gown and gently put his fingers near her vagina to see if she was wet. He had heard it hurt the woman less if she was wet. He couldn't tell, but he was ready. He pulled his nightshirt up and gently pushed his hardened penis into her. He thrust once, twice, a third time, and then he groaned. He paused a minute to catch his breath and withdrew from her. It was over.

Hannah felt liquid drip down her leg onto the bed. Hannah remembered what her sister had told her. *This is what the fuss is all about?* She thought. *It was pleasant enough, but so fast. I guess I can get used to this. It wasn't so bad after all. Agnes didn't tell me about the short pain and the sticky stuff Saul ejected from his penis. I think that is what makes babies, the sticky stuff.*

As Hannah fell asleep, she thought about the last words Saul's mother said to her: "I expect grandchildren as soon as possible." *Oh my God,* Hannah thought. *He may want to do this every night until I get pregnant. Well, on second thought, maybe it gets better.*

By the end of the voyage to America, Hannah felt an emotion akin to liking Saul. She decided it was not terrible, as she feared, to have a man around. She enjoyed the attention he paid her, and she discovered that she liked being held. Her family was not demonstrative and hugging was reserved for special occasions like birthdays or returns from trips. Although Saul embraced her every night, Hannah was delighted he only approached her for sex three times on the trip to America. Overall, it was a pleasant honeymoon.

As they disembarked from the ship, hand in hand, Hannah realized that as a married woman in America, she would have more opportunities than she ever would have had as a spinster in Germany. *Maybe my parents were right after all*, she thought.

Chapter Six

For over fifty years, German and Italian immigrants settled in Saul's New Jersey neighborhood. Concrete sidewalks lined with oak trees ran parallel to the front of the tall brownstone buildings. In Saul's building, the white staircase walls looked freshly painted. His third floor apartment was spartan and functional. The wooden floors were polished to a shiny golden brown. Windows opened to the street where you could see vendors and residents passing by. The blue-green walls and white ceiling were clean, but the apartment lacked warmth.

Each room had minimum furniture. A refurbished couch and two armchairs were arranged around a large coffee table in the living room. The dining area consisted of a wooden table and four high-back chairs that didn't have cushions. The kitchen had the basic appliances. A gas stove, a small icebox to refrigerate food, and a small butcher block in the middle of the room. There were no paintings hanging on the walls, and the curtains were dirty brown from dust and dirt that blew in from the streets through the open windows. Their bedroom had a full-size bed with a pale blue and green print bedspread. It also had a dresser and two end tables that were made of the same wood as the dining room table.

After assessing the apartment, Hannah said, "Saul, I can make some new curtains for the windows and knit a better blanket for our bed. The sofa could use pillows and maybe a few green plants in the windows. Is it okay if I do this?" She asked carefully as to not offend Saul about his home.

Saul smiled, happy that Hannah liked the place and wanted to make it more homelike. "Yes, Hannah, anything you want. Come see the second bedroom. That's for the baby when we have one." He smiled, imagining a small child living in the room—a small boy dressed in blue pants and a white shirt playing with a wooden train set.

He watched Hannah's face for any sign of her approval. "You can decorate it any way you like. But... Well, maybe we should wait until you are pregnant. Okay? For now, we can put a table in there for your sewing machine. I'll find one for you to use so you can continue your work as a seamstress. Would this make you happy?"

She threw her arms around him and said, "Yes. That would make me very happy."

***

Before Saul went back to work, he spent three days teaching Hannah how to say important words in English so she could function without him during the day. He also gave her a dictionary he had bought at a local market to help her translate words from German to English when he was not home. He'd asked his neighbors if they would help Hannah with her English. Luckily, many of the Jewish ladies Saul knew in the neighborhood spoke Yiddish, which was very close to German, so Hannah was confident she would get by while improving her English.

Saul notified people he knew in the neighborhood and at synagogue that Hannah did high quality custom design, sewing, and knitting. Ladies from the local synagogue who heard about Hannah arrived at her door, asking her to mend clothes and design new dresses.

One day, as Hannah hemmed a dress for a customer, she excused herself and ran to the bathroom. Dizzy and light-headed, she kneeled on the cold tile floor with her head over the toilet. She gagged, knowing she would throw up. And then, she did vomit. After three days of this, she worried that she was ill. Not knowing who else to turn to, she asked her new friend, Marie, a Catholic woman and a skilled nurse whom she met at the corner grocery, what she should do.

Laughing, Marie told Hannah, "You're pregnant? How exciting! You must tell your husband right away. He'll be thrilled!"

"Pregnant!" Hannah said. "I am pregnant. I hope Saul will be happy."

That evening, as soon as Saul took off his suit jacket, Hannah blurted, "I think I am pregnant, Saul. We are going to have a child."

He flung his jacket on the sofa and walked to her as she stood by the kitchen sink. "I love you, Hannah. You've made me very happy," he said and kissed her on the cheek.

Saul was delighted. He reacted exactly like Marie told her he would.

"Can we wait to write our parents until we see the doctor?" Hannah asked. "I want to be sure about the baby before we tell them."

"Of course, my dear. We can wait, but not too long," Saul sighed, a broad smile on his face. "My mother will finally have a grandchild from me," he replied. "Maybe she'll stop *hocking* me about it."

A week later, after the doctor confirmed their suspicion, they wrote their parents, telling them the good news:

> *Hannah saw the doctor yesterday. He thinks the baby will be born this summer. We have time to turn Hannah's sewing room into a nursery. We aren't sure what color to paint it, blue or pink, so we will do green. We won't buy many things for the baby yet because we know the tradition of not buying clothes for the baby until it is born. The doctor assured us that Hannah is very healthy. There shouldn't be any problems. We hope you can visit us once the baby is here.*

Saul, always a worrier about money, increased the hours that he worked. He knew Hannah would have to stop working soon. He wanted his wife and child to have the best of everything. So what if he was fifty and Hannah thirty? They would be wonderful parents and provide for their children just as well as a younger couple would—maybe even better.

One evening when Saul got home from work around 9:00 P.M., two months after they found out about Hannah's pregnancy, Hannah asked, "Are you feeling all right? You look pale, a little gray. You need to rest, Saul." She shook her index finger at him admonishingly. "You aren't a young man anymore. I want you here to help me raise our baby." She went to the kitchen and hollered back to him, "Stay in bed longer tomorrow. Please try and get home earlier."

"Don't worry, Hannah. It's nothing. It's just a cold. Several men at work have coughs and colds. I won't die from a cold." Hannah placed a plate of warm food in front of him: roast beef, potatoes, rolls, and butter—all of his favorites.

Hannah worried even though Saul said she shouldn't. Although she was an educated woman with a job, she didn't make enough money to support herself and a baby. She needed Saul financially and emotionally. *No one wants to raise a child on her own*, she thought. Even before they married, Hannah worried about marrying someone so much older than her. She knew she could handle the stress of working and keeping a home; she was young. But she was concerned about Saul, fifty, overweight, and a worrier.

Chapter Seven

It was a humid, rainy Monday evening when Marie appeared at Hannah's door. Hannah, who was seven months pregnant, welcomed Marie with a hug.

"Marie, what a surprise to see you," Hannah said. "Give me your coat. It is dripping wet." Before Hannah finished hanging the soaked coat, she noticed her friend's unusual demeanor. "Is something wrong?"

Shaken, ashen, and crying, Marie said, "Hannah, sit down. I have bad news. Be brave." Marie watched Hannah's eyes open wide and her cheeks redden, but she continued. "They brought Saul to the emergency room a few hours ago. It was a massive heart attack. I'm so sorry, but he died in the car on the way to the hospital. There was nothing anyone could do to save him." Marie reached out her arms to hold Hannah.

Stunned, Hannah collapsed onto the couch, a bright blue sofa bed they bought just last week for family members who would come from Germany to see the baby. "No! No! No!" she screamed. "This can't be. How can this be?" She crumbled the white embroidered handkerchief that Marie placed in her hands. "We've only been married eight months. What will the baby and I do? We can't afford to stay here in this apartment. Not without Saul's income. What will become of us?" Her face darkened and fear crept into her voice. "I don't want to go back to Germany. What will I do?"

Hannah wept uncontrollably, gasping for air. Marie, not knowing what else to say, held Hannah in her arms until the weeping stopped and Hannah could breathe. "My dear Hannah, I'll be here and help you." She brushed a lock of Hannah's hair out of her face. "We'll figure this out. You're a strong woman and a smart one. We'll get through this together, if you'll let me help."

"Marie, please stay tonight." Hannah gripped Marie's upper arm tightly. "I have no one. I can't be alone tonight. Will you stay and help me sort through all of this, please?" She was exhausted from weeping.

"I will, Hannah," Marie, who had no family of her own, said as she patted Hannah's shoulder. "I'll stay tonight and every night you need me. Now, let me get you some hot tea and put you to bed. Even if you don't sleep, you can rest." She walked to the kitchen to put on a kettle of water to boil. "We don't want you to lose the baby. You have to take care of yourself even if you don't want to. We'll take care of other things tomorrow."

Neither woman slept that night. Several times, Marie saw Hannah walk into the baby's room. Hannah looked at the green walls that Saul had painted last weekend. She sat in the rocking chair, the only item she and Saul bought before the baby was born. Hannah rocked and cried until 5:00 A.M., when she got up and went to her bed. Marie got into bed with her and held her until they fell asleep.

At 7:00 A.M., the two women got out of bed, drank strong black coffee, and made lists of tasks that had to be accomplished: arrange a funeral, sort through papers, write the families, and look for another place for Hannah to live. Marie volunteered to go through the papers in Saul's chest of drawers while Hannah wrote the letters.

Minutes later, Marie yelled from the bedroom, "Hannah, come quick. I found documents to show you. I think I found Saul's will and insurance policies."

Hannah rushed into the room, carrying the pen and paper. Marie opened Saul's will and handed it to Hannah who read it aloud:

> *I, Saul D. Straus, leave everything I own to my loving wife, Hannah H. Straus, and our baby. The enclosed insurance policy plus my savings, combined with the money Hannah's father gave as a wedding gift, should be enough money for them to get by in America. The bank account is in Hannah's name too, so she shouldn't have any problem getting the money.*

Next, Hannah saw a Manila envelope with her name on it in Saul's handwriting. Thinking that the letter held personal information, Hannah took it with her to the baby's room and sat in the rocking chair.

> *Hannah, my love. Please forgive me for not telling you about my heart condition. I didn't want to scare you away when we met.*

Hannah wiped her hand across the tears as they fell down her chin.

> *Once we were married, I was afraid to tell you because I thought you would leave me and go back to Germany. I knew a day might come when you would be alone and need me to help support you. I have saved money since I first came to America. When I first began saving, it was to have enough money for me to go back to Germany and help my mother. Then, it was because I wanted to be able to bring my mother here. Once we married, I saved for us. Your father gave me money as a dowry to help us start our married life, and I put it in our savings account.*

Hannah hesitated. Her father gave money to Saul and didn't tell her?

> *I regularly added money to the bank account. Between the savings and the enclosed insurance policy I took out when we found out you were pregnant, you should be able to continue to live in America, or go back to Germany, to raise our child. Please forgive me for not telling you any of this. I*

hope you won't be a widow for long. I want you to remarry.

I love you,
Saul

There was a second, shorter letter that Marie found. It was dated last week.

Hannah, if I die before the baby is born, please have the baby in America. I want him or her to be an American citizen. I worry about the political climate in Germany. I don't want either of you caught up in any negative situations. Don't go back to Germany to live. Stay in America, please.

Love,
Saul

Hannah stared at the words on the paper, wishing Saul had talked to her about his health and his concerns about her and the baby. Had he known he was that ill? Had he withheld this information intentionally? She would never know.

Chapter Eight

1922

Hannah, with six more weeks until the baby was due, looked for a suitable apartment for her to rent. It had to be smaller than her current one, if she was going to manage her money and live on it until the baby grew up. Hannah knew she could still work for clients while pregnant or with an infant once her baby was born. Luckily, a one-bedroom apartment in the same building where Marie lived became vacant. The apartment was across the brightly lit hall from Marie and close to the synagogue where many of Hannah's customers worshipped.

The walls were dirty tan and appeared to have not been repainted since the apartment was built. The floor was covered with rugs that were once red, orange, and gold. Now, they were brown with wear. The curtains, dusty and torn, covered windows that allowed bright, direct sunlight to enter two of the rooms. She could put her sewing machine near one window and a few pots of herbs near the other. Her furniture, too sparse for Saul's apartment, fit comfortably in her new one. The closet space in the new apartment was more than she needed for her few clothes and any she made for the baby.

Hannah, with Marie's and several men from the synagogue's help, moved to her new apartment thirty days after they buried Saul. She was glad to be moving because the old apartment only reminded her of Saul and how little time they'd had with each other.

On a hot night in mid-July 1922, Hannah's water broke, and the labor pains began. Marie had done her best to prepare Hannah for what to expect during childbirth. She'd brought Hannah books and pamphlets from the hospital's maternity ward. Marie had never had children, but she was a nurse and had helped deliver dozens of babies. She also hired out as a private duty nurse for wealthy New York and New Jersey women who wanted help with their newborns. These women would never take care of their infants without help. Nurses, like Marie, were employed for three to six months, assisting new mothers to care for their babies.

Hannah wasn't frightened, just in terrible pain. She walked across the hall and banged on Marie's door. "Marie, wake up! The baby is coming! We've got to go!"

Marie was half asleep when she answered the door. She dressed quickly and helped Hannah grab the suitcase that they had prepared days ago and had left by the front door. They hailed a cab, and one miraculously appeared in less than a minute. Hannah and Marie scrambled into the back seat and gave the driver directions to the hospital.

Weeping, Hannah confided to Marie, "Once again, I feel so unprepared. Just like when I married Saul. I had no idea of how to be a married woman." She gripped her stomach in pain. "Now I have no idea how to be a mother. I want to be a good mother, not like my mother, who was demanding and critical. I want my daughter or son to love me."

"There is no reason to criticize yourself," Marie said. "No first-time mother feels prepared. You've got me to help you, no? So, there's no reason to worry." She squeezed Hannah's hand and held it the rest of trip to the hospital.

The baby was born at 11:47 P.M. She was tiny, five pounds and six ounces, with a full head of black, curly hair and pink, rosebud lips. Hannah couldn't tell what color the baby's eyes were, but she expected them to be black, like hers and Saul's. When the nurse put the baby in her arms, she was unprepared for the rush of love she felt for her daughter. It was unexpected, visceral. No one told her about this surge of emotional attachment. She knew this bond she felt with her daughter would last forever. Nothing would ever damage it.

Chapter Nine

As Hannah fed her baby for the first time, she realized that she and Saul hadn't discussed a name for a baby girl. They had listed boys' names. German, Jewish men wanted their first child to be a boy, as if having a son proved their manhood. Hannah and Saul's child left the hospital without a name. She was listed as "Baby Straus."

Baby Straus was finally named three weeks after she was born. "I think I like the name Sophie," Hannah told Marie at dinner one night. "I may call her *Baby* a while longer. That's what Saul and I called her before she was born." This was one connection to Saul she could hold on to, at least for a while longer.

Hannah and Marie pooled resources for food and ate dinner together most nights. A hot meal was on the table when Marie got home from work. Hannah liked having an adult to talk with at the end of the day, especially if all she did that day was take care of the baby, or occasionally deal with a client. After dinner, Marie played with Sophie while Hannah pinned and sewed clients' garments.

The two women delighted in taking *Baby* for walks in the park. They pushed her in the fancy stroller Hannah bought with a small amount from her bank account. People stopped and commented on how beautiful Sophie was with her ink-black curls and dark, penetrating eyes. Sophie was a happy baby and never lacked attention. Within a month, Sophie slept through most nights, which was a relief for Hannah.

"Thank God I have a good baby," Hannah commented to Marie. "I think I get more sleep with Sophie than I did sleeping with Saul, who snored all night."

The house was filled with laughter again after a long period of mourning and tears.

Hannah put her inheritance into a bank account and tried to use only the money she earned with her seamstress, hat making, and knitting jobs. Business was good. Clients appreciated Hannah's attention to detail and high-quality work. Her rich, Jewish customers and the referral business from Marie kept Hannah busy most days.

Hannah stored her sewing machine and knitting supplies in a cabinet that she had found on the street one day. She and Marie sanded and refinished it. The cabinet fit perfectly in one corner of the living room.

Sophie slept most of the day, except when hungry, while Hannah worked. When customers were there and Sophie was awake, she played happily on the floor with her toys and the remnants of rolls of yarn.

"Hannah, what a lovely and well-behaved baby you have," one customer commented. "What is your secret? My children are always running about and fighting with each other. I swear, one day I'll kill them all," the customer laughed jokingly.

"The answer is to have girls," Hannah answered, grinning. "Boys are a different story, or so I've heard. You must quickly let them know who is boss."

When Sophie was one year old, Hannah decided it was time to show Sophie to her grandparents. Hannah booked passage to Germany to see her parents and Saul's mother. Hannah was proud of her baby, and she wanted Saul's mother to see her grandchild before her mother-in-law passed away. She also wanted her parents to see how successful she was as a single mother and how thrifty she was with her inheritance. Secretly, she wanted her sisters and brothers to be jealous of her good life in America.

Chapter Ten

1923

Mr. and Mrs. Horowitz were delighted with the match they had made for Hannah even though her husband had passed away. As far as they were concerned, their daughter's being a widow was far superior to being an unwanted spinster. They were besotted with their beautiful, obedient granddaughter.

"Hannah," her mother started, "It's not good for you and Sophie to live alone in a foreign country where you know no one. Maybe you should move back here. We can help you find another husband. Now that you are a widow with money and American citizenship, I'm sure we can make you a very good match."

"No, Mother. No more matches for me; no more husbands. I just want to have some fun while I am here and for you to get to know Sophie." Hannah modulated her voice so as not to show her mother how distasteful the idea of another arranged marriage was to her.

After several boring weeks with her parents, Hannah needed to get away. My God, she was a widow, with a baby. Why should she have to listen to her parents all day? She convinced her sisters, Agnes and Sarah, to leave their children with their husbands and go on a holiday with her. She left Sophie with her parents.

The sisters made reservations at several well-known spas in the mountains twenty miles away from home—places they hadn't been to since they were teenagers. The first spa, deep in a lush green valley at the foothills of a nearby mountain, was known for its food and wine and its healing mineral baths. Another spa, further up the mountain, amidst the tall pines, was renowned for deep-muscle and hot-rock massages.

One day at breakfast, Hannah announced, "I am bored with the spas. I want to go to the Grand Hotel, the special hotel we went to once with Papa and Mama. There is so much to do there: hiking, fishing, dancing, and swimming. Please go with me for just two days."

"I don't know if I can afford to go there," Agnes admitted. She hadn't bought any new clothes for herself in years. All her allowance went to the house or to the children. "Karl's business isn't doing well. He doesn't want anyone to know we're almost broke. He has a new competitor, you see. He's losing customers."

Hannah waved off her sister's concerns. "That will pass. He'll get new customers. Never mind about the money. I'll treat both of you. I've got money put aside for fun. Traveling with you both means so much to me. We haven't had any time to be together since I got married."

"Thank you, Hannah," Sarah said. "I'll pay you back as soon as I can." She sighed deeply, relieved she could go with her sisters and still not have to ask her husband for money he didn't have. "I appreciate your offer. I need a break from the children and the pressure. Isaac, my dear husband, is driving me crazy with worry. I'll go."

They left that afternoon and arrived at the hotel for high tea. It certainly was a "Grand Hotel" with massive, decorated columns and windows from ceiling to floor. Frescos and paintings adorned the parts of the ceilings that weren't made of glass. Small sandwiches, fancy pastries, hot scones, and tea sat on sparkling sterling silver trays. Hannah chose a spot by the door so the sisters could watch women in their afternoon finery and men in jackets and ties parade by on their way to their own tables.

After the sisters settled into the high backed chairs and placed the starched white napkins on their laps, Hannah flagged down a waiter. "Sir, please bring us a bottle of champagne. We're celebrating!"

"Celebrating what, Madam?" the tuxedo-clad waiter asked as he handed the women the teatime menus.

"Freedom. Fun. Sisters," the women replied.

***

Dinner was served in a magnificent, formal ballroom where the waiters wore tuxedoes and white gloves. By the time the women were seated, they were drunk on alcohol and freedom. They watched couples, the women dressed in flowing summer dresses and the men in black suits, waltz in a large circle around the room on the marble-tiled floor. The music mixed with the sounds of feet moving and couples whispering.

"Do you remember how we loved to dance?" Sarah laughed and took another sip of the French red wine they ordered with dinner. "We were always pestering Papa and our brothers to dance with us, so we would know what to do when a boy asked us to dance."

"Yes, and remember how, at my first dance, I tripped on the hem of my dress and almost knocked over the punch bowl?" replied Agnes, giggling so hard she almost spilled her wine on the white tablecloth.

Hannah shared an incident on the boat to America when she and Saul were on their honeymoon. "Saul was leading and looking at me when he bumped into another couple, who then bumped into a third couple, the captain and his wife. I was mortified."

Spurred by the alcohol and lack of parents and children, the women giggled uncontrollably.

Suddenly, a tall blonde man dressed in a tuxedo appeared at the table. "Ladies, would one of you be so kind to dance with me?" He bowed from his waist as if addressing royalty. "I couldn't help noticing how much fun you were having. One of you would make my evening more pleasant if you shared that fun with me." He was at least six feet tall and stood in front of them with his shoulders pulled back, looking like a soldier ready to march in a parade.

Sarah and Agnes looked at each other. Then they looked at Hannah. "Our sister Hannah will dance with you," Sarah pronounced. They thought it would do Hannah some good to have a man's attention, something she rarely experienced.

Hannah was not a classic beauty. Her nose was too strong and her dark eyes too severe. She could, however, be quite attractive when she dressed to show off her figure and used makeup to focus on her best attributes. Even so, she was still surprised when a man paid attention to her.

"Will you grant me this dance?" the tall gentleman asked Hannah as he bowed and extended his hand to her.

"I guess so. Yes," Hannah answered and rose from her comfortable brocade chair.

Chapter Eleven

One dance led to two dances, and then three. At midnight Agnes and Sarah decided to go to bed, leaving Hannah with the handsome stranger. After the third dance, Hannah's throat was so dry she could barely speak, and she needed something to drink. Heinrich took her gloved hand and led her to the bar next door to the dining room. Red leather booths lined the walls and wispy white curtains fell from ceiling to floor, providing couples an intimate place to talk.

"I know your first name, but you don't know mine. I am Heinrich Werner. I live in Frankfurt." He paused, checking Hannah's reaction to him. "I enjoy coming here when I have time, which isn't often." He sipped his cocktail. "I'm a lawyer who works too much. That's why I don't have a family. No woman would have me. Who wants a man who works all the time and is never home?" He laughed at his own predicament.

"I'm Hannah Straus. I live near New York, in New Jersey, in America. I'm visiting my family who live not far from Nuremberg." She looked into Heinrich's eyes and continued. "I lost my husband a year ago and haven't decided exactly what I'll do next. I came back to Germany to spend time with my family and introduce my daughter to her family."

"A daughter? How nice," Heinrich said in his rich, baritone voice. "A boy would be better of course, to help support you in your old age. You don't need to worry about that now. You are young and beautiful," he teased. "How long are you in Germany?"

"A few more weeks," Hannah lowered her eyes and answered.

Heinrich leaned over and kissed Hannah. He caught her off guard. His kiss was unlike Saul's; it was wetter and deeper. The lust she felt shocked her, made her head spin. She pulled back and stared at him for several seconds. She had no idea she could feel this way. She was torn. Kissing a stranger? In public? Why shouldn't she follow up on her feelings? She was a widow now, not a virgin looking for a husband. She wanted to have fun tonight and forget her grief and worries.

"Let's go some place quieter, where we can be alone," he whispered in her ear. His warm breath sent shivers down her spine. "Will you come with me to my room?" he asked.

"Well, if you do not think badly of me for going with you, I will go for a few minutes. Then, I must return to my room," she said and meant it when she left the bar with him.

As they walked to his room, he thought about Brigette, his steady girlfriend. He promised Brigette he'd be monogamous and, maybe, marry her this year. He'd not had a spontaneous affair in over a year. A long time for him. Even so, Hannah intrigued him. An affair here was safe; no one knew him.

Heinrich opened the door to his room and gently ushered Hannah into the darkened room. As Hannah dropped her shawl and purse on a small table near a couch, Heinrich turned on a lamp and opened a bottle of red wine. Once they settled he offered her a glass of the slightly chilled wine. They sat on the sofa in the small sitting room adjacent to the bedroom. As they made small talk, Heinrich slowly ran his fingers across Hannah's arm and hand and then her neck. Hannah found it hard to think each time he touched her. He leaned over and kissed her, this time more insistently. She loved how it felt to be kissed this way, so purposeful and demanding. Between the champagne and wine and Heinrich's close contact, she found it difficult to think straight.

Hannah was not a virgin, but she was inexperienced in lovemaking. Hannah, like most women of her time, had been taught that lovemaking had one purpose: babies. Not pleasure for pleasure's sake. Sex with Saul had been agreeable, but he had never made her feel the way she felt now.

Heinrich, on the other hand, was a lady's man; known for the pleasure he gave his lovers. Sensing Hannah's positive response to him, he ventured further. Before she knew it, she was on his bed with her clothes off. He kissed her lips, her nipples, her belly, and finally, her clitoris. Hannah was mortified that he would kiss her *there* and tried to pull his head away.

"Relax," Heinrich murmured as he continued to lick her. When he thought she was ready, he positioned himself so he would bring her the most pleasure. He thrust into her until she came. Then he allowed himself to come.

Hannah was frightened, crying. "What have I done? Why did this feel so good and so scary? Wasn't what we did sordid?" she said out loud without thinking.

Heinrich, his blonde hair tousled and sweat running down his chest, laughed. "You just had an orgasm. You're lucky, not every woman can have one. There's nothing wrong with what we did as long as we both enjoyed it." He lifted her chin and said, "You never had an orgasm with your husband?"

"No. It felt good when we made love. It was okay," she stammered. "But not like this. Is this the same thing that men have when they appear to be having a fit?"

Laughing, he said, "It is not a fit, my dear. It's wonderful."

Hannah looked at the clock, horrified at the time. She slid out of bed trying to cover herself. No man had seen her completely naked. Even with Saul, she changed in the bathroom and came to bed in a long gown. When they made love, he merely lifted her gown up enough for him to enter her, and he came quickly. Now, with Heinrich, she was embarrassed. She grabbed her dress and undergarments and put them on while sitting on the bed with her back to him.

"Maybe next time, it will feel more natural," Heinrich said as he lit a cigarette.

"Next time? How can there be a next time?" Hannah asked, perplexed. She and her sisters were leaving the spa early the next morning. How would there be a next time?

"Listen. I work for myself and have a room at the back of the office where I spend the night when I work late." He paused to watch her reaction. "You can visit me there. Do come. Just call me and let me know when you are coming. I'll close the office for you." He reached over to the bedside table and handed her a business card. "Call me when you know you can come." He kissed her. Brigette worked during the day and never came to Heinrich's office. Sex with Hannah wouldn't present a problem for him as far as his fiancée was concerned.

She hurried out of his room and snuck into the room she shared with her sisters. Once she settled in her bed, in the safety of her room, her body pulsing from the aftermath of their lovemaking, Hannah touched her clitoris. She couldn't believe she was capable of the feelings she had experienced from Heinrich's touching her there. *Why had no one told her,* she thought as sleep overwhelmed her. *Why had no one told her?*

Chapter Twelve

During the trip and after the sisters returned home, no one talked about the night Hannah stayed out dancing. Although her sisters were eager to know what happened with Heinrich, they didn't ask. Certainly, she didn't volunteer. Even sisters don't tell each other intimate details of their sex lives. It wasn't proper.

Over the next month, Hannah found excuses to get away from her parents' house. She needed clothes for Sophie. She wanted to see an art exhibit. She was having lunch with a friend she made at the spa. Or she was looking up information for her friend Marie in America.

Hannah knew this might be her only chance for an affair with someone like Heinrich. She became sexually assertive just so she could be with him. She'd walk into his office and ask to talk to him privately in the back room. She'd kiss him and rub him until he had no choice but to lock the door and take her on the small bed that he kept in the back room. He was her addiction. He was the catalyst for her sexual awakening. She never knew she could be this wanton.

When Hannah wasn't with Heinrich, she could think rationally. She knew the reality of her life. Sophie was growing up. For her and her baby to remain American citizens, they had to return to the United States on a regular basis. There was unrest in Germany and much anti-Semitic rhetoric. Hannah didn't want to be stuck in Germany if conditions worsened. So how could this affair with Heinrich be more than what it was? Not serious and just a fling?

As the time for their return to the America grew closer, Hannah panicked. How could she live without Heinrich? How could she go back to being that naïve woman who knew nothing of the pleasures of sex? The only time she had felt beautiful was at her wedding. Never desirable, until now, with Heinrich.

On their last day together, Hannah confessed, "Heinrich, I don't think I can survive without your touch. You've changed me. I can't stand the idea of leaving you here and never experiencing pleasure again."

"Darling, you'll never again be the same person you were," he said during one of their last times together as he stroked her breast and her nipple hardened. "I want you to crave my touch. I want you to be wet with desire. I want you to know what you will be missing when you go."

"Then come with me to America," Hannah begged. "I know you can find work there. We can get married. Raise Sophie. Have children of our own."

"Hannah, you funny woman." His laugh was cold, not one of amusement. "I can never leave my homeland. I am German. You have never told me, but I suspect you are Jewish. Am I right?" His fair eyebrows rose with the question. "I have to marry the right woman. But, you and I, we could be lovers."

Hannah was shocked. She had not told him she was Jewish. Or did she? How did he know? Why did it matter if they loved each other? "You don't love me?" she asked, incredulous. How could a man probe her body as he did with her and not feel love? To do such unmentionable things with her and not feel love? She couldn't process the contradictory thoughts and actions.

"Did I ever say I loved you? This was fun, pleasurable, but you're not someone I could love, let alone marry." He was so matter of fact that she was stunned. Had she missed his callousness? Had she confused sex with love?

Hannah got out of bed, dressed, and left. Not another word was spoken.

Chapter Thirteen

The next day, Hannah booked passage to America. She and Sophie would be back in New Jersey for Sophie's second birthday.

The trip back to America was very difficult. Hannah tried to lose herself in her amazement at all the wonderful things her daughter could do. Sophie was walking and talking. She turned pages of the children's books Hannah's sisters had given her, pretending to read. Sophie tried to imitate Hannah's fast hand motions as she knitted, using her stubby fingers as knitting needles. She was a social child and made friends with everyone on the ship.

"What a beautiful child you have, " one lady said.

"Look how smart she is," said another.

"Where does she get those beautiful, stylish clothes?" the other passengers commented on her daughter.

The captain of the ship, who had a young daughter of his own, let Sophie "steer" the ship one afternoon when she had on her blue sailor's dress with a white collar. Hannah sometimes wondered which side of the family was responsible for her daughter's brilliance, and usually thought it was hers. Saul's family was not as educated or as prosperous as hers.

As the ship drew progressively closer to shore, Hannah promised herself that once she set foot on American soil, she would never think of or talk about Heinrich again.

Chapter Fourteen

Marie, in her nurse's uniform, was at the dock, waving a blue handkerchief when they disembarked in New York. "Oh, my God, Sophie is turning into a real beauty," she said as she took one large suitcase from Hannah.

They walked rapidly through the throng of people leaving the area—a sea of people rushing inland like the ocean waves that brought the weary travelers to shore. Sophie, afraid she would be swept up in the flood of humanity, held Hannah's hand tightly.

"Yes," Hannah said. "Who would have guessed Saul and I would have a gorgeous child? She was a hit everywhere I took her." She squeezed Sophie's hand tightly. "She'll have to go through withdrawal from all the attention she got while we were abroad." Hannah laughed. "I wonder if Saul could have lived longer, would we have had more beautiful children or if my Sophie is an anomaly."

"Hannah, we'll find you a new husband to make more beautiful babies with." Marie grasped Hannah's hand reassuringly as they entered the cab Marie hired for them to get home.

"Not yet, Marie, not yet. I don't want a husband yet." Hannah volunteered nothing about Heinrich and how he broke her heart. How could she ever marry a man she didn't love and desire? Who wasn't like Heinrich? She sat silently in the cab while Sophie jabbered in baby language to Marie.

Hannah, Sophie, and Marie returned to Hannah's apartment and to the life they had created for themselves before Hannah's trip to Germany. Hannah worked all day sewing, hemming, and designing for her clients. Marie spent her days at the hospital and her evenings with Hannah and Sophie. After eating the dinner she prepared, Hannah returned to her sewing, and Marie taught Sophie how to speak English again.

One evening after a full day of nursing, Marie came over for dinner and found Hannah nervously pacing the room. Hannah turned to Sophie and said, "Please go to your room and play with your dolls for a few minutes. I need to talk to your Aunt Marie alone."

Sophie obediently picked up her favorite dolls and took them to the bedroom.

"I'll call you to the table in a few minutes." Hannah closed Sophie's bedroom door behind her.

Returning to the living room, Hannah began. "Marie, I have some...news. Please do not judge me. I don't know if it is good or bad news. I need your help to sort through options."

"Oh. Well, what is this news?" Marie asked as she settled into the overstuffed living room sofa.

"I had an affair with a man in Germany." Hannah twisted the potholder she held in her hand. "I had no idea that sex could be so pleasurable." She took a deep breath. "You would be shocked to know what we did. Things I never did with Saul." Her face flushed as she whispered so Sophie couldn't hear them.

"This is good, isn't it?" Marie commented as she pulled a half finished, bright pink sweater for Sophie out of her knitting bag.

"I am pregnant," Hannah said, whispering in an even softer voice.

Marie was silent as she gathered her thoughts. She continued knitting for a few more seconds and answered, "How could this possibly be good news?" Her normally pale complexion reddened with emotion. "Hannah, you're a widow. People here know you went abroad. You surely didn't come back with a husband. My God, Hannah, think of the shame it will cause for you and your children, if you keep the new baby without a husband."

Surprised to hear such negative judgment from her friend, Hannah continued, "I could say I got married. That my husband will be here soon. Later, I can tell them he died."

Marie, who remained calm during life-threatening emergencies, stammered, "Do you really think people will believe

41

you? These women are all such gossips. Who, then, is this man? Would he really come here and marry you? Is he Jewish?"

"No, he isn't Jewish," Hannah said. "He doesn't know for sure that I am." She paused, trying to remember if she had told Heinrich she was Jewish or not. "I'm sure once I tell him about the baby, he'll marry me and move here." Hannah's palms were sweating. She knew her chances of getting Heinrich to change his mind were slim.

"Oh, Hannah, you're so unrealistic." Marie dropped her knitting on the coffee table. "If he doesn't marry you, you need to be prepared for the scorn you'll get. Your customers will stop coming to a house where a woman who had a baby out of wedlock lives. How will you survive?"

Hannah's eyes shined brightly with tears. "It'll be okay. If he doesn't marry me, I'll tell people he did marry me. Maybe he died in some horrific way. I want this child. I know Sophie will love having a new brother or sister..."

Chapter Fifteen

Neither Hannah nor Marie talked about Hannah's pregnancy in front of Sophie. They tried hard to return to normal life. Marie worked the afternoon shift at the local hospital. Hannah tailored women's clothes and designed fashionable hats during the day. As long as she stayed busy, Hannah didn't think about all the ways her plan could go wrong. As her due date grew closer, she began to doubt her plan. She decided to write Heinrich and tell him about the baby.

When Hannah told Marie about the letter she planned to write Heinrich, Marie cautioned, "Hannah, I think this is news you give in person, not in a letter. Wait until you see him in person." Marie fiddled with the hem of her dress. "Maybe, well, maybe he'll see how much he misses you. Maybe he'll be happy about a child." She stopped and took a deep breath, thinking about the options. "Leave Sophie here. She'll be fine. I can live in your apartment while you are gone. It's easier. All her things are here. You know I love her as if she were my own."

Hannah couldn't believe Marie was willing to help her with her plan to tell Heinrich. She quickly agreed to leave Sophie with her. She wrote Heinrich telling him that she was coming for a short visit without her child, so she could spend time with him. She told her parents she was coming to see her mother, who was losing her memory, and her father, who was having chest pains. She knew her parents would be disappointed that she left Sophie at home, so she manufactured an excuse that their grandchild had a cold and couldn't travel.

Hannah took only loose-fitting dresses and large shawls to cover her body. She didn't want anyone to notice the growing bump in her stomach. She let out seams on other dresses to cover her bulging disgrace. No one noticed, and if they did, they didn't mention it. Once she was home, Hannah spent the first few days visiting with her parents and having discreet discussions with her sisters about options for what to do with their parents, who were both in ill health.

After several days with her parents, Hannah worked up the nerve to contact Heinrich and tell him she was in town. They agreed to meet at their favorite coffee house near the inner city.

While waiting for Heinrich to arrive, Hannah sat at a table near the back of the restaurant and shredded several napkins and coasters, littering the table with pieces of paper. She had no idea how he would react to her news. He had very strong negative opinions about Jews, and she believed he knew she was Jewish. Would knowing it was his child make any difference in how he saw the situation?

She wore her finest outfit, shades of purples, blues, and red. She took an hour to do her hair and makeup. At home, she never found time to put on makeup or fix her hair in a fancy hairdo. She glowed from the pregnancy. She looked even younger than when she met Heinrich less than a year ago.

He arrived at the coffee house a few minutes late. He kissed her on both cheeks, hugging her tightly. "You left so unexpectedly last time. You never said good-bye," he scolded her. "I missed you, especially your body. You know you drive me crazy." He whispered, "I could take you right now if we weren't in public."

"Not now, Heinrich," she replied, laughing, trying to sound light. "Let's catch up with each other first. Tell me what you have been doing."

"I'm a soldier with the Nazis now." He proudly showed her his membership card. "I gave up being a lawyer, for now. My job is to enforce the new rules we have about Jews, Catholics, and those filthy homosexuals." He lit a cigarette and blew smoke away from the table. "We'll have a prosperous Germany again soon, once we rid our country of these people who've caused so many of our problems. But I worry for you. You avoided discussing your religion and let me believe that your family converted years ago. I don't know if you are Jewish or not, and I want to leave it that way." He searched her face for any reaction. A twitch of the eye, a small grimace? "Even so, the new rules can be very strict for how many generations back a family was Jewish. Be careful while you are here."

A moment passed before Hannah began. "Heinrich, I want you to come back to America with me." She sipped some of her water. "Don't stay here. There's too much instability and negativity here." She watched for a reaction and saw none, yet. "Life is better in America. You can be who you want to be and do what you want. They don't care if Jews marry Gentiles. You can be a lawyer there. Make money. Be with me."

He buttered his piece of roll and took a sip of coffee before he answered. "Married? Married? Did I not make myself clear the last time we saw each other? My family has standards. Certain criteria for whom I marry, for my children. I cannot hurt them by marrying a possible Jewess who has another man's child." He gripped the edge of the table. "In fact, Hannah, marrying you is impossible."

Hannah's eyes were wide and moist with tears. He continued, "I married my old girlfriend after you left. Her father is one of Hitler's top lieutenants. It made sense to marry her. I want to stay here and enable Germany to be the best country in the world, back where we belong."

Hannah tried to breathe, but she couldn't. Her throat constricted. Her eyes filled with tears. She gazed into Heinrich's sea-blue eyes and saw only anger. "Heinrich, I am with child, your child. That's why I came back. To tell you and give you a chance to be a father."

"My child? Mine? How could that be? I thought you were always careful. It's impossible to have a child with you. Get rid of it." He waved his hand as if swatting away a fly.

"What am I supposed to do?" Hannah tried to stifle her sobs as she spoke. "I can't go back to America with a child and say my husband died. My first husband died before Sophie was born. No one would believe me. Do you want me to get an illegal abortion? Kill our child? There is a human being inside of me. It is part yours. You really want me to get rid of it?" Tears fell down her cheeks like floodwaters off a mountain.

"I want nothing to do with this child. I don't want it." His face was red with rage, his fists clenched, and his knuckles white.

"All right," Hannah said. She thought about this new baby and what Marie had said. She couldn't come back from Europe with a baby and have a credible story for the people she knew in New Jersey. She understood now that what she thought was love was just sex for Heinrich. She blamed her newfound sexuality and sensuality for creating this horrible dilemma. She would never allow this to happen again. "So, what do you suggest I do?" she asked quietly. "I don't want to kill the baby."

"Have the damn baby. I don't want it. You did this purposely to make me marry you." His gaze was hostile, violent. "Put it up for adoption. If the child is a boy with blonde hair and blue eyes like me, there are agencies that will find a good Christian home for him." Sneering at her with teeth bared, he lost his good looks. "You won't know where he goes. I'll get you a phone number. This is all I'll do for you. If it is a girl, I suggest you kill her." He dropped a few coins on the table, rose, and left.

As Heinrich stomped down the street, he thought. *Why can Hannah get pregnant, and my wife can't?*

What now? Hannah thought. She sat at the table, evaluating her options.

Chapter Sixteen

1924

Hannah struggled with the decision of whether or not to tell her parents about her dire situation. Her father and mother were ill and could possibly die in the next year. She decided against telling them. Why cause them more heartache? Didn't they have enough to deal with?

She told her parents she was returning to America, but wrote Marie to let her know that it would be another few months before she came home. As much as Hannah regretted being away from Sophie, she knew she had to stay in Germany, not with her parents, to have the baby.

The next day, she boarded a train to one of the mountain spas she had visited less than a year ago. There was a small rural hospital nearby where she could have the baby. And a doctor who didn't know her or her family.

She decided to take Heinrich's advice and called the number he gave her. The soft-spoken woman who answered the phone gave her detailed instructions for what to do when the baby was born. Very clear instructions about what to do if the baby was a boy or a girl. Hannah prayed it was a boy. She could not imagine having an abortion or killing the baby. Anyway, it was long past the time needed to have an abortion. She had waited too long.

Hannah spent her days at the spa walking the grounds or sitting alone reading. She chose not to talk with anyone unless it was absolutely necessary. What would she say? "I am here to have and give away a baby"?

Hannah went into labor on a snowy day as cold as her heart felt. Hannah was heavily sedated for the birth, just as she had requested when she completed the paperwork a month earlier. She was groggy when she heard the doctor say, "It's a boy."

"Please tell me what he looks like," Hannah asked the nurse as the woman cleaned the infant.

"Madam, the boy looks nothing like you. His father must be blonde and blue eyed. Hitler would approve of this child," the nurse said as she handed the neatly wrapped baby to Hannah.

After her one and only look at the baby, Hannah said, crying, "I won't be keeping him. Please take him back to the nursery." She wiped her nose with a tissue. "People will come and pick him up. I have signed all the papers. Please call the number listed on my chart, describe the baby to them, and reassure them there is no way this child could be thought of as Jewish."

Hannah made sure she left the hospital before the people from the agency arrived to take the boy to a family that desperately wanted a child. Her son's new family were approved Aryans who supported Hitler. Her boy would be raised as a good Christian, loyal to Hitler. *What irony*, she thought.

Chapter Seventeen

Once Hannah accepted the fact that Heinrich would never marry her and that their baby was safely in the hands of a loving family, she booked passage on the next ship leaving for America. She didn't have to wait long as a ship was leaving two days later. Hannah maintained her composure until she was in her small, stuffy cabin. Then, with no one to watch her, she broke down, sobbing and wailing. She put her face into the soft down pillow and screamed until she fell into a stupor and slept.

She rarely left her cabin except for practice lifeboat drills. All of her meals were delivered to her room. She wanted to die. She thought that if she stood at the railing on the side of the ship, she would jump into the ocean and disappear.

Sophie was what kept her alive. Sophie needed her. She would devote her life to Sophie. *There will be no more men in my life. Sophie will be my only child*, she thought. *This is my punishment for what I have done.*

Chapter Eighteen

1925

One cold, winter evening, a year after Hannah had the baby boy, she announced, "Marie, I'm moving to Florida." They had just finished dinner and were resting before clearing the table.

"Florida? Why?" Marie slammed her fork on the plate startling Hannah and herself.

"I can't stay here. I only came here because of my marriage to Saul. He isn't here anymore. There are too many reminders of things I want to forget. Anyway, I have family there."

"You never mentioned family in Florida before." Marie pushed herself away from the table. "Hannah, how could you withhold such information from me? Why have they been a secret?"

"It's not like I am close to them. I have two brothers who I haven't spoken to in years. When our grandparents died, there was a dispute over family money. My hateful brothers kept it all to themselves." Hannah scowled. "You see, I was supposed to get part of it.

Tears filled Hannah's eyes and she continued, "Because my brothers knew our father would give money to my husband one day, a dowry like he did with my sisters, my brothers thought I shouldn't get any of the inheritance. My parents thought I'd get married and get the money then." She laughed a hollow laugh and continued. "Instead, my brothers took the money and moved to Florida, for some obscure reason. They left Germany several years before I did."

Hannah took a deep breath and said, "My brother, George, divorced several years ago. His former wife, Molly, lives in a place called West Palm Beach." Hannah watched Marie's face and saw growing sadness in her friend's eyes. "We've been in touch since she got divorced. She wants me to come live near her and her children. She has two sisters that live nearby. They have husbands. This way, Sophie can grow up with father figures in her life, with family, if I move there."

"Hannah, I am speechless. How can you leave me here? What will I do without you and Sophie? You are my family." Marie's voice cracked.

"Marie, I love you like a sister, but I can't stay here." Hannah held Marie's hands in hers. "Other than you, I don't have any friends, just clients. Saul's friends in Newark haven't made much of an effort to see Sophie or me." She huffed. "It's warmer in Florida, and there are no big cities. I think it'll be better for Sophie than living here. Saul's money will last longer there than if we stayed here. Come with us to Florida."

"Hannah, I can't. No, I don't want to move. I've lived in this area all of my life. My work is here. All my patients and doctors I work with are here. Florida is a hot, uncivilized swamp. Why would any sane person want to live there?" Marie stood and put the dirty dishes in the sink.

"I'm so sorry you won't go with us. I'll miss you so much. I have to think of Sophie. She needs to know she has other family. You and I'll still see each other. We will come here, and you can visit us."

"I know, Hannah. I know." Marie, overwhelmed with feelings of grief and rejection, hugged Hannah and went to her own apartment.

Chapter Nineteen

1926

Hannah moved quickly once she decided to leave New Jersey. For the first few months after the move to Florida, Hannah and Sophie lived with Molly and her three children. The three-bedroom house was too small for two women and four children.

Hannah, after careful analysis of her financial situation, decided she could afford a small house of her own. With part of the money from Saul's estate, Hannah put a down payment on a two-bedroom and one-bath white stucco house on Flamingo Drive in West Palm Beach, Florida. The houses in the neighborhood had been built twenty years before and were strong enough to withstand the periodic hurricanes that hit Florida.

The Flamingo Drive house had a lemon tree in the front yard and a grapefruit and mango tree in the backyard. There was a patch of sun by the backyard fence for roses, flowers Hannah had always wanted to grow. The Atlantic Ocean and beaches were thirty minutes away by bus, across a sturdy concrete bridge that separated West Palm Beach and Palm Beach. Molly lived two blocks away from Hannah and Sophie. A very distant cousin lived in Boynton Beach, forty miles down the coast.

Between 1926 and 1929, Hannah and Sophie visited Germany several times. Hannah enjoyed being able to see her mother, father, and sisters as often as possible, so she continued working to fund her travels.

Hannah continued as a seamstress, but she had to adjust how she used her other talents. There was very little need for knitted or crocheted woolen items in South Florida, so she converted her skills to more practical items. She crocheted fine table linens and dollies and knitted baby blankets and clothes from lighter-weight yarns. Just as she did in New Jersey, she developed a loyal group of clients and was able to save money to fund her frequent trips back home to Germany.

Because Hannah and Molly worked from home, the women took turns baby-sitting and managing the four children who were close in age. By sharing childcare duties between them, the women saved money, which was a high priority for Molly and Hannah.

Even when Molly's children went to public school, Hannah continued to educate Sophie herself. Because Sophie spent almost as much time in Germany as she did in the United States, Hannah taught Sophie how to read and write in both German and English. This practice made sense until 1929 when the economy went bad. Hannah's income had dropped when women couldn't afford her services, so Hannah enrolled Sophie, age seven, in the local elementary school.

Sophie had a tough first day at school. Even though Molly tried to convince Hannah that school children dressed casually in Florida, Hannah made Sophie wear a lightweight wool skirt with knee-high white socks, black patent shoes, and a crisply ironed white shirt. The other children wore flimsy cotton summer dresses and sandals. They stared at Sophie, and she stared back. She was as strange to them as they were to her.

At lunch and recess, no one sat with her. Her cousins weren't at the same school. They were younger than Sophie. Although Marie and Sophie's cousins had spoken English with Sophie, Hannah had taught Sophie to read mostly in German, the same way Hannah had learned to read. Sophie also had a slight trace of a German accent from spending so much time in Germany and with the Jewish women in New Jersey who spoke Yiddish. English words still confused her. Words that were pronounced the same but spelled differently, like "fare" and "fair" or "for" and "four," didn't make sense to her. The children at school made fun of her when she used the wrong words. She cursed at them in German under her breath. "*Arschlochs,*" she whispered. "Assholes."

It isn't right, Hannah thought when Sophie complained to her about school. Sophie was more advanced than other children in her class. She had experiences other children her age didn't. She'd traveled back and forth to Europe three times, made friends with ship captains and waiters of all nationalities, and met travelers from all over the world. In addition to German, she knew a little Italian and Spanish.

Sophie had also been exposed to more information than the average child, having traveled with her mother, her aunts, and her cousins. Hannah's sisters would take turns teaching their nieces and nephews. They visited museums and attended concerts, as well as practiced arithmetic and mathematics. They read and learned German grammar. Sophie was the youngest of the group, but she caught on faster than most of her German cousins.

"Mama, I won't go back to school again," Sophie said in German at the end of the first day. "I don't completely understand what the teachers are saying. It's so unfair how the other kids make fun of me."

"Yes, Sophie, you'll go back. I'll talk with the principal to see what we can do. I'll fix it," Hannah reassured her daughter.

Hannah knew Sophie's mathematic and logic skills were more developed than the average seven-year-old's. She was an excellent reader in German. Her retention and understanding of what she heard were exceptional.

The South Florida school system just wasn't designed for a child like Sophie. Hannah had a long talk with the school principal. He agreed to have Sophie tested by one of the few educational specialists in the public school system. After the test results came back, the school and Hannah reached an agreement about Sophie's education. The school would give Sophie a chance to learn the first and second grade material, and, if in six months all went well, she would be put in third grade.

It wasn't just Sophie who had to catch up. Hannah also needed to increase her knowledge in English, rather than German. The agreed upon learning process worked out well for Hannah and

Sophie. They spent time every day learning the material the school had assigned Sophie. By the end of the trial period, Sophie passed all her tests and was assigned to a third grade class.

Hannah, if nothing else, was a perfectionist and quite proud of her daughter's intelligence. She told one client, "Yes, my Sophie is only seven years old. And may be able to skip a grade or two."

"I am so proud of my little girl. The school says they have never seen a child like Sophie before. Such intelligence and brilliance," she told another.

In addition to her intellectual gifts, Sophie was beautiful—with long thin legs, beautiful black curly hair, puffy pink lips, and large black eyes. Hannah believed Saul would be very proud of his daughter. She thought, and then hesitated. Did she really know much about Saul when she married him? They were together maybe six months. She had no idea what he would like. It was pure conjecture.

***

When Sophie started school, Hannah wondered what her little boy in Germany was doing. Marie had convinced her it was best if they never spoke of the boy again. It broke Hannah's heart to be unable to tell anyone about him. Hannah had instructed the adoption agency that she didn't want to know where the baby went. She never wanted there to be any record of her giving birth to him.

What does he look like now? I wonder what he is doing today. No, I am not supposed to think about him. She had thoughts of him each year on his birthday. Her heart broke and she was filled with shame each time she thought of him.

"This is too, too hard. I gave him away. I don't deserve to raise him," she said to herself.

She devised a plan to forget the boy. When she was awake and his face appeared in her mind, she made herself think of something awful, to shift her thoughts to something else. She put a thick rubber band on her arm and snapped it hard against her inner wrist. By day, she built a brick wall around her heart to eradicate thoughts about the small boy she gave away. Most days, she was successful in eliminating him from her mind and heart, except on his birthday, when she baked an imaginary cake for him, and at Christmas, when she knitted a red scarf for him that she donated to the Salvation Army.

"I'm sorry, Saul," she said quietly to no one, "that I couldn't have given you a son. A son to turn the business over to when you got older." She sat in the dark in her bedroom, not wanting Sophie to see her like this. "I know that is every Jewish mother's responsibility: produce a male heir. A boy who grows up and gives her grandchildren. Takes care of her in her old age." She rose from her bed and paced by the window. Still talking to herself, she said, "Sophie is a wonderful child, but she isn't a boy. That small act of fate, a girl or boy, has long-lasting consequences in a family. Boys could be rabbis, scholars, doctors, and men of business." With strong feelings of anger and resentment on her face, she said out loud, "And girls could be wives, mothers, teachers, or cooks."

One day, as Hannah made soup for dinner, she thought of her son. A tear escaped her eye.

"Mother, why are you crying?" asked Sophie from where she sat at the kitchen table, doing her homework.

"Nothing, dear. I am just chopping onions for dinner tonight." Hannah brushed the tears from her eye. She thought about telling Sophie one day about her half-brother. Not now. Not yet. It can wait. "Let's have dinner on the porch. It's a lovely evening tonight, not too hot."

Chapter Twenty

Once she was in the right grade for her abilities, Sophie blossomed. She loved to read and draw. Hannah's house was filled with sketches that Sophie produced. Pictures of boats, palm trees, the beach, and her grandparents' house in Germany. With the correct education and support, Sophie moved rapidly from being in the first grade to the third grade.

"Mother, I am now in the third grade. I speak English just as well as the other children do. It'll be much easier to make friends now," Sophie announced one afternoon as she sat at the small table in the brightly lit kitchen.

Hannah knew that she'd made the right decision in pushing the school to allow Sophie to skip grades. "Sophie, I want you to understand how important it is to be the best at everything you do. Not just in school." She turned Sophie to face her. "Your being the best in everything makes you stand out from the other children. You'll meet the right people. And one day, you'll find the right husband."

"Mother, why are you telling me this?" Sophie rolled her eyes at her mother. "I don't understand what a husband has to do with me. I am just a child," she said, confusion and defiance creeping into her voice.

"Because," Hannah said, gritting her teeth, shocked at Sophie's tone. "It's never too early to start being aware of your reputation and how it can be ruined when you are young. Whom you are seen with can make a big impression on people."

"Okay," Sophie said. "I just want friends. People who I can play with. Please let me pick my friends. I promise I will be careful."

By the end of third grade, she had a group of friends who played together at school, ate lunch together every day, and spent the night at each other's houses on the weekend. Sophie spent most of her time with her friends, Julie, Susan, and Ella.

"Sophie, how do you manage to get new clothes for every party?" Ella asked one Saturday afternoon when the girls were at Sophie's house. "Each one is entirely different from the last."

"My mother thinks I should look good every day. She makes me new clothes almost every week. I don't care about the clothes, but she won't listen to me," Sophie responded, the sound of superiority in her voice.

"I should be so lucky. I hardly ever get new dresses. I have two older sisters. All I get are hand-me-downs," Julie sighed.

The girls lived within walking distance of each other's houses. Most mornings, the neighbors watched the four girls holding hands, strolling down the street to school. Sophie was the youngest of the four friends, but none of the other girls cared about her age.

After school, the girls went to each other's houses. They organized plays and dressed and undressed their dolls. Even though Hannah did not want Sophie to play with the neighborhood boys, Sophie and her friends played Kick the Can with them and rode their bicycles until all the children were called home for dinner.

One night at the dinner table, Hannah said, "Sophie, what were you girls doing today with those horrible boys from the corner house? I distinctly told you not to play with them. Do you not remember?" She paused to see if Sophie grasped the importance of what she said.

"Mother, they're not horrible people. They're nice and fun to play with. We don't do anything bad," Sophie explained.

"Well, I don't like it. You are a girl, not a boy. You are limited to once a week for this," Hannah said very firmly, letting Sophie know this was a serious violation of Hannah's rules.

"Another thing, young lady, you need to find some Jewish girlfriends. You can't trust these Christian girls. I've told you the stories I have heard from my family in Germany," Hannah lectured as they sat at the dinner table. "The Christian children will turn on you to save themselves. Now, eat and finish your homework." Hannah said

Sophie felt like crying so she excused herself and went to her bedroom—a room that her mother had decorated. Sophie had wanted a splash of red in the room, maybe the curtains. She also wanted her dolls displayed a special way in the white and glass credenza. Her mother had other ideas. The room would be primarily white with a few details in pink and green. Sophie wasn't allowed to play with the "good" dolls she received as birthday presents. They were for show and might "be worth something one day." They stayed in the boxes on the shelf. *Look, don't touch.*

Chapter Twenty-One

1930

Hannah grew to like Florida's slower pace of living more than New Jersey's high-pressure one. In Florida, traffic was nonexistent. You could clearly see the soft blue sky with white cotton-looking clouds in all directions. Brightly colored flowers and rich green plants dotted the landscape. Palm trees, with their long fronds and green coconuts high in the trees, swayed in the gentle breeze. After years of living in cold climates, Hannah enjoyed the heat.

Hannah also enjoyed being part of a small community. She liked living near her former sister-in-law and her family. Along with other Jews in the area, Hannah helped start a new temple. She enrolled Sophie in its education program where Sophie met and socialized with people her age.

In West Palm Beach, no one seemed to care that Hannah didn't have a husband and that Sophie didn't have a father. There were several other widows in the congregation, so Hannah being one didn't matter.

The only downside to the move to Florida was that Hannah missed Marie. Although Hannah made friends easily, she found no one to take Marie's place as a best friend.

Hannah wrote Marie at least once a week telling her about Hannah's various activities and Sophie's rich social life. In one weekly letter to Marie, she wrote:

Dear Marie,

I miss you. We wish you'd come visit us soon. Sophie has become quite the attractive young lady. You wouldn't recognize her. I worry about you. In your last letter, you told me you had a slight heart attack. There is no such thing as a slight heart attack. More the reason to come see us. We won't be able to get away until July because of Sophie's school and my work. I have so many clients. You wouldn't believe it. Sophie is involved in multiple activities outside of school, which makes leaving now impossible. Please take some time off and come visit. I beg you.

Love,
Hannah

Chapter Twenty-Two

Two days after Hannah mailed the letter to Marie, she received a telegram from her sister, Agnes, asking Hannah and Sophie to come home to Germany. Hannah's parents were not doing well physically and emotionally. Agnes knew Hannah would never forgive her if either of their parents died before Hannah could get home to see them.

Hannah tried to book the same ship for all of their trans-Atlantic trips. She found there were perks for having the captain and the staff know her and her child: sitting at the captain's table, getting extra towels every day, and securing prime time dinner reservations. Luckily, they were able to book passage on their favorite ship for this unexpected trip home to deal with Hannah's parents.

"Good morning, Mrs. Straus," the captain said as he greeted Hannah and Sophie when they boarded the ship. "My goodness, this couldn't be little Sophie. She has turned into such a beauty. How are you doing, Sophie?"

"Captain Harvey, I'm doing great." Sophie curtsied. "I am in the third grade now. We bought a new house. We have lemon trees in the yard. We make fresh lemonade every day." She spun around to show the captain her new outfit. She wore a blue sailor's coat and matching hat that Hannah had made.

"Mrs. Straus," the captain said to Hannah. "This is not your usual time of year to go abroad. I hope there are no problems."

"Thank you for asking," Hannah said, pleased that the captain remembered when Hannah and Sophie usually went back to Germany. "My parents are ill, and we are going home to be with them."

"Well," he said. "I hope they are better by the time you get there." He smiled at Hannah and turned to greet the next person in line as they came on the ship.

***

Whenever they took a trip to Germany, Hannah made sure that Sophie had a new sailor's coat and hat. The ship's photographer always took a formal picture of Sophie standing behind the tire-sized lifesaver with the ship's name stenciled on it.

It never failed that other passengers marveled at Sophie's clothes. "You really made that cute outfit? How marvelous. I would love something like that for my three children," a woman said as she watched Sophie pose for her picture.

Hannah smiled. "Yes, I made them. I also make outfits by special order. Let me know if you want me to make something for your children before we leave the ship. I can make whatever it is you want when I get back home to Florida."

News traveled around the ship that Hannah was an excellent seamstress. If the ship's official seamstresses were too busy to handle all the work, Hannah was given the opportunity to pick up some extra work and money.

***

Seven days after Hannah received the letter from her sister, she and Sophie were in Germany. Hannah was frightened about how ill she would find her parents. Once off the ship and in her parents' house, she got her answer. Her father had lost at least forty pounds and most of his hair since she last saw him. When he stood to walk on his own, which he rarely did, he shuffled slowly across the floor, holding on to the backs of furniture for balance. He mumbled, cried, and moaned as he sat in his favorite chair in the library, in the dark.

Hannah's mother showed signs of aging and dementia. She didn't recognize anyone anymore. She called her daughters by her sisters' names and cried out for her own mother to comfort her. Normally a compliant woman, Hannah's mother had turned mean and belligerent, even screaming at Sophie and threatening to hit her.

"Mother, why is Grandmother acting this way?" Sophie asked with tears in her eyes after Mrs. Horowitz screamed at her. "I didn't do anything wrong."

"It's not your fault," Hannah tried to explain. "This happens to some people when they get old."

"I don't like her. I don't want to be here. And Grandfather smells bad and looks like he's going to die very soon," Sophie added.

"I know. But, that's why we came. To be here before they die. To help out, if we can. Please try and be patient with them," Hannah explained. "Go outside for a walk. That might make you feel better. I need to talk with your aunts."

Sophie readily followed her mother's advice, grabbed her coat and hat, and went outside to the small garden. She took a book with her to read so she could stay away from the death and dying inside the house.

As soon as Sophie left the room, Agnes turned to Hannah and said, "See, I told you how bad he looks. I fear he is dying,".

"I agree. The doctor said he thinks Papa doesn't want to live because Mama doesn't recognize or remember him," Hannah confided.

"Maybe so. He's also devastated because he doesn't hear from his sons. He didn't know if they were dead or alive," Agnes added.

Two of Hannah's brothers had fled to America years ago. Neither of the brothers wrote their parents regularly nor did the men keep up with their sisters. They'd left Germany after a radical, prejudiced politician, Adolph Hitler, began taking over the country and preaching anti-Semitism. The Jewish community was concerned about what would happen if Hitler became more powerful, and some of the young men left to start over in other places like America.

Hannah planned to stay for two or three weeks with her family, depending on how her father felt and what arrangements the sisters could make for her mother. On a Sunday night, one week into the visit, Hannah and Sophie went in to his bedroom to tell him good night. Immediately, Hannah knew that something was wrong. "Sophie," she said softly, so not to scare her. "I think Grandpapa is sleeping. Go tell Aunt Agnes I need to see her, and you go on to bed."

"But I didn't kiss him good night," Sophie whined.

"It's okay. You can kiss him twice tomorrow night," Hannah replied impatiently. "Now hurry and tell Aunt Agnes to come here."

When Agnes entered the room, she saw Hannah holding their father's hand and crying. "He's gone. He's gone," she cried. "We no longer have a father, and our mother is as good as dead."

***

The rest of Hannah and Sophie's time in Germany was taken up with the funeral, *sitting Shiva*, and deciding what to do with their mother. Sarah volunteered to take her mother and let her live with Sarah, her husband, and children. No one was happy with the situation, but there were no other options. They decided to not tell their mother that she was moving until the day before the move. Mrs. Horowitz rarely understood what was happening around her, and her daughters thought there was no point in upsetting their mother sooner than necessary.

The evening before the move, after everyone had gone to bed, Hannah couldn't sleep. She quietly left the bedroom she was sharing with Sophie and snuck into her mother's room to see if she was sleeping. A soft light emitted from the window allowing Hannah to see her mother's face. *How peaceful she looks*, Hannah thought. Her mother's face appeared less wrinkled and her brow less troubled. *I'd like to remember her this way.*

Hannah walked closer to the bed, planning to kiss her mother gently on the cheek. As she leaned over, Hannah noticed her mother wasn't breathing.

"Mother," Hannah said. "Wake up." She shook her and repeated, "Mother, wake up."

Hannah knew her mother wasn't sleeping but was dead. She woke Agnes and Sarah who were sleeping in the guest room and told them, "Mother has passed away. It is probably for the best. I think she knew Father had died, and we are making her leave her home where she's lived for forty years."

"I think you are right," Sarah added. "She didn't want to come live with me any more than I wanted her to. I think it is best she died this way. She had no real life anymore."

"I agree. It's still sad. We are now parentless," Agnes said and began to cry.

The sisters never went back to sleep. They had another body to make ready, another funeral to plan, and decisions to be made about their parents' house and belongings.

Once the second funeral was over, and it was time for Hannah and Sophie to go back to America, the sisters decided to sell the house and to divide the proceeds from its sale and their parents' belongings among themselves. They felt their brothers didn't deserve anything from their parents' estate, as the men had been so thoughtless, rarely getting in touch with their parents after the men had moved.

The sisters had a second reason to not include their brothers in the proceeds from their parents' estate. Each one of them needed the money. Hannah didn't have a husband and was raising a child on her own. Her sisters' husbands were having financial troubles due to the adverse political climate. Either Jewish owned shops were attacked or closed, or non-Jewish customers refused to enter. Why try and locate the brothers when the sisters had done all the work after their parents' deaths, and the sisters really needed the money?

Hannah and Sophie returned to America richer than when they left and with beautiful items from the Horowitz home. Hannah sold as much of what she inherited as she could, not wanting to pay for shipping items to America. She kept several bracelets, a ring, a cameo, a set of fine china, and the family's sterling silver flatware. Little did she know that had her parents lived, all her parents' belongings would be lost to the Nazis when they took over Germany.

Chapter Twenty-Three

Hannah and Sophie returned to Florida as soon as they could after Hannah's parents' estate was settled. One morning, as Hannah made Sophie's breakfast and before Marie responded to Hannah's last letter, Hannah received a phone call.

"Mrs. Straus?" the man asked.

"Yes, this is Hannah Straus," Hannah answered, her voice quivering. People only called you at this hour in the morning when something was wrong. *Who is in trouble? What could be wrong?* She thought as the seconds ticked by.

"My name is Norman Hunter. I am a colleague of Marie Rider. I regret to inform you that she passed away last night while resting in the nurses' lounge. We found your name listed as next of kin," he hesitated as his stifled grief vibrated through the phone wires. "We all loved Marie and are saddened by her passing. Please let me know what we can do to help."

"Marie? Dead? No! That cannot be!" Hannah screamed into the receiver. "I just wrote her and told her to come here." She sobbed and tried to talk simultaneously. "What can I do? Where do I make arrangements? I will get there as soon as I can." She said as she sat down on a kitchen chair.

"My condolences. I know this is a difficult time. If you call the Sacred Garden Funeral Home, they can give you more information," he replied.

Hannah wrote down the contact information that Norman Hunter gave her. After talking to the funeral director, securing train tickets, and arranging for Sophie to have a place to stay, Hannah moved to the living room and lay down on the sofa. She remained in that position for most of the day, weeping. Before Sophie got home, she went to her room to sob into her pillow. She didn't want Sophie to see her like this—emotionally out of control and unable to stop crying.

Sophie got home from school and went into her mother's room to tell her about her day in school. Sophie saw the old brown suitcase, open on the floor. Clothes were flung on the bed, the floral-patterned high-back chair, and the dark mahogany nightstand. "Mother, what is it? Where are you going? Why are you packing? Why are you crying?" Sophie implored.

Attempting to maintain some sense of control, Hannah replied, "Your Aunt Marie died this morning." Her voice broke, and she wept. "I am going to take the train to New Jersey to take care of her things." Finally able to talk without crying, she added, "You'll stay with your cousins until I get back."

"I loved Aunt Marie. Can't I come, too?" Sophie asked.

"No, you have school. You can't miss it. You've already missed too much from when we went to Germany." Anyway, Hannah wanted to be alone on this trip. She wanted to be able to mourn openly and to not have to restrain herself for Sophie's sake.

"I've never been alone without you. I'm afraid." Sophie began to cry.

Hannah reached out and pulled Sophie close, something she rarely did. "Sophie, you will be all right. I promise. I'll be home as soon as I can. Now, don't argue." She let go of Sophie and added, "I don't have the energy to quarrel with you right now. For once, please just accept my decision."

The next day, Molly took Hannah to the train station while Sophie was at school. On the train, Hannah found her seat and pulled out a handkerchief. She had reserved a sleeper car for the trip so she could try and rest on the two-day trip to New Jersey. She barely slept and cried most of the way there and back. Even the loss of her father wasn't as painful as losing Marie.

Chapter Twenty-Four

1934

"Mama, I don't want to leave Germany. I don't want to go to America," Leopold argued as he sat on the tattered and faded red sofa in the small living room of their apartment over the butcher shop. Leopold, a tall, black-haired boy, had just turned seventeen.

"We've discussed this enough. The decision is made. Papa and I have the money and the papers. You will go!" Golda, her thinning white hair pulled back in a loose bun, insisted. She had been packing Leopold's suitcase and had folded the last garment, a white shirt. She placed it gently in his small valise.

"Mama, I'm worried about you." Leopold searched his mother's wrinkled face. "You only just started your leukemia treatments. You're so frail." He reached out to hold her hand. "What if you get worse and I am not here? Please let me stay. Maybe I can get my old job back. Earn enough money for you and Papa to come to America with me."

"Leo, my baby," Golda said, holding tightly onto Leopold's hand. "You know as well as I do that there is no work for you here, a Jewish boy. And you must promise me you'll go back to school when you get to America. You dropped out of school to work, but a ninth grade education is not enough. Our cousins will make sure you get more education. Then, you can earn money to bring us over," his mother answered slowly.

"Shouldn't we send my brother and sister who have children? Shouldn't the families with children go first?" Leo said.

Golda's face was hidden by the evening shadows. "Enough of this nonsense. Finding enough money for a family of three or four to go is impossible." She, too, had considered this originally, but circumstances dictated otherwise. "Our American cousins sent only enough for one person. You'll go, work hard, and send for us. You are strong, my love, and a hard worker. You are our best chance." She turned away, so Leopold couldn't see the tears running down her face. She pulled herself up from the sofa, pushed her thinning hair back into its bun, and went to the kitchen to finish preparing dinner.

Leo walked to the small room he shared with his three nephews. The room barely held his bed and a small wardrobe, and now a second mattress covered the rest of the floor. His sister Ester and her family had moved in with them six months ago, when Ester's husband had lost his job. The boys were playing in the living room. Leo could smoke in his bedroom without his older sister yelling, "Stop smoking. You'll make Simon's asthma worse."

A few minutes later, Otto, Leo's father, came home. He was the only one in the family still working. Otto had been a handsome man, dark eyes and hair like his son, Leopold's. In the last six months, he had become stoop-shouldered and his face more wrinkled. He went into the dining room that also served as the schoolroom and sewing room. Golda, who had moved the papers, pens, fabric, pins, and sewing machine to the large credenza, was setting the table with the only set of dishes, glasses, and silverware left that hadn't been sold to buy food for the family or Leo's ticket to America.

Otto hugged Golda, feeling the tears on her face. "Don't look so sad. It'll all work out. We are Germans, we have been Germans, and we will always be Germans. This Hitler thing will pass. We will all be reunited." He pulled her closer, feeling her bones through the threadbare woolen dress and heavy sweater she wore to ward off the chill.

Looking with dull, brown eyes at her husband of thirty-five years, she knew neither of them really believed what he said. "Oh, Otto, we are losing our baby. He's only seventeen. He doesn't speak English; he's never been out of Germany." Her tears fell freely now. She watched Otto hang his coat in the cramped closet and look around the bare, dark apartment. His eyes went to the empty places where silver candlesticks used to stand next to elegant lamps. Now, only torn, frayed table liners were visible. Otto released Golda and walked down the short, dark hall to his youngest son's room.

Otto knocked on Leo's door. He heard, "Come in," and opened the door and walked into the room.

"Leo, I want you to know that I don't really expect you to be able to save enough money to get all of us out of Germany. It is not your fault we are still here. We ignored the signs of what was to come." Otto took a cigarette from his pocket and lit it as he continued. "Even though we had seen people battered in the streets, store windows broken, and homes confiscated, we thought this would pass." His eyes brightened with unshed tears. He took a long breath, contemplating what he just said. "We have been in Germany as long as I can remember, so we stayed. We were wrong."

Leopold, who had not been close to his father, found this conversation uncomfortable. He had never heard his father say this many words at one time.

Otto continued. "You are young and strong, and you will carry on the family name in America. If you can just raise enough money for your sister and her family to leave, that would be more than enough. Your brother will try to get out any way he can. He doesn't want me to know what his plans are in case your mother and I are taken away and tortured." He patted his younger son on the shoulder. "Let's go to dinner now."

Tonight was the last night before Leo sailed to America. His older brother and his wife and child, and his older sister, her husband, and their three children gathered at the dinner table. Otto raised his glass and proposed a toast for Leo's safe travels and for Golda's improved health. "May we be together very soon. May we be healthy this next time we dine as a family."

After the Kiddush, Leo's mother and sister brought in bowls of vegetable soup, freshly baked challah bread, and a large platter of cheeses and served everyone. His mother barely touched the food. She split her bowl of soup among the three young boys, all under the age of eight.

"Thank you, Grandmother," they said in unison.

Golda fed the boys more soup and cheese than the adults. She knew the boys had to be very strong if they were going to survive. If they were taken to one of the concentration camps people were discussing, her grandsons had to have physical and mental strength. At least they were still allowed to go to school. For the last year, girls were forbidden to attend school.

After dinner, the family sat around the table, talking about the older days, the days before Hitler.

"Let us focus on the positive tonight," Otto said as he took off his glasses and wiped them clean with the white handkerchief he always kept in his back pants pocket.

"My favorite was ice cream," volunteered the youngest grandchild.

"Mine was playing soccer," said the oldest.

The conversation continued until it was time for the family members to go to sleep. None of the adults said it out loud, but they knew it might be the last night the family would be together.

***

The following morning, as the sky changed colors with the rising sun, Leo's mother made a breakfast of boiled eggs, leftover bread, and sausages for everyone, and extra food for Leo's trip. No one spoke. Silence was better than the sounds of weeping. Each person knew all it would take was for one person to start crying for the rest of the family to dissolve into tears.

Although he knew it was irrational, Leo still wanted his parents to tell him not to go, but they didn't.

Leo checked his suitcase and backpack to ensure he had all of the necessary documents and enough money, food, and clothes for a week. He hid more cash sewn into a coat seam and in a pocket in the backpack. A few small pieces of family silverware were wrapped in his clothes in the suitcase. This was all he had to live on until he got to New Jersey where he would stay with one cousin on his way to his final destination in Georgia. He hoped to find work in New Jersey to earn enough money for the final leg of his journey. To his Atlanta cousins who had paid to get him out of Germany.

He tied a sturdy brown rope around the suitcase and carried it to the front door where his overstuffed backpack waited. His eyes glistened with tears as he hugged each member of his family. His mother clung to him as he tried to pull away; finally letting go when her husband pulled her away from her baby.

As Leo walked down the cobblestone street, away from the only home he'd known, he turned and saw his parents in the window. He waved good-bye. He was seventeen. For such a young man who had never ventured twenty miles from home, this trip would be a test of his survival skills as he learned to negotiate a new land in a foreign tongue.

He didn't know if he would ever see his family again.

Chapter Twenty-Five

Leo's trip from Germany to New Jersey took longer than he had imagined. He had to stretch the money he brought. He booked passage on the least expensive part of the ship, several levels below deck. The room was a dark, large open space with bunk beds, cubbyholes, and little else. There were two dorms, compartments like this; one for the men and one for the women. The walls were dirty from age, with layers of old moisture and candle smoke. The smell of body sweat and urine filled the air.

Leo quickly learned to never leave his valuables in the dorm. Late at night, men roamed the large room, sneaking into cubbyholes to take other passengers' valuables. Leo kept everything he owned on him or with him.

He also knew not to speak up if he saw anyone stealing. When a fellow traveler asked, "Has anyone seen my black coat?" or "Who took my socks? Everything I own was in there," Leo clenched his hands and stood silently, just like the other men did.

"I'll give a reward for the return of my socks and my mother's blue broach. It's all I have to remember her by," one man begged, obviously crushed by the loss of the last connection he had to his family.

There was silence. No one offered to help. Each man was afraid he would be the next victim.

Leo just wanted to get off the ship as soon as possible. As much as he loved the new experience of being on the water and seeing birds, whales, dolphins, and fish he had never seen before, he yearned to be on land. At home in Germany, he was used to open spaces with mountains in the distance. Not cramped in a dark, smelly room filled with scared and anxious men.

He feared the group of young men who also booked passage in the large, unsupervised room. He knew what could happen when you put dozens of men together for a long period of time. Rumors fly. Fights start. People get hurt. He saw too much of this happening in Germany. He wanted no part of this on the ship to America.

In Germany, he witnessed men and boys called *Brownshirts* beat a man in the street just because he was Jewish. Leo saw shops and homes burned and destroyed, young girls raped. These images danced through his dreams at night and filled his daytime with anxiety. He hated the sight of it on the streets at home, but he didn't step in and fight.

He didn't intervene on the boat either. He was his parents' only hope to get out of Nazi Germany before the situation deteriorated even further. They had heard the stories of families torn apart and sent to various camps. Rumors about the very old and very young not making it to the camps; their bodies thrown into mass graves. Leo remained silent during most of the voyage and kept his head down. He wanted to survive.

Leo spent his days exploring the various levels on the giant ship. As he strolled from deck to deck, women quickly noticed him. Not just women from the below-deck dorm, but ladies from the upper-class cabins. He had a strong, chiseled chin, a nose that didn't betray his heritage, and piercing black eyes framed by long, dark lashes. His smile portrayed innocence and understanding, and his sincere interest showed on his face.

His mother and sister had taught him manners, which helped him avoid difficult situations. "Leo, please come sit with me," one of the first-class women asked when she saw him walking the deck.

"No, Ma'am. I can't. I am on my way to run an errand for my mother," he lied, just to get away from any temptation. He didn't want any shipboard rumors to diminish his chances for achieving his mission.

"I won't take up much of your time," voiced another young lady. "You are the most handsome man on board this dreadful ship."

"Maybe another time," Leo replied as he quickened his pace. He decided to avoid this part of the ship on his next walk.

Leo grew hungrier by the day. Even in Germany, he didn't get enough to eat and now he had even less money for food. He was thin by nature so day by day his face became more angular and emaciated. By the time he arrived at Ellis Island, Leo was so thin his hip bones protruded.

***

When his ship finally landed at Ellis Island, Leo was overcome by the sight of long lines of people waiting to be admitted into the United States. Never had he seen so many people in one place. He stood frozen, not knowing what to do next.

"Please show me your papers," an American passport official, whose job it was to help the bewildered immigrants find their way to the right check-in station, requested.

"Yes, sir," Leo said, trying to control the quiver in his voice, and handed the official a crumbled wad of paper.

"I do not speak much English," Leo said as he tried to understand what the man was telling him.

"You need to go to that line over there, the one marked 'German' please," the man said.

The official pointed to a line farther down the dock, where hundreds of people stood with their meager belongings, waiting to be given permission to enter America. He stood in a line that was marked "Speaks German Only".

"Your name, please," the man asked in German, eyeing Leo with indifference.

"Leopold Wolfgang Rosenstein," Leo said.

"Your name will be Leo Rosen here in America. It'll be easier for you. Do you have family here that will vouch for you?" The official asked. All new arrivals were asked this question. Immigrants had to have a family member or friend to vouch for them in America.

"Yes. Here in New Jersey short term, but eventually in a place called Atlanta, Georgia." He pulled a tattered letter from his pants pocket to show the man. "See, here is the letter they sent for me to come here. Is there a problem?" Leo said in German. His voice cracked; he was afraid. Maybe the people in America were just like the people in Germany. Maybe they would put him in a concentration camp here.

"No, go over to that other line and get your injections," the man answered, nodding his head towards an area where nurses in starched white dresses and stiff hats gave shots to people sitting in lines of metal, folding chairs. "We don't want you bringing in any diseases from that ship. Too many people are sick when they get on the boats. Then, they get off here in the USA and make everyone else sick."

After getting the required shots, Leo sighed in relief and carried his suitcase and backpack to another long line of people who were waiting for the ferry into New York. Once off the ferry, he stood in another line to take a bus to New Jersey. He had an address and a phone number for a distant cousin there.

"Excuse me. Can you drop me near here?" he said in broken English and showed the bus driver the address.

"Yes. I will tell you when to get off the bus." The driver nodded his head and pointed to a seat behind him. "Stay there 'til I tell you." The driver picked up enough of these German immigrants to understand a few words of German. He took pity on them and their situation and did what he could to help them.

Chapter Twenty-Six

By 10:00 P.M., Leo found himself in front of a tall, brick building. He located the correct name on the list of tenants and rang the bell. A short, bald man in plaid pajamas and a dark blue bathrobe came to the front door of the building.

"Leopold?" The man asked before he opened the doors.

"Yes," Leo replied. "I am Leopold."

"Oh, my God," the man exclaimed in German, and he opened the front door. "Come in. You look half dead," Alfred Waxman said. "We were expecting you two days ago and had almost given up hope." He pulled Leo into the brightly lit front hallway.

He took Leo's arm and led him to a first floor apartment. "Come in. Please come in. Sit down. I'll get you something to eat and drink. You look starved."

"Thank you," Leo said as he dropped his tattered belongings on the floor by the front door. "I do not want to make your home dirty." He looked around the front entryway and noticed the furniture, seemingly new and unscarred. "Where can I put this to avoid making a mess? I also should not sit on any of your beautiful furniture. I have not bathed in a long time, and I am filthy." He lowered his dark eyes with embarrassment.

"Just leave your bags on the floor." Alfred pushed Leo towards a straight back chair in the dining room. "Come sit on this chair. I will put a towel down for you to sit on."

As Mr. Waxman placed a brown towel on Leo's chair, he yelled to his wife, "Bianca, wake up! He is here. We need food and coffee."

For the first time in years, Leo felt he could let down his guard. He was in a place that was safe, and there was food and drink. Plates of cheese and cured meat. Freshly baked bread and real butter. Red wine. A wave of pent-up emotion overwhelmed him, and he began to weep. Sobs of fear, pain, anger, and loss filled the room. He tried to hide his tears from his hosts, but it was impossible. He laid his head on his arms and wept, unashamed, for ten minutes before he could drink or eat. He had reached the first milepost of his journey.

"So, they shortened your name to Leo Rosen?" Alfred quizzed him as Bianca, Alfred's wife, poured hot coffee into Leo's cup. "They do that, you know. At Ellis Island now. Change people's names. There are probably hundreds of men with shortened names like 'Leo' or 'Willie' in America that came through Customs." He faked a laugh. "Ha, they think they are doing you a favor, but who knows? They may be right," his host continued, speaking in German still for Leo's sake. "When you are through eating, there is a bathroom at the end of the hall with clean towels in the closet. Your clothes are too dirty to salvage. I can lend you a few things until we can take you shopping tomorrow, if you are up for it."

"Please, don't take the clothes yet. I must get some things out of them first," Leo said, worrying about his valuables.

"Don't worry, Leo. We all know about sewing valuables into our clothes." Alfred patted Leo's arm reassuringly. "How do you think we managed to get and settle in here?" He gestured to his wife. "Bianca and I will make sure we get everything of value out before we get rid of your clothes. Don't worry." He laughed again. This time, a real laugh. "We won't keep any of it."

Leo ate and drank as Alfred continued. "We know you will need all the money you have plus more to make it to Atlanta. You'll also need a job here before you can move to Atlanta. Everything is expensive in the United States. Many Americans are being bankrupted by The Great Depression, so everyone is being very careful with their money."

"I will pay you back for any money you spend on me," Leo said and continued rapidly in German. "I want to earn my way. I must save for my mother and father, to get them out." He switched to broken English and said, "Also, tomorrow, I want to learn to speak English. After tonight, we will speak no more German. Only English."

After his late-night meal, his host showed him to his room. Clean sheets. Fluffy pillows. A real bed. *Thank you, God, for bringing me here. Now, just keep my family alive long enough so I can save them*, he thought. For one minute, he felt secure. Then reality crept back into his thoughts. *I have a job to do*, he remembered. *My family is counting on me. How can I be here with the gifts I have been given when my mother and father and sister and brother and all their families are fighting for their lives? They are starving and being beaten—and I lie here, satiated and clean. Safe.* He felt relief and shame. He was safe, warm, and full, but he knew his family felt none of these things. Only hunger, fear, and pain.

The last image he saw before he fell asleep was of his mother. She stared back at him with eyes exactly like his. "My son," she said, "Please try hard to convince your cousins in Atlanta to send more money, at least to get all the children out. Then you can earn money to get me and Papa out. I love you, my baby boy." She faded away.

He dreamt of men and women being shot. Babies and young children crying out in fear. Young girls raped. Blood everywhere. When he woke at dawn's first light, his head hurt, and he had dried tears on his face. There was no peace, even in his dreams.

At seven o'clock in the morning, he tiptoed into the kitchen, not wanting to wake anyone. His hosts were already up, however, and they smiled when they saw their frail, young guest.

"Leo, how much sugar and cream do you take in your coffee? How about warm pastries with butter and jam? A boiled egg?" Bianca asked as she filled his cup with steaming coffee.

"Yes, I would love all of that. I haven't had real cream and butter in years. The coffee smells wonderful. I will have some of everything," he said as he grabbed a Danish and slathered butter onto it.

"Leo, slow down. It's not going anyplace," Alfred said as he touched Leo's arm. "You will be sick if you eat too fast and too much of this rich food. Your stomach can't handle it. Trust me, I know. We were like you when we arrived here." He looked at Bianca, and they smiled knowingly at each other.

Chapter Twenty-Seven

1932 - 1934

Sophie loved everything about her life in West Palm Beach. She had three best friends, her own yard, and always wore beautiful clothes. She earned very good grades, and her teachers called her a "model child." To placate her mother on the topic of religion, she made friends with the girls from her Sunday school class and went to mother-daughter luncheons at the Temple. She knew what to do to keep her mother off her back. She could have fun and appear to comply with Hannah's rigid rules.

Most of Sophie's friends were one or two years older than she was. As hard as she tried to mature as fast as her older friends did, she couldn't overcome nature. Boys weren't interesting to her or in her. She still liked to make clothes for her extensive doll collection and to design outfits for her paper dolls. Whereas her friends' bodies were transforming from girls to young ladies, hers was still a little girl. Julie, Ella, and Susan got their periods. They were twelve and thirteen. She was only eleven. When her friends talked about what it was like "being a woman now," she felt ignored and left out.

"Does it really hurt like my sister told me?" asked Ella.

"Sometimes it does for me," Julie replied.

"What about it smelling or boys knowing when you have it?" Sophie asked.

"I don't think people know just by looking at you or being near you," Rachel explained.

"When it does hurt, I take some aspirin," volunteered Julie.

"Do you remember that talk, the school offered for girls, that our mothers took us to that last year about how once you get your periods, you can become pregnant? It was too vague. I still don't understand how the whole thing works. I asked my mother, and she said I was too young to worry about such things," Ella said.

Wanting to be part of the discussion, Sophie offered, "I'll go to the library and find some books. We can figure it out ourselves, seeing how no grown-up wants to explain it to us."

She knew her mother would never give her a truthful answer on any subject she felt was inappropriate for a girl Sophie's age. Sophie tried talking to her mother about her father or about any other men in Hannah's life. Why Hannah only hung around with women and why her mother was one of only two women she knew who didn't have a husband. Hannah would just give her a stern look and walk away.

The next afternoon, the girls met in Sophie's backyard.

"Here is what I found out by reading two reference books," Sophie told them. "I had to sneak the books out of that section of the library because the librarian keeps these books hidden, so only grownups can see them."

"Okay, okay," rushed Ella. "Tell us."

"Your period is called 'menstruation.' It's what happens to your body around once a month. It's a mixture of blood and the lining of your uterus."

"What is a uterus?" Julie interrupted.

Sophie took a large tablet of paper she had carried outside and drew what she thought was a good replication of what she read in the book. "An egg comes from here." She pointed at a small object on one side of the picture. "The egg and the lining and the blood come out of you, and that is your period."

"So, what's the big deal, then, about once you have a period, you can get pregnant? If this stuff comes out of you, you can't have a baby," Rachel interrupted.

"You can get pregnant if your egg is in process of going to your uterus, and a boy puts this stuff in you at the same time," Sophie continued.

"A boy puts what in you?" Ella was wide-eyed.

"He puts his pee-pee place in you and something comes out called 'sperm.' That's what makes a baby. But you can't have babies until you are married," Sophie replied.

"Well, I am not getting married any time soon. Definitely, no boy is going to do that to me," Rachel concluded, pointing at the crude picture that Sophie had drawn.

A few months after the girls' educational session, Sophie started her period. She was delighted. She was now like her older friends.

Chapter Twenty-Eight

"Sophie," Hannah said one Sunday morning as they were cleaning the house. "We need to talk about what it means to be a proper young lady."

"Mother, I know all about that. I went to the library and researched what it means to have a period and become a young lady." Sophie stopped dusting and looked at her mother.

"Well, there is more to being a proper young lady than what you can read in a book," Hannah huffed and glared at Sophie. "Did it talk about your reputation, how important it is to see to it that you have a good one? It's about how you dress and how you act, and who your friends are. It means you listen to your mother and other adults and behave in a way to make your father and me, if he were here, proud. Did the book tell you about these topics?" Hannah's voice grew louder, agitated.

***

"No, Mother." A tinge of sarcasm crept into Sophie's voice. "I figured you would tell me about that, just like you have been doing all my life." She plopped down onto the rattan sofa. "I know I need to dress a certain way and be seen with certain people and not with others. I know you want me to learn to sew, knit, and cook, so I can get a good husband. You did all those things and got a good husband, and he died." She paused to let her comments sink into Hannah. "Why haven't you dated anyone since my father died?"

Hannah paused to catch her breath. She was furious with Sophie's tone of voice and the lack of respect Sophie showed for her opinions. She also wanted to tell Sophie about Heinrich and her baby brother, but she knew she could never tell her daughter that. She didn't want Sophie to bear the burden of a mother who had an affair and had a child out of wedlock.

Instead of reprimanding Sophie for her disrespect, she answered, "I had lived without a man before I met your father. When he died, I knew I would be okay without another husband." Hannah looked at Sophie to gauge her reaction to what Hannah was telling her. "I had you and my friend, Marie. Now we live here, where we have family and friends. I like our life and don't see how another husband is necessary." Hannah wanted to add, "And I had another man, but he didn't want me." This was not something you told your daughter.

"What was my father like?" Sophie asked as she picked at her fingernail. She still bit her nails, a habit her mother tried to curtail by putting a bitter ointment on her fingers.

"I wish I could tell you more than the little I know." Hannah sat down on the sofa next to Sophie. "He was a second or third cousin on my mother's side. He was a kind, nice man who worked hard. I knew him less than a year when he died. He knew I was pregnant with you." She bit her tongue so she wouldn't say any more about Saul or Heinrich. "Now, go back to work. The oven is still a mess from the burst sweet potatoes from dinner last night. You need to finish cleaning it before you go out and play."

***

As the years passed, Sophie excelled academically through elementary, middle, and high school; she was always at the top of her class. She socialized with children older than she was who didn't mind if she was a year or two younger than they were.

Her problem was her mother. Hannah never let up on her. It was, "Sophie, do this," or "Sophie, do that." "Good girls act this way" and "Bad girls act that way." Sophie could never be the way Hannah wanted her to be: perfect.

"Sophie," Hannah said, "Make sure the purse you use matches your shoes. Be polite to everyone. It's better to ask people about themselves than for you to talk about yourself. Only socialize with the proper people."

"Mama, what do you mean by proper people? All my friends are nice people. They don't get into trouble. So, I don't understand. What are you trying to say?"

"I mean, what kind of family do they come from? What does the father do for a living? Do they live in the right side of town? I would prefer your friends to be Jewish. But not from one of those Russian Jews. God forbid that you marry one of them. German Jews are in a higher class than other Jews," Hannah pontificated.

"Mama, do you hear yourself? Why are German Jews better? That is like the Nazis when they talk about Aryans being better," Sophie said, challenging her mother.

"How can you say that to me, your mother? When my family is either destroyed or lost because of them?" Hannah raised her hand as if to slap Sophie, but she didn't. "I never want to hear that kind of talk again from you. Do you understand me?"

"Yes. I am sorry for saying that." Sophie's face reddened. "I do have Jewish friends. Two of my friends are Jewish, Rachel and Ella. Isn't that enough?"

"That is a good beginning," Hannah said. "It is my responsibility to teach you right from wrong. As long as you understand the rules in this house, I won't bring it up again."

Sophie knew it was best to just agree with her mother when they had arguments like this. She nodded her head, went to her room, and quietly shut the door.

Chapter Twenty-Nine

1937

At breakfast one morning, Hannah announced that they would be celebrating Sophie's fifteenth birthday in Germany.

"Mother, don't you read the papers? It's 1937, not 1927." Sophie, who was putting on her bathing suit to go to the beach with her friends, reacted. "Don't you hear about what is happening in Europe? And especially in Germany? It is too dangerous for us to go this year. Maybe we should wait until this blows over."

"Don't be ridiculous. We are going, and we'll be fine." Hannah thought, as many Americans did, that the stories coming out of Germany were exaggerated. Even so, she wanted to see her sisters, to see if they were okay. If they weren't, she wanted to help them get out of Germany. "Nothing is going to happen to us while we are there. We are American citizens. You're just making up an excuse. You just don't want to leave your friends for the summer."

In spite of Sophie's warnings and her sisters' letters telling her to wait until Germany returned to normal, Hannah booked passage to Germany. When they boarded the ship, Sophie noticed a difference immediately. The captain was not as jovial and friendly as usual when he greeted Hannah and Sophie.

"Hello, Mrs. and Miss Straus. I hope you have a pleasant voyage this year, and I hope you don't have any difficulties when you visit with your family. I don't approve of what the Nazis are doing, but there is not much one person can do. Please be careful. We want you to be back on next year's summer voyage."

"What do you mean by difficulties?" asked Sophie. She didn't have on her usual blue sailor coat and hat this year. Instead, she wore a form-fitting tan dress and deep brown coat.

"Miss Straus, don't worry that pretty little head of yours. I don't mean to frighten you," the captain answered, bowing. *My God*, he thought. *What a sexy young lady Sophie is now. It's hard to believe she is only fifteen.*

"Please tell me. I must make sure we're safe. I can handle it. I am much more mature than other girls my age," she urged.

"A few of the so-called Brownshirts have broken windows of Jewish-owned stores. They will sometimes stop a man on the street and beat him for no apparent reason." He wondered if he was saying too much, but he continued. "Occasionally, they take people from their homes and move them elsewhere. But this is not a common practice, so please forget I ever mentioned this." He coughed and changed the subject when he saw the frowns on Hannah and Sophie's faces. "I look forward to seeing you tonight at dinner."

"Does that mean we will be sitting at your table tonight?" Sophie asked, trying to mask her fear and to appear to be more sophisticated than she was.

"Yes, dear. You and your mother and a few of the other return passengers will dine at the captain's table. There will be a young gentleman at our table. I'll make sure you are seated next to him so you have someone to talk to that is closer to your age. Now, I must go and greet the rest of my passengers." He kissed her hand and moved on to the next people, who were beginning to show signs of impatience as they waited for the captain to finish flirting with the teenager in front of them.

Chapter Thirty

"*Mein libeling!*" exclaimed Sarah, Hannah's older sister said when she saw Sophie—a tan, confident young woman in a brilliant blue dress, off-white shawl, and deep blue shoes. Sophie's aunt hadn't seen her in seven years. During those years, Sophie changed from a little girl to a young woman. "So beautiful," Sarah repeated.

"Yes, Sophie has turned into a real beauty," Hannah said, shrugging off her sister's compliments on her daughter. "I have to constantly tell men that she is only fourteen, going on fifteen, and she is not available."

"Aunt Sarah, Mother exaggerates." Sophie leaned over and kissed her aunt on the cheek. "There are no older men in my life, just some jerky boys who make fun of me because I have breasts. They are such juveniles."

Later that day, Hannah's other sister, Agnes, and her family came over to Sarah's house for dinner. The conversation at the table was stilted because everyone was afraid of scaring the young children with stories of the incidents that had been happening in the last six months.

The next day, when Hannah and Sophie explored Hannah's hometown, they saw evidence of the incidents alluded to at dinner. People wore yellow Stars of David on their clothing. They saw broken windows in the shops they had frequented seven years ago. People stared at Sophie and her mother, looking as if they were trying to figure out if they were Jewish. Were their noses too long or their facial structures like the pictures that the Nazis had distributed to show how Jewish people supposedly looked? Were these women the ones who should be reported to the Nazis? Or were they just staring because Hannah and Sophie were dressed in more stylish clothing and looked more beautiful than the average German women in town.

One day, in spite of Hannah's family's warnings, Hannah invited her sisters and their children to lunch at a favorite restaurant in town. When Sophie, Hannah, and Hannah's sisters and daughters went to the local ladies' lunchroom, the maître d' asked, "Aren't you some of the Horowitzes' girls? I believe I know you, Hannah. We were in school together many years ago."

"Yes, Peter, we went through grammar school together," Hannah replied, surprised he remembered her. "How are you? Did you marry your high school girlfriend, Gerta? Do you have children?" She paused for a second and continued, motioning to Sophie. "This is my daughter, Sophie. Sophie, please say hello to Mr. Berg."

"Hello. I am pleased to meet you. Today's my birthday. We're celebrating at lunch," Sophie explained.

There was silence for several seconds. Peter's face went through a series of expressions as he contemplated what to do. His orders were to let no Jewish people in. But here was his friend, Hannah, and her family. How could he turn them away?

"Hannah, I am in a very difficult position." His face reddened and a fine line of perspiration appeared on his upper lip. "My orders are to not let any Jews into the lunchroom. But I know you and your family and don't want to have to embarrass you by turning you away," he explained.

Sophie's face burned with shame and anger as she listened to the man talk to her mother like this. "Excuse me, sir," she broke into the conversation. "My mother and I are American citizens. These rules do not apply to us! These are my aunts and cousins, so they should be allowed in with us. It is my fifteenth birthday today. You wouldn't want to ruin it, would you?"

The maître d' hesitated as he thought about what Sophie said. "Okay. I'm letting in two Americans with their German relatives. Please sit in the back where no one can see you from this door. My manager stops by unexpectedly, and I don't want to get in trouble."

Once the group was seated and the menus distributed, Hannah's sister Sarah said in a low whisper, "Hannah, I told you what it is like here now. I don't know why you had to bring us here." She, Agnes, and their daughters looked uncomfortably down at their plates.

"We could have gone to one of the Jewish-owned restaurants to celebrate. You always want to do whatever you want, even if it causes other people problems," Agnes chimed in. "This is not America. We're in Germany, and whether you want to face it or not, we are always in danger when we go out in public."

One of the babies started crying. Sophie picked up the little girl and rocked her on her lap. She didn't want to call any more attention to their table than was necessary. They ate quickly and left the restaurant as soon as possible.

Chapter Thirty-One

Hannah planned a second event to celebrate Sophie's birthday. She had reservations at the fanciest dinner-and-dancing club in the city. Because she and Sophie were Americans and had American passports, she believed no harm would come to Sophie and her. She had fashioned Sophie an elegant lavender dress with purple trim along the bottom of the skirt. The dress showed off Sophie's mature figure. Hannah's outfit was black and fell to her ankles. The top had a high collar and lace sleeves with a ruffle that hit the edge of her black gloves. As they entered the dining room of the club, people turned to watch them. Sophie felt her face redden.

"Mother, I'm afraid." Sophie gripped her mother's arm. "See how they look at us? Do you see the table of Nazi officers by the door?"

"Sophie, you worry too much. They are looking at us because you are so beautiful. We have nothing on that distinguishes us from all the other women here." Hannah pulled her arm away from Sophie's fingers. "Please don't act nervous or uncomfortable. They will become suspicious if you keep looking like you have seen a ghost. We're here to celebrate."

They were seated at a small table near the dance floor. As she sat in her seat, Hannah had the feeling of déjà vu of coming to a different place for dinner and dancing. A fancy hotel in the mountains. Of meeting Heinrich. Of her baby boy. She brushed those thoughts away like a maid sweeping dirt from the front doorstep.

As they waited for their appetizers to arrive, a young Nazi officer came over and turned to Sophie.

"I would very much like to dance with you," he said with his blue eyes riveted on Sophie. "Madam," he said, turning to Hannah, "Do I have your permission to dance with your lovely daughter?"

"Of course, if she says yes," Hannah replied.

He turned to Sophie and asked, "Would you please accompany me to the dance floor? It would be a great honor to be seen dancing with a lady as beautiful as you."

Sophie was shaking when she stood up to dance with the solider. "Of course, I will dance with you."

Sophie stumbled and the solider caught her by the arm. "You seem nervous. What in the world could you be nervous about? I won't hurt you. I only want to dance with you."

"It's my new shoes," Sophie lied. "I'm sorry I stumbled. Please forgive me," she stammered and tried to smile.

"What is your name?" he asked.

"My name is Marie," Sophie lied again.

"And what brings you to this place tonight?" he asked as he held her tightly. "I've never seen you here before."

"It's my birthday," she answered, trying to keep her voice from quivering.

"Let me guess. You're nineteen?"

"No, I turned fifteen today."

"Fifteen? You look much older than you are. Have people told you this before?"

"Yes," she said. She was beginning to calm down just as the song ended.

"I'll escort you to your table. Thank you for the dance." His attitude had changed since Sophie told him her age. "I look forward to meeting you again one day when you are a few years older."

Sophie sat down and said to her mother, "Please, let's go as soon as we finish dessert. I am afraid of these people. I don't want to dance with any more Nazi soldiers."

"All right, Sophie," Hannah agreed. "We'll leave as soon as possible, but I am not going to let your fear ruin our expensive meal."

On the way back to Hannah's sister's house, Sophie begged her mother, "Mother, please let's leave Germany and go home. I think the worst is yet to come, and I don't want to be caught up in what I fear will happen."

They had one more week left in Germany. Sophie and Hannah's sisters finally convinced Hannah that it was very dangerous to be Jewish in Germany. Hannah spent most of that week helping her sisters and their husbands try to think of ways to get their respective families out of Germany. Multiple obstacles stood in their way. Money to buy visas, to pay for bribes for authorities, and to book passage. In addition, they had to locate a family member in America to vouch for them. It was an impossible task to accomplish in seven days.

Regrettably, when Sophie and Hannah's ship sailed a week later, solutions to save Hannah's family had not been found. With great unease and fear, Hannah and Sophie boarded the ship. The two had bid a tearful good-bye to the family the night before. No one knew if they would see each other again. Hannah wished her family had believed the rumors years before and that she had listened to Sophie all the times her daughter had warned her about the coming disaster. She didn't want to think about never seeing her family again. It was just too much to bear.

Chapter Thirty-Two

Hannah was very proud of her daughter. Although she was a year younger than her classmates, Sophie managed to complete each grade faster than her older girl friends. In addition to her academics, Hannah made sure that Sophie learned all of the skills a good wife and mother would need. Not only did she instruct her daughter in cooking, cleaning, sewing, knitting, crocheting, ironing, and baking, she gave Sophie assignments to complete to make sure Sophie could perform these tasks to her mother's perfectionist standards.

Sophie never knew when her mother might say, "I want you to bake two plum pies for us to take to Mildred's for dinner Friday night." Or Hannah would demand that Sophie iron all of their clothes, even their underwear. If Sophie made any mistakes, she would have to redo whatever it was that Hannah wasn't happy with.

Hannah was very active in the Conservative Temple that overlooked Lake Worth. A lake that is part of the Intercostal Waterway. She joined the Temple Sisterhood and the local Hadassah chapter. Through the Temple, she met a group of women, and they met once a week to play Canasta at each other's houses.

Ostensibly, the reason these women got together was to play canasta, but what they really did was gossip.

"Did you hear about the Goldman girl? I heard she got pregnant and had to drop out of school." One woman said.

"Did you see Myra's new diamond ring that Al gave her for their anniversary?" Said another.

"Would your son Ronnie be willing to take private dance lessons with Sophie at the Towers for five weeks this summer?" Hannah asked a friend.

"You know that my daughter already needs a size C bra!" Hannah told another woman at the table.

Sophie hated hearing her mother and her friends criticizing almost anyone not in their group. She was especially appalled when her mother disclosed personal information about her as her mother often did.

"Can you believe Sophie asked me about intercourse last week!" Sophie heard Hannah tell her friends one Wednesday as the women played their first hand of Canasta. "I didn't tell her. I just said she was too young to ask such things."

Hannah's friends laughed and continued to play cards. Sophie was red with embarrassment. She thought, *I'll never ask her anything again!*

***

Summers were Sophie's favorite time of the year. Her mother and her friends belonged to a beach club on the Atlantic Ocean in Palm Beach. It was the only public club in Palm Beach. It allowed anyone to become a member, unlike the clubs that restricted Jews, Catholics, and people of color. There was a large pool with low and high diving boards and a baby pool. Blue and white cabanas surrounded the pool on one side of the street. A tunnel ran under the street to the beach.

Parents let their children play all day while the mothers played Mahjong or Canasta. The men came on weekends and sat shirtless around tables, playing Poker and Gin, drinking beer or Tom Collins. The women gossiped; the men smoked cigarettes and cigars while talking about sports or politics.

Sophie heard her mother talk to Molly, her sister-in-law, about various girls and their families in a disparaging way. "That family has no dignity. The mother works all day and a maid takes care of her children." "Did you see the dress that woman had on at the Mother-Daughter Tea? It made her look so fat."

Sophie was aware that she was one of the only children there who didn't have a father. In fact, she never had a father figure even though Hannah hoped there would be one or two when they moved to Florida. Not even an uncle; she'd never met her mother's brothers. All Sophie knew was there had been a dispute between Hannah and her brothers over money. Hannah felt her brothers cheated her out of money due her. This topic, like many others, was taboo to discuss.

"Mother, why do you never see your brothers anymore?"

"I don't want to talk about it. It's over and done. Please don't ask about this again."

"Mother, do you know why your brother and Aunt Molly got divorced?"

"Sophie, that is none of your business. We don't ask people questions like that."

"But, Mother, I hear you talking about this and other things to your friends, but you tell me not to ask about them. Why can you talk about it to other people but not me?"

Hannah's reply was usually, "You are still just a child. You don't need to know the answers yet."

Another secret, Sophie thought. *Will I ever get a straight answer to a question from my mother? Will I always wonder what the truth really is?* .

"One day, when I am older, you can tell me about these things," Sophie said.

Hannah replied, "Maybe one day when you are older. Now leave me alone. I have work to do."

Chapter Thirty-Three

1938

By the time Sophie was sixteen, most of her girlfriends were those she met in the Temple. Although she was still friendly with the non-Jewish girls at school, it was easier to have friends of which Hannah approved. A group of four girls spent most of their time together: Ruby, Connie, Dotty, and Sophie. They spent weekend nights at each other's houses, went to parties together, and hung out on Sundays after Sunday School at the Temple.

Hannah was delighted with Sophie's choice of friends, even if they were all older than Sophie. When Sophie was sixteen, Ruby and Dotty were in their freshman year of college at Florida State College for Women. It was a two-hour drive from Gainesville, where the boys' college was. Sophie regularly corresponded with Dotty and Ruby, who happened to live in the same dorm and who had pledged one of the two Jewish sororities at FSCW.

Dear Sophie,

> *You wouldn't believe how hard my classes are. I thought we got a great education at Palm Beach High School, but college is much harder. Dotty and I pledged Delta Phi Epsilon and are going through pledge week. If you don't join a sorority, you are considered a nobody here. You would not believe some of the things the sisters make us do. We had to go to class once in our nightgowns under our raincoats. If we got caught, we could have been suspended from school. We have a big dance coming up. Why don't you and Connie come*

up for that weekend? We will have a blast. You can stay in our room. We'll figure out beds somehow once we know if both of you are coming.

Love,
Ruby

After school the next day, Sophie dropped her school bag on the kitchen counter and sat at the formica kitchen table while Hannah prepared dinner. "Mom, I have a question. Ruby asked Connie and me to come up next weekend to visit. It would be fun. We would take the train. I promise we will be very careful. Please say yes, please," she begged.

Hannah continued to baste the beef roast and hesitated before she spoke.

"Sophie, don't you think you are too young for this?" Her back was to Sophie, making it difficult for her daughter to read her mother's face. "You are only sixteen years old. I'm not sure you can handle being there without me or another adult coming with you." She turned and looked at her daughter. "What does Connie's mother say?"

Sophie looked Hannah straight in the eyes and replied, "Connie's mother said she could go if I go. That way, if we have each other, we will be safe on the train." She tried to control the excitement in her voice and added, "The sorority has a housemother on the premises all the time. I can give you her phone number. Please let me go. You know I have never done anything to get in trouble."

She rose from the chair and stood next to her mother at the stove. "I get good grades and never smoke or drink like some of the other girls I know do." She went to the drawer that held the silverware and began setting the table for dinner. As Sophie placed the two dinner plates on the table, she continued. "This would give me a chance to check out the college for when I go to college. I swear I'll be a good girl."

"All right, Sophie, you can go. I want you to be super careful and watch out for each other." Hannah waved the wooden spoon in the air for emphasis. "If you get into any trouble, you won't ever go there again until you are in college."

Sophie threw her arms around her mother and hugged her. Hannah was startled. She didn't believe people should display physical affection to a child once they were no longer a baby. Sophie noticed her mother was not hugging back, but she was used to this with her mother. Hannah was not one for showing love that way.

Early the next week, Hannah took Sophie shopping. "I want you to be stylish and attractive so the boys notice you," she explained when they entered the local dress shop. She selected three dresses, two skirts and sweaters, and one blue blazer for Sophie to try. She handed them to Sophie over the dressing-room wall. "We can get you an outfit that makes you look a bit older. But not too old, so it will not make the boys think you are not a good girl, if you know what I mean."

"Yes, Mother," Sophie said with a sigh, "I know what you mean. You want me to attract boys but not do anything with them."

"Yes," Hannah answered, not hearing the sarcasm in Sophie's voice. "Now let's pick the clothes out that you want so I can fit them to you. I'll need to take in the waist and let out the bust. And definitely hem them. You are so petite; you are barely taller than I am."

"Thank you, Mother," Sophie said. "I'll try on a dress and skirt for you to alter. I am really lucky you are such a good seamstress. My friends just wear their clothes the way they come from the store. Their mothers can't even do a hem properly."

Hannah smiled. Sophie rarely showed appreciation for what Hannah did for her.

"Sophie," Hannah said. "Thank you."

Hannah stood by Sophie and gave her a quick hug. "Hurry if you want me to finish in time," Hannah added as Sophie went to the dressing room to change.

Chapter Thirty-Four

The week flew by and before they knew it, Connie and Sophie were at the train station with their small suitcases. Connie wore a brown tweed skirt with a long-sleeved white blouse. She had a light brown jacket slung over her arm that she could wear for the cooler Tallahassee nights. Connie's dark brown hat, handbag and shoes matched in a softer brown shade. Sophie wore a red and blue plaid dress with a dark blue patent belt and black patent shoes. She carried a navy blue blazer that fit her like a glove, which Hannah had made to accentuate her assets and cover the few physical defects Sophie had.

The girls' train arrived in Tallahassee at 9:00 P.M. rather than 8:00 P.M. as planned. Dotty and Ruby were no place to be seen. Sophie and Connie stood on the platform, waiting patiently with their bags.

"Do you think she forgot we were coming?" Dotty asked after twenty minutes had passed.

"No, I don't think she forgot us. Something could have happened. I am sure she will be here soon," Sophie said reassuringly.

Just as Sophie finished her sentence, a large blue car drove up. The doors flew open and Ruby and Dotty ran to the two waiting girls.

As Dotty hugged Sophie, she began to cry. "I missed you so much. I am so happy that you are here."

"Then why are you crying?" Sophie asked as she dabbed at her own eyes with a tissue she pulled from her dress pocket.

Within a few minutes, their suitcases were in the trunk and the girls piled on top of each other in the car. A young man with red-blond hair and a scattering of freckles sat in the driver's seat.

"This is Lenny," Ruby said as she pointed at the driver. He turned and smiled at the two new passengers. "He is a friend of ours who had a big enough car for you both and your luggage."

The girls hugged each other and held hands on the trip back to the college. Only with her friends did Sophie have any physical affection. Her mother was so rigid and uncomfortable with physical contact.

Lenny dropped them at the sorority house. The girls made their way to Dotty and Ruby's room. It was tiny, maybe 10' × 10', with two dorm beds and sleeping bags rolled up in the corner. There were two small desks that had been stacked on each other to make more room. The two closets in the room couldn't hold another item of clothing, so Sophie and Dotty draped their clothes over the top of the stacked desks.

"Tell us everything. What do you have planned for us? Where will we go? Will we meet boys?" Sophie asked as she removed her hat and put her gloves inside of it. "God, how I hate these gloves. I wish I didn't have to wear them."

"It's not as strict here as it is at home. Because it is an all-girls' school, they are not as worried about what we wear as long as no boys or parents are around," Ruby explained.

The girls had a great weekend of parties and just hanging out and catching up with each other. The freshmen boys visiting from the University of Florida paid attention to the high school girls while the senior boys from the same school were focused on the college freshmen, to the consternation of the senior girls. It always seemed that the boys were looking for girlfriends who were younger than them. None of the boys wanted to date girls their same age.

On Sunday morning, Lenny picked up Sophie and Connie to take them to the train station. There were tearful good-byes among the girls and promises to see each other soon.

On the train home, Connie asked Sophie, "What was the best part of the weekend for you?"

"I don't know because I loved the whole weekend from the time we arrived to now," answered Sophie. "If I were forced to answer your question, I would say seeing Dotty and Ruby was the first best thing. The next best thing was meeting the college boys. It was refreshing to have a boy to talk to who wasn't an idiot like the boys back home."

"I would have to agree with you. I hope we can do this again," Connie sighed.

"Me, too," Sophie said and yawned. "I think I will close my eyes for a few minutes. "

Then both girls fell asleep and slept most of the way home, dreaming of parties and boys. In another year or two, Connie and Sophie would be old enough to go to college and have fun like they had this past weekend.

Chapter Thirty-Five

New Jersey was supposed to be just a stopover on Leo's way to Atlanta. His goal was to reach Atlanta by 1936, contact his relatives who paid for his journey out of Germany and secure a job. Instead, Leo lived with the Waxmans for almost two years while he learned to speak English and work to make extra money for his trip to Atlanta. He took odd jobs, such as working for a moving company, waiting tables, or washing windows, and anything he could do that didn't require a high school education. His employers, to his surprise, generally complimented his work ethic and his ability to connect with other people. Although he spoke little English, he projected sincerity and warmth no matter the circumstances.

When the time came for Leo to leave the comfort of the Waxmans' home, he made sure the Red Cross had descriptions of all of his family members and that they had his cousins' Atlanta address and phone number. Just in case any of his family survived and was looking for him.

"If you need us, we are here. Please keep us up to date on how things progress. Call collect. We will pay for the call," Mr. Waxman told Leo.

Bianca hugged Leo. He felt her tears as he bent to kiss her on the cheek. "You have become my other son. I know I can't replace your mother, but consider me your American mother. I couldn't love you any more if you were mine. We are always here for you. We love you."

The morning sky was dark and rain fell in large drops. The Waxmans and Leo stood in the same hallway Leo entered two years ago. A lonely, frightened, and hungry boy arrived and a healthy, determined, and focused young man was leaving. Leo extended his arm to shake hands with Mr. Waxman, but he pulled Leo into his bear-like arms and held him tightly.

Leo walked out of the front door. The tears and the rain blinded him as he hailed a cab to the train station.

Part II

The Second Generation

1936 – 1941

Germany and America

"What is past is prologue."

William Shakespeare
The Tempest

Chapter Thirty-Six

The train ride from New Jersey to Atlanta afforded Leo the opportunity to see sundry parts of America. Through the moving train's windows, he saw New York, Washington, and Richmond on his way to Atlanta. As the train got closer to Atlanta, the conductor announced, "Welcome to the hill country of Georgia. On our way to Atlanta, you will see everything from mountains to scenic rivers. We'll pass graveyards from the Revolutionary War to the Civil War and fields of cotton and tobacco. For those of you who will depart at our Atlanta station, you will be in the biggest city in the South. Sit back. Enjoy this last part of your train ride. We hope you have enjoyed your time on the railroad and that you will speak kindly of our service and accommodations."

Leo pulled his new suitcase off the shelf over his seat and put his backpack on. Although he didn't sew his valuables into his clothing like he did when he left Germany, each piece was wrapped carefully and placed in his backpack. He sold some of his jewelry in New Jersey to a pawnshop owner, a friend of Mr. Waxman's. He received more than adequate payment for the pieces. His cash was in a money belt wrapped securely around his waist.

A few hours after Leo left for the train station, Mr. Waxman called one of Leo's cousins in Atlanta, Jack Bernstein. Jack and his sister, Carol Kohen were part of the family that owned the biggest and most prosperous furniture and home decorations operation in the Southeast.

"Jack, this is Alfred Waxman from New Jersey," Mr. Waxman said to Leo's cousin Jack on the phone. "We are sending Leopold Rosenstein your way on the afternoon train. He's Leo Rosen now, compliments of Ellis Island. He should be there in about ten hours, give or take. You never know how the trains will be running. If I were you, I would check on how late the train is going to be before you go to the station."

"Al, it's been a long time since we have talked. So, you are sending Leo to us. Please be honest. How is he doing? Anything we need to know?" Jack Bernstein quizzed.

"He is a charming and sensitive young man who has been through hell for someone his age," Mr. Waxman began. "Although, so many Jews in Europe are experiencing worse. Families torn apart. Barbaric practices or torture. Treating people worse than livestock." He paused to catch his breath and hold back tears. "I wish there was more we could do." He believes he's done as much as he could, but he wished the rich Jews would do more. "I know you're trying hard to get other members of the synagogues and temples in Atlanta to sponsor more people to come here. I am sure you are aware of all the restrictions placed to limit how many people are allowed to emigrate."

Alfred Waxman didn't give Jack a chance to answer. "If you ask me, many Americans, and in particular, politicians, are just as anti-Semitic as the Nazis are. It makes me so angry." He paused for a while and continued. "Our synagogue has sent applications to sponsor many more immigrants. But, damn it, we are running into walls."

He finally asked the question that had plagued him since Leo arrived. "What happened that you could only get one person out of Leo's family? I understand his mother is quite ill, and there are three young children caught up in the nightmare over there."

Jack coughed and hesitated. "We were originally shooting for four slots, which would have covered Leo's sister and her three boys, but only one visa came through." Jack and his grandmother, Leo's mother's sister, had been devastated when they couldn't get more family members out. "The cost associated with four people is astronomical," he continued. "With us trying to establish and grow the business, the family decided to bring over one at a time. We asked them to pick the first one, and they picked Leo. He's the youngest." Jack pulled a dining room chair closer to the telephone and sat down. "They thought he had the best chance of getting out of the country and finding work. I am personally working on my grandmother to loosen her purse strings and send for at least two more."

Alfred and Jack continued talking about the situation in Germany and the United States' lack of support for the plight of European Jews. Like many American Jews, the Bernsteins and the Waxmans believed the stories about Germany's "ultimate solution," whereas politicians and non-Jews thought the stories coming out of Germany weren't entirely true.

"Jack," Alfred said as the conversation was ending, "We really should get together more. Our families need to know each other better."

"You're right," Jack replied. "We need to support each other now even more than before. Maybe next summer, you and your family can come to Atlanta."

Laughing, Alfred replied, "From what I hear about the heat in Atlanta in the summer, you all should come to New Jersey. Please call me as soon as you get home from picking Leo up at the station. We want to know if he safely made it down to you."

"I promise I will call," Jack said. He hung up, moved the chair back to the dining room table, and went to the kitchen to find his wife. He wanted her to be prepared when Leo arrived, to be prepared for the sad young man they had promised to help.

Chapter Thirty-Seven

Leo moved to Atlanta in 1936. It was a city of rolling hills, thousands of trees, and large mansions that reminded him of some of the castles in Europe. He roamed the city to familiarize himself with its various parts. The poor and affluent neighborhoods and where the whites and the colored lived. He always said "yes" when one of his new friends asked if he wanted to get out of town in the fall to see the leaves change colors in the North Georgia mountains. He felt right at home in Clayton, Georgia, the Appalachian Trail, or the Kennesaw Mountain outside Atlanta. Back home, he had spent summers in the mountains in Bavaria hiking and picnicking with his friends. He couldn't help but think of his German friends and wonder what happened to them. Whether they were dead or alive.

He spent his first two weeks living with his cousins in their mansion in Buckhead, a rich suburb of Atlanta. The house had five bedrooms and three bathrooms, an elegant living room, two dining rooms (one more formal than the other), three acres of land, and a two-car garage. He felt uncomfortable in his cousins' extravagant home, having grown up in a three-bedroom, one-bathroom apartment.

Two weeks after he arrived in Atlanta, he moved into an efficiency apartment over a barbershop near Spring Street and close to downtown where he worked at Rich's Department Store. He furnished his apartment with used furniture and housewares from his cousins' house, items they were going to donate to charity. He had a small, framed picture of his family on his nightstand, next to his alarm clock. The walls were dingy white and the hardwood floors were covered with throw rugs he found at a neighborhood flea market. Although his apartment was small, it suited his needs better than a bedroom in his cousins' house. If his family in Germany had to live in desolate environs, he could manage in an efficiency apartment.

"Whatever I have to live in is better than what I believe my family is enduring," he said to himself each night when he prayed for their safety.

Leo checked with the local Red Cross every month to find out if there had been word about anyone in his family. Information about the Jews in Europe was sporadic and often inaccurate. He left his new address and his cousins' phone number with the organization in case any information surfaced. Sadly, he heard nothing. It was unbearable to believe his whole family was dead, that he would never see any of them again.

After each time he checked and was told "no," he went back to his apartment and wept. He sat on his sofa for hours in a catatonic state, staring at the wall, trying not to think of the atrocities he was sure his family was experiencing. Even so, after a night of worrying and weeping, the next day he got up and went to his three jobs. He had to work for the money he was saving to either find out what happened to his family or to bring anyone out.

Each month, on a Friday, he ate dinner at his cousins' house, where the cook prepared dinner and the maid served it. Platters of rare roast beef and onions, noodle kugel, green beans, and hot rolls and butter, followed by pie and ice cream. Leo didn't say anything, but he wondered, *If these people can afford a maid and a cook, why can they not afford to pay for one more visa for my family?*

When he called the Waxmans once a week to check in, he asked, "What am I missing? My cousins seem to have as much money as royalty does, but they say they have no money to pay for getting my mother or my sister and her children out." He brushed his black hair from his face and adjusted his wire-framed glasses. "They got me a job. I work very hard, but I don't make enough money for what I do. Sometimes, I get so angry that I want to shout at them, but that is not in my nature. What do you think about all of this?" He knew he could count on the Waxmans to answer truthfully and give him useful advice.

Alfred and Bianca Waxman were each on separate phones, one in the living room and one in the upstairs hall, so they both could talk to Leo. "Leo, we don't know what is going on inside of the family or how well the business is doing. We don't know if they have given money to another family, maybe the wife's family. I know it is hard, but try not to judge them too harshly," Mrs. Waxman said in her soothing voice.

"Leo, you know, Bianca may be right. We don't know their circumstances." Alfred stared out of the window in the living room. "Being angry and resentful only hurts you. We must continue to have hope." He paused a moment to let his statement sink in to Leo. "There are stories every day about how people have escaped from the Nazis' occupation. Some are about people finding other members of their families. We will keep looking. You can't give up," he urged. "Tell me about your jobs. Your letter said you added a third one. I don't know how you do it and find time to sleep and have fun."

"I don't have a social life," Leo said in a matter-of-fact tone. "I work in the stockroom at Rich's, because my English isn't good enough yet to be a salesman. I work at a liquor store, and I translate a letter or two for any people who have German relatives and need a translator." He counted his fingers as he listed each job. "It sounds silly for a German who doesn't know much English to translate letters or write letters for Americans, but it seems to work. I am improving my English every day and making extra money." His voice grew lighter, and he added, "I have been studying for my GED so I can say I graduated high school."

"Leo, you are an amazing man. May God grant you some peace of mind and a social life. All work and no play..." Alfred said.

"I know that one: makes Jack a dull boy," Leo said and laughed. He always felt better after his weekly calls with the Waxmans. They had become his American family more than his Atlanta cousins had.

Leo joined a young people's social club at his cousins' Temple on Peachtree Street, which was a newer Reform congregation, very different from his family's traditional, Conservative one. He attended the dances and baseball games sponsored by the Temple's Sisterhood and Brotherhood groups. Slowly, he began to meet people and to date. As his depression lifted, his natural personality emerged. He was sensitive, danced well, knew how to treat a lady, and was a great baseball player. Soon, he became one of the most eligible bachelors at the Temple.

His personality and innate abilities enabled him duties beyond his employers' expectations. He related well to customers, listening carefully for what each wanted. His customers referred friends to him when they wanted to buy new furniture for their homes or businesses. As his grasp of the English language increased, his confidence and his commissions increased enough so he could drop one of his jobs: working in the liquor store.

Jack's sister, Carol Kohen, bragged about Leo to her friends. One day Carol told her bridge club, "Leo has the looks of Clark Gable, the personality of Robert Young, and dances like Fred Astaire. Everyone is in love with our cousin Leo. You know, the one we brought here from Germany."

Chapter Thirty-Eight

While Leo was settling in to his new life in Atlanta, Sophie breezed through high school. The courses that seemed too easy to her were the same ones her friends complained were too hard. Sophie, a voracious reader, wanted to experience adventures like those she lived vicariously through books. Meet painters in Paris. Look into the chasm of the Grand Canyon. Make a contribution to society. She believed she could do something special with her life, not just get married and have children.

Hannah, on the other hand, had other aspirations for her only child. Sophie will graduate from high school, go to college long enough to find an educated man, preferably a doctor, a lawyer, or a business owner, marry, and have children. Hannah saw herself as the live-in grandmother and nanny.

She didn't discuss this directly with Sophie, but Sophie knew what her mother wanted. Hannah told her canasta friends, "Sophie will go to college and meet a good man to marry. If she goes to college, she can meet a higher-class man, one who has done more than graduate from high school." At a Temple luncheon, Hannah described Sophie's future to the other women at the table. "I think she will meet a doctor or maybe a lawyer. They could settle here in West Palm. I could babysit the children." Hannah's friends nodded their heads approvingly. They all wanted similar lives for their daughters.

Sophie just wanted out of the small stucco house in a neighborhood of similar small houses where all of the families seemed to be the same. The wives had prescribed roles, and the husbands went to work each day to support their wives and children. Sophie wanted to be away from her mother and to be able to have space to decide who she was and what she wanted.

Right now, most of her actions and decisions were based on doing the opposite of what her mother wanted her to do.

Hannah had an opinion on every aspect of Sophie's life:

"Sophie, that dress is inappropriate for going to the movies with your friends. Go to your room and put the blue short-sleeved blouse on with the pleated khaki skirt. And your black patent shoes with the straps."

"Sophie, you need to spend less time with your friends and more with our family."

"Sophie, you shouldn't hunch your shoulders over. Stand up straight. And pick your feet up when you walk."

"Sophie, you need to start applying for scholarships now even if no one else is doing it so soon. You'll make a better impression."

***

One afternoon, as Sophie was doing her homework at the kitchen table and Hannah was rolling out dough for an apple pie, Sophie asked, "Mother, where does your money come from? Did my father leave you enough for all these years?"

"More or less," Hannah answered as she wiped flour from the front of her favorite broadcloth apron. "I also worked as a seamstress among other things during the years when you were young. And hats. I loved designing hats that coordinated with my customers' outfits." Hannah smiled as she carefully laid the piecrust into the glass pie plate. "And, based on good advice from people I trusted, I invested the money your father left us." She paused to see Sophie's expression and continued. "When my father died, and then, my mother so shortly after, I inherited more money. I also made money from selling the valuables from my parents' estate."

Hannah carried the finished pie to the oven and placed it on the center rack. She turned to Sophie and added, "I have been very frugal, as you know. We don't waste money in our house."

Sophie hesitated before she added, "Mother, I admire you for what you have been able to do to provide us a good lifestyle. It couldn't have been easy."

Hannah was surprised at Sophie's compassion. She took Sophie's hand and added, "Now it is time for you to find a good man. One who can support you and me. Once you have children, I can live with you and take care of them. With the scholarship I know you will get, you can attend college long enough to meet the right person..."

Sophie's voice rose. "You have it all worked out, don't you? What if I can't find a rich man to marry me? What if I don't want the same things you want? What if I want to wait to get married, like you did? Does it even matter?"

"What you want?" Hannah stepped back from Sophie. Her hand twitched. She wanted to slap her daughter. "Haven't I given you everything you wanted? I have devoted my life to you." She felt wounded, confused. "Do you think I can continue giving you the life you want?" She didn't wait for a reply and continued. "Didn't I let you go on trips with your girlfriends, unchaperoned, to Tallahassee? My friends thought I was crazy for letting you do that, a sixteen-year-old, but I trusted you, and you were a good student, so I let you go."

"Yes, Mother," Sophie said quietly. "You did let me go. But please, let me have a chance to decide my life after high school. I showed you I could handle myself when you let me go to FSCW without Connie. Didn't I?"

"Sophie, I know you think you can handle everything, but you can't. You're still a child." Hannah sat down at the kitchen table. "I am still responsible for your safety and well-being. Whether you like it or not, I still have a say in what you can and can't do."

Sophie didn't argue with her mother. She picked up her schoolbooks and escaped to her bedroom so she wouldn't have to listen to her mother anymore. She sat on her tightly made bed and thought about what her mother had said. Hannah had sacrificed to provide Sophie a good life. They owned a home, were able to live comfortably, traveled occasionally, and wanted for nothing. "I am ungrateful," Sophie said, berating herself. "I should be more appreciative of what my mother has done for me. I guess I can go to college and find a man to marry me. Maybe, just not on my mother's terms."

***

After the conversation with her mother, Sophie reminisced about a trip to FSCW, when she went without Connie to see Dotty and Ruby. It was on this trip that she met Richard, a college junior who was one of Ruby's cousins. He could be marriage material, down the road, after she had a chance to travel and explore. He attended the University of Florida, was in premed, and was one of the most handsome boys Sophie had ever met. Sophie, Ruby, and Richard spent the weekend together going to parties, going out for a sandwich, or just walking around the campus.

Before Sophie finished packing her bag to go home from that particular trip, she asked Ruby, "Does Richard have a girlfriend?"

Looking up from her history book, Ruby said as she shook her head, "I'm not sure. I think he has a steady, but who knows? Why? Are you interested in him?"

"Yeah, I think I am. I have never met anyone like him before. Intelligent, fun to be with, interesting, kind, a great listener..." Sophie answered.

"Well, you should be aware that he is known as a ladies' man," Ruby cautioned. She gave up on trying to study until Sophie left for the train.

"What do you mean by that?" Sophie asked.

"Supposedly, he 'loves 'em and leaves 'em.' He has broken many a heart," Ruby continued. "There is a rumor that he got a girl pregnant once, but no one really knows." She waited until Sophie was looking directly at her. "I am not sure he is the right guy for you. I'd stay away from him if I were you."

"He seems like a nice guy to me. Maybe when I am in college, he will ask me out on a real date," Sophie said wistfully.

"It might be better for you if he doesn't ask you out," Ruby said, ending the conversation so she could study.

Chapter Thirty-Nine

It was inevitable that Sophie would go to Florida State College for Women. Her mother approved of it because it was an all-girls school and because Sophie got an academic scholarship from the school. Sophie loved it because her friends were there, and Richard, her dream-man, was not far away at the University of Florida.

Sophie spent the summer before college helping her mother with various tailoring projects. She helped knit and crochet items her mother sold to friends at the Temple and in the neighborhood. And she babysat for extra money to spend on school clothes. Having grown up in South Florida and never needing a coat or warm sweaters, she knew she had to supplement her wardrobe with clothes more suitable for North Florida.

One night, before Sophie and her friends left for school, Ruby called, saying, "Sophie, you'll never guess who is in town. Richard!"

Trying to sound nonchalant, Sophie said, "Oh. That's nice."

"We've called a bunch of people to meet at the park on Singer Island. You know the one where everyone goes to party?" Ruby continued.

Sophie's heart skipped a beat when she thought of the tall, brown-haired, blue-eyed guy she met last year and with whom she had spent an innocent weekend. "Sure. I'll come if my mother will let me. See you later." She hung up the phone and took several deep breaths before she asked her mother. Hannah was in the living room, knitting a baby sweater for a friend's grandchild. "Mom, is it okay if I spend the night at Ruby's tonight? They are having a small get-together because her cousin is in town."

"Is this the boy Richard I have heard stories about?" Hannah looked up from her knitting. "He is supposed to be quite handsome and known for taking advantage of young girls. I also know about the wild beach parties on Singer Island." She hesitated, put her knitting down, and motioned to Sophie to come sit on the sofa next to her. "Sophie, we have worked very hard to make sure you have a good reputation. I don't want you getting drunk and doing something with him that would ruin all that we have worked for," Hannah said, and added, "By the way, does he know you are only seventeen?"

Sophie asked, controlling her voice as best she could, "What do you mean by 'we'? I've worked hard at school; I made good grades. I have a good reputation." She rose from the sofa. "What is it you are so worried about? Did you do something when you were young that got you into trouble?" She glared at her mother and asked, "Why would you say such terrible things to me?"

Hannah realized she might have gone too far, but she had to guide Sophie in the right direction. Not in the direction she had gone. "Yes, you can go. I just want what's best for you, Sophie. You still need me to help you know what is right and wrong..."

"I don't need you dictating my life anymore," Sophie said defiantly. "I have my scholarship and my own spending money. So leave me alone." She stormed out of the house and slammed the front door.

Ruby was in front of Sophie's house in her parents' car. Sophie opened the backdoor and threw her small suitcase on the seat.

As Sophie got into the car, she said, "I hate my mother! I can't wait to go to college and get away from her."

"I know," Ruby replied. "You don't have to deal with your parents as much once you get to school. You'll be there soon. Let's talk about the party tonight."

"Who's going to be there?" Sophie asked.

"I'm not sure. I just know Richard is going. He said we could come," Ruby said.

"Will other girls my age be there?" Sophie asked beginning to worry about how she'd fit in with the people at the party.

"I don't know about your age, but a few of the college juniors and seniors will be there," Ruby explained.

As they reached the beach where the party was, a long line of parked cars covered one shoulder of the road. Ruby had to park behind the last car so they had a long walk down the beach to where the other people had gathered. As they traversed the dry sand, the girls passed people they didn't recognize. When they got to the outer ring of people surrounding a small fire pit, Ruby saw Richard and waved at him.

He walked over to the girls and said, "Hi. Glad you could come. I don't think you will know most of the people here, but make yourselves at home."

"Thanks," said Ruby. "You remember Sophie, don't you?"

"Sure," he said. "Hello. Good to see you again."

Sophie hesitated before she spoke. She wanted to say "the right" words to him, but all she said was "Hello."

Richard walked away and joined a group of couples. He put his arm around the only girl standing by herself.

Sophie and Ruby walked around to see who else was there. They didn't recognize anyone.

"I'm sorry, Sophie," Ruby said. "It looks like everyone here is older than us. Let's just go back to my house. Is that okay?"

Sophie took one last look at Richard and the tall, blonde girl he was hugging, and said, "Sure. Let's go back to your place."

The girls walked back to their car and left, having been at the party less than an hour. Sophie was quiet as they drove home. She was disappointed Richard had paid so little attention to her, but didn't want to tell Ruby that she was. It was best to forget about Richard, just like Ruby had told her.

Chapter Forty

FSCW's semester started on the first week of September. Hannah was never much of a driver; she stopped driving when she decided she couldn't afford a car. Luckily, Connie's parents, Mr. and Mrs. Finegold, volunteered to drop Sophie off when they drove Connie to school. At 7:00 A.M. on the first Saturday of September, Sophie, Hannah, Connie, and her parents loaded the girls and their belongings into the car.

"Let me at least give you some money for taking Sophie with you," Hannah said to the Finegolds as she pulled a twenty-dollar bill from her dress pocket.

"Heck, we are driving Connie up there. There's plenty of room in this old car. All of us can fit. Think nothing of it," Mr. Finegold said, refusing Hannah's money.

The trip from West Palm Beach to Tallahassee was more than twelve hours of driving if they drove without stopping.. Instead of trying to do it in one day, they decided to stop at a motel to spend the night.

Early the next day, Connie and Sophie sat in the backseat of the car and talked softly to each other while Connie's parents talked to each other about household and family issues.

"Are you scared?" Connie asked.

"A little," Sophie admitted. "Are you?"

"Yes, me, too. Do you think we will get to room together like we requested?" Connie was worried they wouldn't.

"Yeah, I think so. I think they told my mom that they grant freshmen's rooming requests because it makes adjusting to college easier than placing us with a stranger," Sophie reassured Connie and gently squeezed her hand.

The girls and their parents counted on this rumor being accurate. Sophie and Connie purchased the same twin bed sets with curtains to match. They knew the basic layout of the dorm rooms because of their frequent trips to visit Dotty and Ruby.

After two grueling days in the car with the windows open, the girls and the Finegolds were tired and ready to be done with the trip. As the car drove onto the campus, everyone perked up. Mrs. Finegold read the map to Mr. Finegold enabling him to focus on the road. Even though only freshmen were checking in that day, cars, trunks, and teary-eyed parents and students covered the dorm area.

It took several hours to get all of the girls' belongings into their room on the third floor. Luckily, the building was one of the new ones that had an elevator. Had it not, the girls' trunks would have stayed in the stairwell.

"Go on, Mom and Dad," Connie urged her parents. "We can take it from here. You have a long drive back, so why not get on the road now?"

"You're right, honey," Mr. Finegold said as he hugged his youngest child. He turned to his wife and said, "Come, dear. Let's leave these college girls alone so they can finish setting up their room."

Mrs. Finegold tried not to cry as she squeezed her daughter, but she couldn't help it. "You're my baby and in college! I'm officially an empty-nester."

Chapter Forty-One

"Do you realize that only eight percent of all girls go to college," Sophie told her friends one afternoon as they ate lunch in the school's large dining hall. "My sociology teacher told us that in class today." Sophie stopped talking and drank a sip of her steaming hot chocolate." It is really unique that all four of us are here, in college, statistically I mean."

The other girls laughed. "Of course, we are special," Ruby said as she slowly found and removed all the red onions she had specifically asked the staff to not put in her salad. "Maybe that is why we have been friends for so long. We aren't like the other girls we knew in high school."

"Yeah, that's true. Look at all the weddings and baby showers we've been invited to by our high school friends," Connie added. Her older sister, Betty, dropped out of school three years ago, in eleventh grade, to marry her boyfriend, a senior who also dropped out before graduation, because she was pregnant. Betty had two small children now, and her husband worked in his parents' dry goods store.

"Well, I want to get married and have babies now," Dotty added, "I want to find an older guy. One about to graduate from college. So, I can get married soon. I don't really care about getting a college education, but don't tell my parents I said that."

"Isn't that what we all want? To find a college man to marry?" Ruby asked. "My parents made it very clear to me that college was only for me if I promised to try and find a nice Jewish man to marry me. A man with more earning potential than the boys we know in West Palm Beach."

Sophie was silent. She loved college. Her courses, while more difficult than those in high school, barely challenged her, and she still made all A's. Her professors encouraged her. They were used to seeing girls who didn't take college seriously. Girls like Sophie's friends who wanted to meet a man and never graduate. Her professors saw something different in Sophie. Of course Sophie wanted to get married, just not immediately like her friends did. Maybe she'd be like her mother and wait until she was older to marry.

As she sat at the small round, formica table, Sophie had the dizzy sensation that she stood at the precipice of her life. A life separate from her mother, at least to some degree. She wanted to use her intelligence and college degree to be more than just a housewife. Hadn't her mother's skills been necessary for their survival? Sophie wanted to be prepared like her mother was, just in case one day she too had to support her family.

***

Dotty and Ruby's sorority, DPhiE, pursued Sophie, and she accepted their invitations to join. The fourth member of their group, Connie, was not in a sorority because her family couldn't afford the extra dues and fees associated with pledging. The four girls still saw each other, but Sophie, Ruby, and Dotty were together daily because of sorority activities and events.

On several Saturdays during her first two semesters, Sophie ran into Richard on campus. He was always with a different girl, but was cordial to Sophie when she saw him.

"Hey, Sophie," he said one Saturday when he happened to be alone. "I hope you like being here. Ruby told me you had joined a sorority." He straightened up, puffed out his chest like a strutting peacock, and added, "Did you know I am president of my fraternity? If you ever get to Gainesville, you ought to come by the TEΦ house sometime, and I will show you around."

"Yeah, I made it here, like I told you I would. And, I am a pledge this year." She brushed her hand through her black curly hair and gazed up at Richard, who stood almost a foot taller than she did. "They make us do some of the most ridiculous things in order to get our sorority pin. Really dumb, but it's the ritual. My days are very busy. Keeping up with my courses and doing sorority activities." She blushed, fearing that Richard must know she had a crush on him.

"I know all too well about the stupid things we made our pledges do," he grimaced. "Glad you got into a sorority, especially with Ruby. I really like her." He looked at his watch and said, "I'm running late. Gotta go. See you around," Richard said and walked toward Sorority Row.

I won't chase him, she thought. *If he wants to see me, he can call me and ask me out on a proper date.*

Chapter Forty-Two

1936 - 1939

After years of working for *Rich's* Department Store in the shoe department and in his cousins' furniture company, Leo still hadn't saved enough money to get any of his family out of Germany. He hadn't heard from them since he left Germany, in spite of his efforts to locate them. Although he didn't want to give up all hope of finding them, he spent less and less time looking for them. Every time he'd moved to a new city, Leo filed a new address with the American Red Cross and the United States Army. These organizations were most responsible for tracking German Jews with American relatives and getting them in touch with each other.

Leo took English lessons at the Atlanta Reform Temple that were offered to newly arrived immigrants from Germany. He spoke and understood English, but he still had a strong German accent that lingered. When he spoke, "work" sounded like "verk" and "want" sounded like "vant." The accent didn't bother most people, although occasionally, people would ask him if he was a Nazi. He told them, "Absolutely not. Those terrible people destroyed my family."

Each week, he used part of the money he earned to pay off the money his cousins had loaned him for his passage to America. He'd recently made the final payment and a great wave of relief overcame him. Now his savings would go to getting his family out of Germany.

Leo knew if he was going to eventually own a business, he needed to specialize. He had an opportunity to work as a traveling salesman for a nationwide furniture manufacturer, but it meant he had to move. Florida would be his territory and the company wanted him to move to Tallahassee, their regional headquarters.

At one of the monthly Friday night dinners with Jack and his family, Leo said to them, "I want all of you to know how much I appreciate what you have done for me since I moved here." He hesitated before he continued. "Although I've been unable to make enough money to pay for additional members of my family in Germany, I feel I have done my best. I will move to Tallahassee next week and begin my new job. Thank you." It was the longest speech he had ever given.

The day before Leo left for Tallahassee, a letter from the Red Cross arrived. His hands trembled and his heart boomed in his chest. It was posted six months before.

Dear Mr. Rosenstein:

We found the enclosed letter in a large bag of mail that had never been posted at one of the Nazis' concentration camps. I believe the letter was meant for you. The Red Cross helped us locate you as well as other survivors whose relatives died in the camp. Please accept our deepest condolences and our commitment to end the war with Germany and free all living concentration camp individuals.

Leo pulled out a thin piece of blue writing paper. He recognized his mother's handwriting immediately.

My dear, Leopold, my baby,

Conditions are not good here at the camp we were sent to after every one we knew was rounded up, and all of the Jews were put on trains to various camps. Luckily, your brother Simon escaped before they came for us, taking his chances with an underground group trying to save as many Jewish men as possible. His wife and baby should have been safe, as they were not Jewish, but they were taken anyway. We heard through others who were rounded up with her that your poor brother's wife was shot. The baby was given to a non-Jewish family to raise. Your sister, her husband, and the boys were sent to a camp not far from where we are, but that's all we know. I worry for those three children. They are so young; I don't know how they will survive.

Please thank our cousins for getting you out. You are not to worry about saving us. It is too late. None of this is your fault. My health is poor, and I am fairly certain I won't make it through the winter. They won't send me to a hospital because all the beds are reserved for Nazi soldiers. Papa sends his love, too. He is on the men's side of the camp, but we manage to see each other once in a while if we get to the fence separating the two camps. We must be careful in doing this, as the last couple caught talking at the fence was shot to death by the guards.

—Your loving mother

Leo was stunned by the information in the letter. It had to have been written not long after he fled to America. It had taken years to get to him. He wondered if there were more letters waiting to be delivered to him. He made sure his cousins in Atlanta knew how to find him and where to forward his mail. He knew in his heart that his parents were dead, but he held out hope for his brother and his sister and family. Maybe letters from them would bring hope.

Chapter Forty-Three

It was a sunny Sunday afternoon in Tallahassee when Sophie's secret dream came true. She ran into Richard, and he asked her if she wanted to come to Gainesville for a party at his fraternity the next weekend.

"This should be a great party. We have a live band coming. A few guys pitched in money to buy kegs of beer. Are you free on Saturday?" He paused and realized Sophie had to find a way to get to Gainesville. "I can find you a place to stay. Can you get there? I know a bunch of my fraternity brothers invited girls from Tallahassee. I can find you a ride."

"Sure. I can do that," Sophie said, trying to sound nonchalant. "Call me and let me know the arrangements."

When Sophie returned to her sorority house in Tallahassee, she told Dotty and Ruby the news. "I saw Richard. He invited me to a party next weekend." The words cascaded from her mouth, causing pools of pink to fill her cheeks.

"Just be careful," Ruby said, seeing her friend's excitement and wanting to save her from heartache. "I heard he just broke up with a girl he's been seeing. Rumor has it that she thought he was going to marry her. He dumped her as soon as she started pressing him to settle down."

"Don't worry," Sophie replied, shaking her head rapidly back and forth. "I know him and his reputation. I can handle him. I am more mature than I was last year. He's just someone to date."

Since beginning college, Sophie had dated several guys, but none of them held any interest to her. They were very childish and immature only wanting to get drunk and mess around. None of them could hold an adult conversation. If she were honest with herself, she would admit that she only wanted to date Richard.

***

Richard called on the afternoon before their date to let her know the plans. "The party is going to be at Crystal Lake, about ten miles outside of the city. We plan to roast hot dogs and have chips and beer. Bring pants and a sweater; it may get chilly. I have you set up to stay at a friend's sorority house with another girl from Tallahassee. She's got a car and will pick you up at 3:00 P.M. outside your sorority house."

"Okay," Sophie answered, forcing herself to speak slowly, unexcitedly. "I'll be ready to go. I'll bring a few things to spend the night. I'm looking forward to seeing you."

Sophie didn't own a pair of pants, so she walked downtown and bought a pair of pants like she had seen in a fashion magazine. Her mother would never approve of such an item of clothing. The act of buying the pants made her pulse race—a symbolic break with her mother. She bought a bright red, casual cotton cardigan with buttons down the front. By unbuttoning the top two buttons, she exposed the tops of her firm, large breasts. She planned to wear her trench coat over her outfit to avoid getting into trouble with the housemother who would demand Sophie take off the pants and put on an acceptable outfit. Sophie wanted to fit in with Richard's friends and look like the girls he hung out with in Gainesville.

In Gainesville, Richard was fifteen minutes late picking her up. "Sorry about that," he said. "I ended up having to pick up one of the beer kegs before I came here."

"That's okay," Sophie replied. "I didn't think you stood me up, yet. Maybe if you were five more minutes late, I would think you'd forgotten me." She laughed. "I need to be back by twelve. You know that, don't you?" she asked.

"Sure, I know. I will have you back on time. Don't worry," Richard said as he took her elbow to help her into his car. She held a blanket, one her mother made, on her lap.

It took twenty minutes to drive to the party at the lake. Cars were parked on both sides of the dirt road. When Sophie got out of the car and took off her trench coat, Richard said, "Wow. You look really good in that outfit. I'll need to stay close to you all night so no one tries to steal you from me."

"How flattering. Would you be jealous?" Sophie teased him, trying to sound sophisticated.

He waved to a man who was walking by their car. "Hey, George, can you help me carry this keg down to the lake? It takes more than one guy to lift this."

As they walked to the beach, Sophie noticed the other people were seniors or graduate students. She didn't see anyone she knew, which was puzzling because she thought freshmen girls might be there. It didn't matter. She looked older than she was and knew how to act with people older than her. She had done it most of her life.

Richard handed her a plastic cup filled with cold beer and a hot dog covered with mustard and relish that she ate while standing near the fire the men built. Richard was on his second or third beer.

"Let's walk around the lake," he said as he filled Sophie's cup with more beer. He refilled his cup, and they walked away from the crowd of people. As they approached where they had parked the car, he grabbed Sophie's blanket from the car. "Is it okay if we use this to sit on the beach?" He didn't wait for an answer and just carried it with them as they moved farther and farther away from the others.

When they reached a private spot on the beach he asked, "How about sitting here for a little while?" He shook the blanket out and placed it gently on the dark sand. "Wouldn't want to get sand all over that pretty outfit, would you?" he added.

"Sure," Sophie replied as she dropped down onto the right edge of the blanket. She placed her beer in a small hole she dug in the sand.

Richard sat next to her and placed his cup on the other side of the blanket. They sat quietly for a few minutes, looking at the stars.

"You can't see stars this clearly back in town," Sophie said. "Thanks for bringing me tonight. This is great."

Richard leaned over and put his arm around Sophie. With his other hand, he turned her face to him. He kissed her gently on the lips. She had never felt such soft, warm lips. He probed her mouth softly with his tongue. Sophie felt light-headed as she kissed him back.

The kisses deepened. Richard's hands roamed her body, stopping at her breasts to pay extra attention to them.

"Let's lie down," he said as he moved carefully to position her on her side, facing him. His large, strong hands found her legs, her bottom, and between the legs of her pants. Sophie pulled away slightly and said, "Please, let's not move so fast. This is our first date and I think we should go slower."

"It's not really our first date. You have known me a long time," he corrected her while he ran his fingers down the side of her face. "Ever since I met you at Ruby's house two years ago. Come on. I'm not going to do anything you don't want me to do. I promise."

Sophie didn't reply. She went back to kissing him. As his hands followed the contours of her body, she quivered. She was overwhelmed with unfamiliar emotions. Tingling, pulsing, panting. She loved how it felt to be so close to another human, a man. She was unaccustomed to physical affection. Being held and touched melted her inside and out.

But she heard her mother's voice in her head: "Sophie, remember your reputation. Don't do anything to jeopardize your good name."

Richard's hands moved up her back under her sweater. He unhooked her bra. "Just let me touch your breast. You'll see how good it feels."

135

She let him. He was right about how good it felt. Her nipples hardened and moisture coated her panties. Everything moved faster now. They were naked except for their underwear. Sophie felt something hard against her leg. She knew what it was from the information she found long ago from the library.

"Sophie, please, let me put this in you," he said as he placed her hand on his erection. "I'll be careful. I promise. I assume you are a virgin, right?"

"Yes, I am a virgin. I want to save this for the man I plan to marry."

"Come on, Soph, it's okay. I know many girls who don't wait until they are married." He continued to caress her nipple. "What are you concerned about? You know I really like you, don't you?" He stopped talking and searched her face for an answer. "How about we become boyfriend and girlfriend? Would that make it better?"

"I guess. But you can only put it in once. I don't want to become pregnant. My mother would kill me," Sophie replied, comfortable that they were a real couple and sex was allowed if you were in love, going steady.

As impossible as the request was, Richard agreed to do what Sophie requested. Just as he was about to enter her, she said, "Stop. I've changed my mind. I'm sorry. Please don't put it in me." Her voice shook as she added, "Please don't be mad at me."

"What am I supposed to do with this?" He held his throbbing, erect penis in his hand. "I guess I'll have to take care of it myself." Angrily, he proceeded to masturbate watching Sophie's reactions.

"Look at me," he commanded getting more excited knowing Sophie had never experienced a man masturbating. "Watch me."

Sophie couldn't take her eyes off Richard as he yanked and pulled on himself. He came shooting sperm on his hand and Sophie's blanket. As he climaxed, she felt her own body shutter.

How he hated dating innocent women and having to complete the act with his hand. Those days had ended when he was fourteen. Sure, he masturbated when he was alone, but having to when he was with a woman was beneath him. Maybe he could train Sophie, ease her into having sex with him. "Sophie, I want to show you something. I won't go inside of you with my penis. Just lay back and give in to the feeling."

Sophie, thankful for Richard respecting her wishes, lay back on the blanket. She was so turned on by watching Richard. It took only a few minutes of him rubbing her vaginal area and pushing his fingers in and out of her that she felt tremors of pleasure wash over her. This must have been what the books called an orgasm. She had her first one. "Wow," she said. "That was incredible. Is that what it feels like for you?"

"I don't know," he said and laughed. "I've never been a woman so I don't know how it feels for you." He glanced at his watch. "Oh, I didn't realize how late it is. We better get back if I am going to have you home in time."

They picked up the blanket and shook out the sand. Richard folded it and carried it back to the car. They drove back to the sorority house in silence. Sophie was thrilled; Richard was now her boyfriend.

Chapter Forty-Four

1940

Spring semester was almost over, and Sophie needed a job to earn more spending money. Her scholarship covered tuition, books, and part of her room and board. Her mother paid for the rest of the costs, but Sophie was responsible for paying her sorority dues and buying new clothes. She applied for a bookkeeping job at the local department store, *Weinstein's, Tallahassee's Finest*. She had always been good with numbers. She told her prospective employer about her grades in all of her math courses, and she was able to pass a short bookkeeping test the human resources employee gave her. Sophie took three, rather than four, classes for the summer and continued an on-again, off-again relationship with Richard.

While classes and work were going smoothly, things with Richard were getting very bumpy. She suspected Richard was seeing other women. She didn't see him every weekend, because one Saturday a month, she had to work. She understood Richard needed constant attention from women. Even if he promised her that he was her boyfriend, he would still have sex with other women. Sophie didn't like this. It made her very angry.

I hate him for this, she thought. *He said he's my boyfriend, but then, I don't see him for weeks. What a jerk.*

One afternoon, Sophie went to the department store's tearoom to grab a quick bite to eat. In line stood a tall man with ink-black hair, kind dark eyes, and an endearing grin. She heard him ask the cashier, "Where do you keep the sugar?"

She recognized the accent immediately. "Excuse me," she said to the man getting his change and two packages of sugar. "Are you from Germany? I noticed your accent. I was born here and traveled to Germany multiple times with my mother to see her family."

He turned to look at her and said, "Ya, I have been in America six years." Leo looked at the stunning young lady in front of him and asked, "Would you like to sit with me while we eat? We can talk some more."

Sophie looked up into the man's large black eyes and smiling face and replied, "Yes," and they walked to a corner booth with their lunch trays.

"My name is Leo Rosen." He placed his napkin on his lap and added, "Actually, Leopold Wolfgang Rosenstein. They made me change my name when I came to America."

"I'm Sophie Straus. I was born in New Jersey, but my parents both came from small towns near Frankfurt. I only know my mother's family, not my father's." She paused, thinking about how strange it might appear not to know one's father. "My father died before I was born. They married late in life. My mother lives in West Palm Beach."

"Frankfurt? That is not too far from where I was born and raised. I left before the war and lived in Atlanta for four years." He finished his sandwich and was totally focused on Sophie. "I worked for a furniture company, traveling from town to town. Mr. Weinstein met me when I called on him to buy our new line of sofas. He offered me a job here selling furniture. I'm so lucky to have met him. He and his family have been very kind to me."

"I only work here part-time as a bookkeeper. I go to school the rest of the time. I'm a sophomore at FSCW," Sophie explained as she finished her soup and salad.

"A college girl. I figured that. Do you have a boyfriend?" Leo said, and then added, "I'm sorry. I shouldn't ask you that, as we just met."

"It's okay," Sophie said, laughing. "Yes, I have a part-time boyfriend. He thinks I don't know, but he sees other women besides me. I don't like it, but what can I do? I guess I could ask him to stop, but I am afraid he would stop dating me if I do." She had no idea why she shared so much information with Leo, someone she just met.

"If you were my girlfriend, I'd only date you." Leo smiled at her. He liked her openness and how quickly she confided in him. He hadn't had a close friend since he left Germany, and this young lady made him feel at ease. "I wouldn't need to see anyone else." He looked at his watch. "I have to get back to the floor. Maybe we could have lunch together some other time when you are working." He left her sitting at the table, finishing her lunch.

Sophie walked back to the office area on the second floor. She thought about how nice it was to have a man's full attention, to not feel like she was competing with other women all the time. Leo's face, with his strong, square chin, and his perfect nose and evenly spaced eyes, looked like he could be a model. He didn't appear to be aware of how attractive he was, which added to his appeal.

Leo had moved to Tallahassee permanently after Mr. Weinstein offered him the full-time position. He lived in a one-bedroom apartment near the store and furnished it with items from the store that were marred or damaged.

"Leo," Mr. Weinstein had said, "I donate furniture all the time to German and Polish immigrants who join our Temple—people who came here with nothing but the clothes on their backs. It's my way of helping people out, of doing a mitzvah. And I don't want you telling me that you will pay me back. It's a gift."

Leo selected only what he absolutely needed. A fake wood bedroom set, wooden dining room table and chairs, a blue couch with overstuffed pillows, and a large living room chair and ottoman. He felt he had his own home for the first time since he left Germany.

Although he liked living in Tallahassee, it seemed like such a small and backward town after living in Atlanta. People were kind and friendly, but there was less for a single man to do who was not affiliated with the college. Meeting Sophie was an emotional boost after feeling alone for so long.

Leo still hoped to find members of his family alive. He made more money than he had in his life, so he put part of each paycheck into the bank savings account. Visas and ocean passage tickets were expensive. Just communicating with his family in New Jersey and Atlanta via phone calls was expensive, and mailing letters overseas was costly.

He had not received any more mail from Germany. At night, after work, lying in his bed, he would try not to think about what happened to his family. When he thought of all the horrible possibilities, he became sad and felt like a failure. "It is my fault. I shouldn't have left them there," he lamented. "I should have stayed with them. I shouldn't be alive if they are dead."

On his worst days, if he didn't have to work, he sat in a chair in his living room. The shades drawn; no light in the small room. His head pounded. He prayed for death. "Why did God let me live and take the rest of my family? Why am I left to suffer? Does my being here have any meaning?" No one could console him, not the rabbi, not any of the congregation, and not any of the other Holocaust survivors he met who had made it to America. In his nightmares, he heard his mother saying, "Leopold, Leopold, save me, save me." He couldn't save her in his dreams or in real life.

Chapter Forty-Five

By day, Leo stayed busy and didn't have any time to fret about what might or might not be. Although his headaches came more often, he was able to function. No one at work knew about his headaches; he suffered silently. He didn't even tell Sophie. She brightened his life, and he didn't want to scare her away with his dark moods.

Two days a week, they had lunch together at the store. Once a month, they went to the movies together after the store had closed. They weren't dating; she had a boyfriend—a fraternity boy from the University of Florida. He couldn't compete with that, so he was content just being her friend.

Leo felt he could talk to Sophie. Slowly, he began telling her bits and pieces about his life, his family, and his hopes and dreams. Sophie told him about her domineering mother, her early life going back and forth to Germany, and what it was like being an only child. She envied Leo's having had a big family and understood how horrific it was for him to believe he had lost them all.

Chapter Forty-Six

1940

Sophie had been dating Richard for almost a year. Predictably, each date ended with the struggle over how far she would go. One weekend, they planned a trip to the beach with several carloads of couples. Sophie had to lie about where she was going to the sorority housemother because girls were not allowed off campus with men, only with family or family friends who had been cleared by the university. She told the housemother that she was going away with an aunt and uncle.

As soon as Sophie and Richard reached the beach houses they rented with the other couples, Richard's attitude changed. In their bedroom, he increased the pressure on her to her to finish what they had started at the lake party outside of Gainesville. "Come on, Sophie. You know I care about you." He kissed her on the ear, licking the lobe softly with his tongue. He knew she liked this from all the petting sessions they had. Sessions that always ended with Sophie not letting him go all the way.

"You know I wouldn't do anything to get you in trouble. Please, let's do it right. We have this great room and bed. It would be a shame to waste it." His fingers ran up her leg under her skirt, under her panties, to her clitoris. She shivered with anticipation, trained by him to know the pleasure of what comes next when she let him rub her until she climaxed.

Panting, not wanting him to stop, she consented to going all the way, but not before adding conditions. "All right, Richard, but I need to know if you love me. I said I would save myself for the man I love and will marry."

"Of course I love you, sweetie," he said as he gently pulled off her shirt and bra and helped her take off her skirt. He was down to his underpants. When he pulled them off, she was taken aback by the size of him. She had not seen him completely naked before now. She was familiar with the feel of his erect penis and how it felt to make him come with her hands. But, she had kept her eyes closed, not wanting to see what she was doing.

"Come here," he commanded, pulling her down onto the bed. He took off her panties and kissed her on her mouth. His hands traveled up and down her small body. She squirmed under his hand. "When did you last have a period?" he asked as he fondled her clitoris again, knowing how much she loved this.

"Why? I guess last week," she said, breathing rapidly.

"I just want to be safe. I don't want you to get pregnant." He continued to tease her with his finger.

"I think we are okay. Did you not bring any protection?" Her sorority sisters had warned her about having sex with a man without a rubber. She had almost given into him without asking.

"You're okay. We will be fine." He made sure she was very wet before he entered her. He wanted her to enjoy this, too. Before he began thrusting hard in to her, he teased her by slowly pulling himself out just to the tip of his penis. He heard her moan, so he pushed back in.

"My God, Richard, don't stop!" she demanded.

He continued, doing all the things he knew women liked. He held back, moving in and out of Sophie, paying attention to the moans that escaped her mouth. He knew she was a virgin, but he also knew she could climax. He felt her begin to shutter, and he moved faster and faster. They came together. Richard was proud of this: a simultaneous climax. They lay drenched with sweat on the bed, bodies entangled.

"Do you love me, Richard?" she asked.

"Of course I do. Didn't I just show you I did?" he said as he started to excite her again. He had no idea this little girl would be so responsive.

144

***

After each of the many times they had sex over the weekend, Sophie made plans in her head for their engagement. Richard, on the other hand, tried to figure out how long it would be before they could go away together again.

The weekend flew by, and soon they were back in Tallahassee. Richard remained in the car when Sophie removed her suitcase from the trunk. She leaned over the open driver's side window, and he kissed her. "I'll call you this week," he said and drove out of the parking lot.

Sophie went into the sorority house and unpacked. She had to get ready for school and work on the next day. She hadn't done any homework while she was with Richard, so she had to catch up on her reading and finish a paper for her English class. As she sat at the small desk in the corner of the room, her body throbbed and her vagina felt bruised from all the weekend's activity.

It was hard to study. All she thought about was Richard and how close they were now. How he loved her. How they might get married. When she finally went to sleep at 2:00 AM, she dreamed of her future with Richard.

Back at the store on Monday afternoon after classes, Sophie ran into Leo.

"How was your weekend, Sophie?" he asked.

"It was great," she said without giving him any details. Leo was a kind man, and she knew he liked her. She had mixed feelings about him. As long as Richard was in the picture, Leo would be just a friend.

Even if Sophie wasn't interested in Leo, other women were. He attracted women. He had a natural charisma that drew people to him. When he first moved to Tallahassee, he joined the local Temple and attended most of the singles' social events. He was a great dancer and could whistle any tune people asked him to do. He never had a problem getting a date, and he had casual sex with several of the women he met through the Temple or from work. There was no one special, except for Sophie, but she was taken.

Chapter Forty-Seven

1940

During the Christmas break, Sophie went home to West Palm Beach to spend a few weeks with her mother. She had not seen her in months.

"On the first morning of her being home, Sophie woke at 6:00 A.M., feeling like she needed to vomit. She sat on the cold bathroom floor, close to the toilet, just in case. After a few minutes the nausea passed, Sophie went to the kitchen and said, "Mother, I'm not feeling well this morning. I think I caught the flu or something on the train down here,"

"It's okay, dear, to rest. After all, you've been working so hard. Between school and work at the department store and all your sorority activities, I am not surprised you are sick." Hannah stood outside the bathroom door. "You can take it easy today, but only today."

Hannah planned social events almost every day of the first week Sophie was home. She wanted to show her friends and family how well Sophie was doing at school: Dean's list for her freshman year, most popular sorority pledge, having a full scholarship plus working to earn extra money. Hannah was so proud of what she and Sophie had achieved, without a husband for her and a father for Sophie.

The next morning, when Hannah opened Sophie's bedroom door to check on her, she found her daughter still in bed. Sophie raised her head from the pillow and asked, "Can I just go back to sleep for a few more hours? I know you made luncheon plans for us with Molly and her daughters. I promise I will be up and dressed by the time we need to leave." She hoped the dizziness and nausea would pass by then.

As soon as Hannah closed the bedroom door, Sophie began counting. "I've missed one period, but it might be two. My period is so damn irregular." Her head swam as she tried to calculate days. "It's hard to keep exact track of my cycle. Oh, God, please don't let me be pregnant. Please. My mother will kill me." She rolled over and went back to sleep until her alarm went off.

Hannah poked her head into Sophie's bedroom again later in the morning. "Feeling better, dear? It's about time we leave if we are going to be on time for lunch." She surveyed the messy room and her daughter's rumpled bed. "You haven't spent time with your Aunt Molly and her children. They want to see you."

"I don't think I can go and eat anything," Sophie replied. Then, with the need to make more excuses, she added, "I just don't have anything in common with them anymore since I went to college. They'll just gossip about people I don't know or care about. Why don't you go without me?"

Hannah was startled, beginning to be impatient with Sophie. "Exactly what do you mean you don't have anything in common anymore? They are your family. Is this because you think you are too good for them now?" She sat on the edge of Sophie's bed. "Just because you are a college girl? Or is it about your relationship with that boy who I told you was no good? That Richard person? Ruby's cousin?" She rose from the bed and walked over to the window near the head of Sophie's bed. "I've heard stories about the girls he's ruined, and I don't want you lumped into the same category as them."

Sophie sat upright and leaned against the white headboard. She needed support and backing from the strong, solid wood to handle her mother's heated reaction.

Her mother continued. "I will not tolerate your ruining your reputation as well as mine. You need to find a nice man and get married. What nice man would marry you if you have a bad reputation?" Hannah was almost out of control, yelling at Sophie.

She took a deep breath and continued ranting. "I have given you everything you needed and wanted. I did this without a husband. Your poor father worked so hard that it killed him." She wanted to grab her daughter and shake her. "He would not have liked to see how you have turned out. So mean and nasty."

Sophie said angrily, "Maybe I never did have a father. Maybe you made that up." She glared at her mother, wanting to see if her arrow had hit the target: her mother's ego. "Maybe you were never married. Maybe I was one of those children born out of wedlock."

At that point, Hannah slapped Sophie. They were both stunned.

Sophie began to cry. "Get out of my room! Get out of my room!"

Hannah stormed from the room. She was dumbfounded. She wondered. *Where had all of this anger and resentment come from? Had Sophie always been this way or had college changed her?* It couldn't have been Hannah. She was a great mother, sacrificing everything for Sophie.

For the first time in many years, she thought about the baby boy she gave away. *He'd think I was a good mother. He wouldn't yell at me.* Sometimes, he appeared in her dreams, his sweet face smiling at her. *I'll not think about him. It does me no good. He is gone, and it is best I don't think about him. But Sophie. What about Sophie? I need to get to the bottom of this.*

Chapter Forty-Eight

By the third week she was home, Sophie accepted the possibility that she was pregnant. She made an appointment at a women's clinic in Lake Worth to make sure before she told anyone. She told her mother that she was going to visit an old friend from high school and took the bus to Lake Worth, an even smaller town than West Palm Beach, where she knew no one.

Once the doctor confirmed she was pregnant, Sophie knew she had to tell her mother and that she couldn't go back to college the next quarter. As she rode the bus home, tears ran down her face, but she didn't make a sound. She, who had been starving herself to look thin, knew she had to start eating. If she ate as much food as she craved, the baby would grow and begin to show. Her mother was bound to notice. It was not something she could hide on a petite body.

She looked around at the other people on the bus. *I know they can tell I am pregnant*, she thought. Then she thought about the names her mother would call her—*Slut. Whore. Unwed mother.* There was nothing her mother could say that she hadn't said to herself.

As she walked home from the bus stop, she thought about her relationship with Richard. They had made love dozens of times. She couldn't get enough of him and how good it felt to be so close and intimate with another person. To have someone's hands touch her. His body next to her. To be hugged and kissed. Feelings she had not experienced before. Now there was the harsh reality of what the payment was for the pleasure she had experienced.

Sophie hadn't bothered to tell Richard when she missed her periods. She knew he was losing interest in her. She heard he had a new girlfriend, and she and Richard rarely saw each other. She knew this was his way of breaking up with her, seeing her less and less until the relationship was over. She knew nothing was going to come of their relationship. She knew he wouldn't marry her.

Sophie did not come out of her room for the rest of the day. She rehearsed what she would tell her mother. Late in the day, Hannah knocked on the door and asked if Sophie wanted something to eat.

"No, thanks, Mother," she answered and then lied. "I ate a late lunch with Connie. I'm really tired, so I think I will read a while and then go to sleep early. See you in the morning."

The next morning, Sophie got up before her mother and made coffee. She took a cup to her mother's room and knocked on the door.

"Mother, can I come in? I brought a cup of coffee for you."

"Sophie, how thoughtful. Please come in." Hannah had calmed down since their argument and since Sophie had promised to visit all of the people Hannah wanted her to see. Hannah sat on the edge of her bed, putting on her bedroom slippers.

Sophie handed the hot coffee to her mother and blurted out, "I have something I need to tell you, and there is no easy way to say it. I think I am pregnant. Richard is the father. He's ruined me, just like you said he would." Her head was down and tears ran down her face. Shame flamed red on her face.

"You are what?" Hannah's voice rose. "You are pregnant? You slut! You whore! How could you do this to us? Have you told him?"

"No, Mother, no one knows." Sophie knew what her mother's reaction would be, but preparation didn't cushion her from the pain.

"Not him or any of your friends?" Hannah's reputation radar awoke.

"No, Mother. No one knows but you and me. Oh, and the doctor I saw in Lake Worth. Don't worry. I gave him a false name." Exhausted, yet relieved she had told her mother, Sophie wanted to go back into the cocoon of her bed.

Hannah sat numbly on the corner of the bed. "I bet he told you that he loved you. Didn't he?"

"Yes, Mother. He said he loved me." Sophie hung her head.

"I will not let you ruin everything we've worked for. Now, go to your room and let me think. Don't come out until I call you." Hannah bounded off the bed. She went to the dresser drawer, pulled out her address book, and flipped through the pages, looking for the right name and number.

As Hannah walked to the kitchen to use the phone, she felt like she was breathing under water. *How could Sophie do such a thing? Why would this smart child make such a stupid mistake?* She poured another cup of coffee and added cream and sugar. Her thoughts swirled in circles. *Like mother, like daughter? Surely not. Was making wrong decisions about men inherited?*

One question led to another. *Was it because Sophie never had a father?* It couldn't be that. Hannah had a father, and she still got pregnant by the wrong man. *Well, no use worrying about why she did it,* she thought as she picked up the phone to call her cousin in New Jersey.

Meanwhile, Sophie was glad to be in her room. She didn't want to see or listen to her mother any longer. The truth was out. At this point, she knew all she would get from her mother were accusations. And the typical response: "Why did this happen to me?" To Hannah, it was always about what happened to Hannah. Why, when Sophie needed her mother's support and understanding, was her mother so incapable of giving it?

Dinnertime came and went, and Hannah didn't call Sophie out to eat. By 10:00 P.M., Sophie knew her mother wasn't going to tell her it was okay for her to leave her room. "She's punishing me," Sophie realized. She left her room and went to the kitchen. She was ravenous. She had starved herself for months, trying to hide her pregnancy. There was no reason for her to starve anymore. Her mother knew. Her size didn't matter.

Chapter Forty-Nine

The next morning, the phone's shrill ringing jarred Sophie awake. She dragged herself from her warm, safe bed and walked to the kitchen in time to see her mother carry the phone, with its extra-long cord, to her bedroom. Sophie fixed herself a cup of coffee and slathered a hard roll with butter and orange marmalade. She took her breakfast with her and stood by her mother's closed bedroom door, listening.

"Yes," Hannah said to the person on the other end of the line. "I can get her ready by then. Which train do you suggest we use? Okay. Okay. I think we can be ready the day after tomorrow." She hung up the phone. "Sophie," she yelled. "Please come in. I can see your feet under the door."

Sophie came in and sat on the chair in the corner of the room. Her eyes were swollen from crying all night.

"This is what we are going to do," Hannah said, coldly calm. "We are taking the train to Newark on Thursday, where you will live with our cousins, Edwin and Martha Blum." She paused and watched Sophie's eyes. "You may not remember them, but you met them years ago. You'll stay with them until the baby is born, and then you can come home."

Sophie's eyes filled with tears of hurt and anger, but she didn't interrupt her mother. *I deserve whatever my mother does to punish me*, she thought.

"There will be no further discussion on this matter, ever," Hannah continued. "You'll agree to tell no one, not even your best friends, about this baby. I am very serious about this." She pointed her index finger at Sophie to make sure she understood the rules. "You and I will never speak of this child again. The baby is not yours. It is going to a distant cousin. They are being kind enough to do this for us. You will be courteous and do anything your cousins

153

Edwin and Martha ask you to do." She stopped talking and looked at Sophie directly in her eyes, and said, "Do you have any questions?"

Sophie put her cup of coffee on the edge of a small table next to her chair. "Do I have any say in this matter?" She knew the answer to the question, but she had to ask. To ascertain how firm her mother's resolve really was.

Hannah gritted her teeth and answered firmly like a judge sentencing a prisoner to death row. "Absolutely not."

"Can I know if it is a boy or a girl? Can I at least know what sex the baby I am giving away is?" Sophie begged.

"Yes, you can know that. I want you to know for the rest of your life what you gave up." Hannah was condemning Sophie to a life not different from her own: a torturous truth about a baby she couldn't keep. She envisioned the beautiful baby boy she gave up so many years ago. The pain of giving up her child had kept her from ever having sex with a man again. Now her own daughter had made the same mistake she had made: having sex with a man who would not marry her. She had to ensure that Sophie returned to being a good girl.

Hannah had plans for Sophie's life, and as her mother, she had the right to manipulate it. She had to find a man for Sophie who would marry her and make "an honest woman" out of her. "Go to your room and pack. Don't try to contact the man who did this to you. He can't know that you are pregnant. And don't tell your friends. They gossip. The less people who know, the better," she said, ending the conversation.

Chapter Fifty

The summer of 1941 was an ordeal for Sophie, not just because she was pregnant. She was a prisoner. Sophie was not allowed out of her cousins' house except to go to her doctor's appointments. She wore a raincoat to cover her shape. Edwin and Martha didn't want anyone to know that they had a pregnant cousin in their house. It wouldn't look good to the neighbors.

Edwin and Martha were polite to Sophie, but it was obvious they were doing this for another reason besides helping her mother out of a tough situation. She suspected these were the cousins who would keep her baby. They were in their late thirties and had not been able to have children of their own.

When her labor pains began, Sophie told Martha. Martha reassured her there was nothing to worry about and that Edwin would drive them to the hospital in plenty of time for the baby to be born.

"Martha, it hurts so much. Please ask Edwin to take us now. There is medicine they can give me so it won't hurt so much," Sophie pleaded.

"I am sorry, Sophie, but your mother made us promise we wouldn't allow them to give you pain meds. It is supposedly best for the baby not to have narcotics in its system." Martha felt awful about the promises she had made to Hannah.

Martha and Edwin had tried for years to have a child, but never did. Adopting Sophie's baby was the answer to all of their prayers. Sophie could never know that the cousins who took care of her during her pregnancy would be the child's parents.

As another labor pain gripped her body, Sophie pleaded with Martha, "Please, let's go. I beg you. It hurts too much." Sweat poured down her face. Her thin cotton shift was soaked with perspiration. "I think something is wrong with the baby. I read that when girls under a certain age have babies, their hips and bodies may be too small or underdeveloped."

"Oh, Sophie, your mother warned us that you would try to use your intelligence to manipulate us. I can see what she means," Martha replied while she avoided looking at her niece by folding the clean sheets and towels.

"I am not manipulating you now. I think something is wrong because it hurts so much," Sophie said weakly.

By the time Edwin drove them to the hospital, Sophie was so fatigued she could not stand up and walk. A smiling, young nurse approached them with a wheelchair.

"Get in here, honey. I'll take you to your room." As the nurse wheeled her to the maternity ward, the nurse asked, "Why did your parents wait so long to bring you here? We could have helped you with some medicine. We usually give young, first-time mothers this."

"These people are not my parents," Sophie said with no further explanation. She knew her mother had planned it this way. She wanted her to be punished as much as possible for her transgression. God, she hated her mother.

The baby was a girl. Before her cousins could stop her, Sophie asked the nurse quickly to show her the baby before they took her to the nursery. She knew this would be the only time she would see her daughter. The baby was so beautiful, with black curls and a small, pink mouth. Her eyes were deep black. Although unlikely, the baby appeared to look right at Sophie when the nurses placed her on her chest.

Sophie wept as she handed the baby back to the nurse.

"It's okay, honey," the nurse said quietly. "You'll see her again later."

Chapter Fifty-One

1941

Sophie returned to West Palm Beach with just enough time to pack to go back to college. Ruby and Dotty came over one day to hang out with her. Both girls commented on how thin Sophie was and how much they had missed her while she was away from school. They couldn't help but notice how sad she seemed, too. She wasn't eating, going out with the girls after work, or smiling.

"No, I didn't do anything special to lose weight. I've just been so active for the last few months, helping my aunt with her children," Sophie lied. "I guess I'm just sad I had to leave the children." This was the lie Hannah had concocted to explain Sophie's absence. She supposedly had been in New Jersey, helping her mother's cousin with a new baby and two other small children to earn money to continue college. However, it was true that Sophie missed "a baby," her baby.

"Sophie," Ruby said, "I know something else is wrong. Why can't you tell me? What could be so horrible that you can't tell your best friend? The only thing I can imagine being that bad is that you were you pregnant? Is that why you left for the summer?"

Sophie hesitated before answering. She wanted to confide in her friend, but she promised her mother she wouldn't tell anyone. "Ruby, please stop asking me. I told you what I can tell you. I was with my mother's cousins. I had to earn money. They got, I mean, they had a new baby. I helped them with her." She turned away from Ruby so she wouldn't see her eyes watering. "Now leave me alone about this. Let's just get ready to go back to school."

When it came time to go back to Tallahassee, Ruby's parents offered to drive Sophie back to college when they drove their daughter. Everyone noticed the icy good-bye between Sophie and her mother, but no one dared to ask about it.

Chapter Fifty-Two

1941

Leo's small apartment was close to downtown, so he walked to work at *Weinstein's Department Store.* He loved the walk and being outside, having spent so many years in cars and motels when he was a traveling salesman.

He ran into Sophie as they went in the employee entrance. "Sophie, I haven't seen you around all summer. Did you go away?"

"Yes, Leo. I, um, went to New Jersey and helped a cousin out with her three young children. I needed to earn some money to be able to continue school, and they paid me." She didn't smile or offer more explanation about her summer. She had trouble lying to people so she said very little about what she had done for the last few months.

"That was very nice of you to do. Are you close to these relatives? I am jealous because I have no family here," Leo told her, his sad eyes looking into hers.

"I am so sorry, Leo. I forgot that you told me about how your family was trapped in Germany." Sophie didn't want to take her bad mood out on Leo, who had been such a good friend. "My mother and a few of her family members got out before things got too difficult for the Jews in her town. Her parents died before the war. She has two brothers who both got away, but she hardly ever sees them." She opened her employee locker and put her hat and bag into the small space. "We aren't very close to them. My mother is angry with them about an inheritance they didn't share with her." She looked up at Leo and said, "She can really hold a grudge." She added, "How awful it must be for you to not know what happened to your family."

Leo changed the subject. He had no desire to talk about his grief. "So, how is your boyfriend? Did you get to see him while you were away?"

"Oh, things are over with him. We haven't seen each other in months." Sophie tried to sound unfazed by her break-up with Richard.

"Then, I can ask you out," Leo said, smiling broadly. "How about Saturday night? I finish work at 5:00 P.M. I assume the office is closed on Saturdays."

"They started closing the office every Saturday rather than one Saturday a month. And, yes, it would be nice to go out with you, Leo. Thanks for asking," Sophie replied, actually glad he asked. *I need to forget about Richard and the baby. To move on with my life. To find a decent man to marry me.* She thought.

Sophie took the stairs to the offices, and Leo walked downstairs to the furniture department.

During the day, Sophie thought about Leo. He was very handsome. She knew other women flirted with him, trying to get him to ask them out. The women in the store gossiped over lunch, and Sophie heard about various women's short-lived affairs with Leo.

Soon after, Leo and Sophie began dating, and in a few weeks, everyone in the store knew they were a "couple." Leo reluctantly talked to her about his family and how concerned he was about them. "I don't like having to talk about what happened and how I got out. I failed them. I couldn't make enough money to get any of them out." Hurt filled his eyes as he continued. "I couldn't convince my cousins in Atlanta to lend me any more money, so now I have no one in this country. They may all be dead," he said as a tear escaped down his cheek.

"Leo, I will be your family here. You can meet my family when I go home again. I know they'll like you," Sophie said without knowing the true implication of her statement.

Leo was an affectionate man who liked physical contact. He held Sophie's hand as they walked. He put his arm around her when they were at the movies. His touch was calming and reassuring, not like Richard's, which always seemed demanding. She and Leo easily progressed from kissing and hugging to petting.

One night when they were in Leo's apartment on his bed kissing, Leo, a sensual man by nature, gently caressed Sophie over her clothes. He slowly tugged at the bottom of her shirt, and Sophie pulled back from him.

"Sophie, what's wrong? Do you want me to stop what I am doing?" He quickly moved his hands away from her and sat upright on his bed. "You feel like you are tensing up. What's going on?"

"I'm just a little afraid," she explained.

"Are you afraid I will hurt you?" he asked. "Don't worry. I won't push you to do anything you don't want to do." He thought for a second and added, "Are you a virgin? It's okay if you are. It's okay if you are not. I love you and accept you any way you are."

"No, I am not a virgin." She sighed as she said this. "I'm just a little scared. I only had one man before you. Richard, the guy I dated." She looked directly at Leo. "I felt he used me." She sat up and kissed him. "It's okay. Let's keep going. But you must use protection." Her voice shook.

"Of course, I always use protection. We wouldn't want to have a baby before we were ready to be parents," he replied, unaware of the meaning of what he just said.

Sophie thought Richard had been a good lover, but Leo was so much more. He took off all her clothes, kissing each part of her exposed body. He lay her gently down on the bed and undressed himself. He was tender, more in tune to Sophie's desires than Richard ever was.

"Sophie, do you like this?" Leo asked as he tried different techniques. "Does this feel better?" It was obvious that he'd made love to many women by how and what he asked. He wanted Sophie excited. He kissed, sucked, and massaged her body until she was writhing on the bed. He asked her, "Can I enter you now?"

"Yes, hurry, I can't stand it anymore," she whispered hoarsely.

Leo took his time. He wanted her to be desperate for release. He waited until she was grabbing him, pulling at him, wanting him inside her. Only then did he enter her.

That night, Sophie discovered she could have multiple orgasms with Leo. He melted her physically and emotionally. Never had she felt so connected to a man.

After seven nights together, a feeling of love for Leo began to grow in Sophie. She decided she would take him home to meet her mother.

Chapter Fifty-Three

Leo and Sophie took off work and went to West Palm Beach over the Christmas holiday, so Leo could meet her mother and her cousins. Hannah was at the train station with Molly, Sophie's aunt. To Sophie, it appeared her mother had taken extra effort in how she looked. Rather than a cotton housedress, which is what Hannah usually wore due to the constant Florida heat and humidity, Hannah had on a bright, navy blue and white shirtwaist dress and matching thin white belt. Her white shoes looked to be new or recently polished.

Sophie supposed her mother wanted to impress Leo, a man Hannah had heard about over the past year, who had befriended Sophie. Several times Hannah had remarked, "Sophie, your friend Leo sounds like a better man than Richard. I don't understand why you aren't dating him."

"He's just a friend," Sophie had said. "I don't feel drawn to him like I did to Richard. Anyway, its none of your business."

Once Hannah and the rest of Sophie's family and friends met Leo, they were taken with him: his friendliness, his smile, and his drive to be professionally successful. He showed interest in Sophie's family and friends and displayed old fashioned, European manners. Even Hannah warmed up to Leo and showed him more kindness than she had recently showed her daughter.

One night, when it was just Sophie, Leo, and Hannah at the dinner table, Leo said, "Mrs. Straus, it would be my great honor if you would allow Sophie to marry me."

Sophie had no idea Leo was going to ask her mother for permission to marry her. She had mixed feelings about Leo's doing it this way. *Shouldn't he have discussed it with her first? Asked her if she even wanted to marry him?* She thought as she sat quietly, her face reddening. *He is old fashioned, so he probably thinks he has to ask my mother first.*

Hannah was delighted. A nice Jewish man wanted to marry Sophie. Hannah was willing to overlook his lack of money and family; she just wanted her daughter married. It was positive that Leo was a German Jew, as in her mother's view a Russian or Polish Jew was of a lower class.

"Leo, if Sophie wants to marry you, I give my permission." Hannah smiled broadly. "I'd be very happy with you as my son-in-law," she sighed in relief.

After dinner, Sophie and Leo sat in the living room. He said to her, "Sophie, I love you very much and want you to be my wife. Sophie Straus, will you marry me?" He caressed her hand. "I don't have a nice ring for you yet, but I promise I will buy you a diamond ring as soon as I can." He sat up very tall and straight. "I'm going to make something of myself. I plan to open a business. I'm not sure what type it will be." He looked at her beseechingly. "I'll be able to take care of you and our children. I assume you will want children. Will you? Will you marry me?"

"Yes, Leo Rosen, I will marry you. I just wish you would have discussed it with me first." She smiled and leaned in to kiss him. "But, I forgive you. You can get me a ring later," Sophie said, knowing that she really did love Leo. He kissed her deeply. He wanted her to remember this kiss to be able to describe it to their future children. "I will support you in any way I can," she added.

Later that night, Sophie was in her room, and Leo was settled on the couch that was made up into a bed. Hannah went to see Sophie. "Sophie, remember your promise. Do not tell him about the child. You can never tell him about the baby you gave away."

"Mother, I don't want to start my marriage with a lie. I don't want to keep it from him," Sophie argued.

"Sophie, be practical. Do you want to marry him?" Hannah sat on the bed. "If you tell him, you are taking a chance on how he might react. He may decide he doesn't want a woman who had a child out of wedlock." She paused and watched her daughter's face for any reaction. "He's going to want his own children and not think about the child you had with another man. Do not tell him," she warned as she left the room.

Sophie fretted as she tossed and turned in her bed. *Maybe my mother is right,* she thought. *I don't want to risk losing Leo. If I don't tell him now, I can never tell him. He would never trust me if I wait and tell him later. He'll want to know why I didn't tell him up front.* Her mind was in turmoil, trying to sift through all of the possibilities. *I'll do what my mother says. Not because I agree with her, but because I can't take a chance on what Leo might do.*

Part III

The Third Generation

America

1941 – 2005

*"Life can only be understood backwards;
but it must be lived forwards."*

Soren Kierkeguard

Chapter Fifty-Four

In 1940, the US Army Air Corps assumed control of the Palm Beach County airport and established a flight training school and command headquarters there. They renamed it Morrison Field. By 1941, there were hundreds of job opportunities. Leo decided to enlist in the Army, and Sophie, who had permanently dropped out of college, applied for a bookkeeping job at the base. With the war in Europe escalating and the uncertainty of the future, they decided to marry as soon as possible.

They wed on New Year's Eve, 1941, at the new Reform Jewish Temple. Only three people attended: Hannah, Ruby, and a friend of Leo's. Sophie was nineteen and Leo was twenty-four. Sophie didn't wear a wedding dress. Her dress was off-white with tan accents and a brown belt that showed off her tiny waist. Her hat was off-white with a bow and fake flowers. It didn't seem appropriate to wear an expensive, fancy wedding dress. No one had the money to spend on such a luxury. Years later, when she looked at the photograph taken that day, she noticed how no one was smiling.

Chapter Fifty-Five

1942

Leo was sent to basic training in South Carolina. When he completed his training, he returned to Morrison Field in West Palm Beach where Sophie waited for him. His job was to guard Nazi prisoners, ones the Allies thought might be of use during the war, men who had been secretly flown in from England to the prisoner-of-war camp in West Palm Beach. Leo was considered a huge asset to the Army for his ability to speak and write both German and English. His job was to serve as a translator for the Army or any other branch of the service that wanted information from the German prisoners. Leo's superiors had no idea of what had transpired with Leo's family back in Germany. Therefore, they showed no sensitivity about the task they assigned to him.

"Sophie," he said one evening when he returned home to their tiny garage apartment which they rented near the base. Leo's face was drawn and his eyes dull with sadness. "It's so difficult for me. Sometimes, I want to shoot the people I have been ordered to guard."

"I know. I know," she replied. "I can't imagine what it must feel like for you." She reached out and touched his arm. "Why don't you tell your commanding officer about your past? Maybe he'll understand and give you a different assignment."

"You know I don't want to talk about my family with anyone except you." He shook his head and sat up ramrod straight in his chair. "No. I won't let them think that I am too weak to handle my situation."

"No one would think you're too weak if you tell him what you have been able to do since you arrived in the United States,"

Sophie said as she knelt in front of him. "I hate to see you suffer like you do. I'll bring you some coffee. Sit. Rest." She rose and walked to the kitchen to brew fresh coffee.

She returned with a steaming cup of black coffee sweetened with two teaspoons of sugar. In her other hand, she carried a small container of milk that she poured in Leo's cup. She sat down in a chair opposite Leo and continued in a soft and gentle voice, "I think the terrible headaches you get are caused by the stress of your job, being around those horrible Nazis. And not knowing if your family is dead or alive."

He rose and paced the room. Sophie watched his face transform from sadness to stoic resolution. "Never mind. I don't want to talk about it anymore." He changed the subject. "How was your day?"

Sophie worked in the commandant's office pool where classified information passed her desk every day. "Leo, you know I can't tell you what I am doing. We had to swear to tell no one, including our spouses and families, what we do every day. Let's stop this whole conversation." She reached over and held his hand. "It only upsets you. By the way, Mother asked us to dinner, and it's time to go. We can talk later."

Over a dinner of roulade, a dish made with slices of beef rolled around vegetables, mashed potatoes, and a green salad with fresh tomatoes, Hannah approached them with a proposition. "I have plenty of room in the house. It makes no sense that you spend money on your own place. You can have Sophie's bedroom. You can pay me a little rent and help pay for the food. I think this solution benefits everyone. Don't you?"

"Mother," Sophie said, miffed that her mother didn't ask her first, "Let Leo and I discuss this. Thank you for the offer."

After dinner, Hannah and Sophie sat and knitted baby blankets for Sophie's friends who recently had children. Leo drank coffee and smoked cigarettes while he listened to the women talk. At 8:30 p.m., Leo told Sophie, "It's time we get home. I've got to be at the base very early."

Sophie and Leo gathered their belongings and thanked Hannah for dinner.

Hannah replied, "Think about my offer, and let me know what you decide."

Later that night, when Leo and Sophie were at home, sitting together on their small sofa in the living room, Leo said, "Soph, I think that was a very kind and generous offer your mother made. I think we should do it." He pushed a curl of hair out of her face.

"Leo, I have mixed feelings about living there with her," Sophie said as she held his other hand. "I feel like everything she does has an ulterior motive. Sometimes, I think she is too much in our lives." She watched Leo's face for any reaction to her statement. "But it makes sense monetarily. We have the car payment for another year. We can start saving for a home of our own." She was quiet for a minute or two, and then added, "As long as she doesn't become too demanding and too invasive, I can go along with her idea."

"Okay. We'll tell her in the morning. Come to bed, dear. I know something we can do that will help both of us relax," he said as he started fondling her breasts. "Is your diaphragm in?"

"Of course," Sophie said with a smile on her face. "I put it in before we went to Mother's house for dinner."

Sophie walked to the bedroom, shedding her clothes as she went. Leo followed getting more and more excited as Sophie revealed her naked body. He quickly removed his work clothes and grabbed Sophie from behind. He kissed her neck, her shoulders, and her back. Slowly she turned to face him. He kissed her mouth and her breast.

Leo moved Sophie to the bed, positioning her on her back. He knew she was ready for him by her soft moans.

Ramming into her, he whispered in her ear, "I hope soon, we'll do this to make a baby."

After both of them were satiated, Leo rolled off of Sophie's warm body. He grabbed a cigarette from the bedside table and looked at her. He noticed Sophie had tears in her eyes.

"Why are you crying," he asked as he lit the cigarette.

"Oh," she said. "I sometimes cry after I have an orgasm. It's normal. Don't worry." But she thought, *it was because he said "baby". I just couldn't help think about my other baby.*

Leo put out his cigarette and gathered Sophie in his arms. They fell asleep entwined and slept this way until dawn.

In the morning, while Leo was in the shower, Sophie called her mother. "We will take you up on your offer. However, I don't want you interfering in my marriage, and I don't want you telling Leo what to do all the time. He is my husband, not yours, and not your son, so please treat him as such."

Hannah was drinking her second cup of coffee when Sophie called. She listened to Sophie and answered, "Of course I won't meddle in your affairs. You haven't told him about the child, have you?"

"No, and will you please stop asking?" Sophie raised her voice. "Just drop it."

"I was just asking for your own good," Hannah answered with a hiss. "You are such an ungrateful child. It wasn't anything I did wrong. I gave you too much."

"Gave me too much? Too much what?" Sophie's voice got louder. "You have to be—"

"Sophie, what's all the noise about?" Leo asked as he entered their kitchen.

"Nothing, dear. I am on the phone with Mother," she answered. To Hannah, she replied, "Thank you, Mother, for your offer. I have to go." She hung up and left for work with Leo.

Chapter Fifty-Six

1945

When the war in Europe and Germany finally ended, information about the concentration camps and the surviving victims became more available. The Red Cross tried to help people find relatives who survived the camps. Sophie and Hannah knew what had happened to Hannah's sisters and their families; they had died in the camps. Hannah's two brothers were in America and her parents had died before the war. Hannah, as was her character, chose to bury her feelings about her sisters and never talked about them again to Sophie or anyone else.

For Leo, the lack of information was excruciating. On a weekly basis, he contacted the Red Cross and other agencies that might have information about his family. Due to the circumstances of war and the Nazis burning records, information was spotty about who was dead and who was found alive. As time passed, he became more and more certain that no one from his family survived. The thought was overwhelming.

"How can it be that not one member of my family survived? Why did God do this to me?" Leo wailed to Sophie. He took to bed with horrible headaches and lay silently for days. Sophie and Hannah tried everything to comfort him.

"Let's go to Temple and pray for your family," Sophie suggested. "Or you can find out if the Army offers any kind of support to people who lost family. What can I do to make it better for you?"

Leo said nothing. He shrugged off any of Sophie's suggestions, seeming to prefer to grieve in silence and alone. He was unable to allow anyone, even his wife, into the black hole that was his sorrow.

Over time, Leo began to adjust to his new reality. He was discharged from the Army at the end of his assigned term, and he began looking at businesses that might be of interest to him. Sophie, who gave up college after marrying Leo, continued to work as a bookkeeper so that they had money to pay Hannah for rent, food, and other necessities.

"Don't you think it is time to start having children?" Hannah said to Sophie when she got home from work one afternoon. "We know you are capable of having a child. Have you and Leo at least been trying? Do you think there is something wrong with him? I would like to have a legitimate grandchild."

Sophie, who exerted continuous control over her emotions related to her lost daughter, gritted her teeth before answering Hannah. "Mother, first of all, it is none of your business about when we decide to have children. Second, and it really is none of your business, I used birth control so we wouldn't have children until the war was over."

Leo and Sophie had discussed starting a family, but they agreed to wait until Leo found a new job. Leo took advantage of the Army's G.I. Bill for veterans of WWII to attend courses at the local junior college. It helped improve his English, and he began taking courses on how to start and run a business. He kept an eye on the want ads in the newspaper for job opportunities and kept in touch with his Army buddies in case any of them had business connections for him.

Chapter Fifty-Seven

1945

Leo wanted his own business, but he didn't know where to start looking for one to buy. He explained to his friends and the members of his Temple, "I know what I want to do with my life, to support my family. I want to start or take over a business. Do you know anyone who might be interested in talking to me?"

One day, his persistence paid off. An Army friend's father owned a moving and storage company. The father's dream was to have his son run it. The son, Michael, who had higher aspirations than his father, had no desire to run this business. He wanted to go back to school and become a lawyer.

One evening just before dinnertime which was at precisely 5:30 PM, Leo's friend called. "Leo, I hope I'm not disrupting your dinner, but I think I've convinced my father to consider you taking over the business, maybe," his friend said. Leo had met his friend's father on several occasions, and the two men developed a strong affinity for each other.

Michael continued, "Maybe his knowing that a friend of mine wants the business will make him get off my back about my not wanting his damn business. What I mean is the business is a good one. I just don't want it. What do you think?"

"Michael, that's wonderful. When can we meet? Can you set it up," Leo was so excited that his German accent became more prominent.

"I'll set it up for tomorrow if that isn't too soon," Michael said. He was as determined as Leo was to make this deal work.

"Thank you, Michael. I appreciate your doing this for me. Sophie has dinner on the table so I must go." The two men arranged a meeting time, and Leo calmly went to the dinner table. He didn't want to bring it up to his family yet, not until the there was a firm deal.

After meeting with Michael's father the next day to discuss the details, Leo decided that he wanted to buy the business. Michael's father made him a good offer. He just had to find a way to get enough money for a down payment. He knew that as a veteran, he could get a low-interest loan. He just needed a down payment.

That night, when he and Sophie were in bed, he asked Sophie what she thought of the idea.

"I want to buy this business, but we need money as a down payment. I know we have money that we saved while we were both working, but it's not enough for the down payment." He hesitated before he spoke again.

Sophie had learned not to interrupt Leo when he was talking. He needed time to organize his thoughts clearly.

"Do you think your mother has any money she can lend us?" he continued. "Would you mind discussing the idea with her? We can pay her back, a little each month, like we will with the bank."

"I'll try." Sophie had mixed feelings about asking her mother for money. She and Leo needed the help, but giving Hannah another toehold in their lives worried her. "I have no idea how much she has or what she does with her money. She's always had enough for us to live on. Let me see what I can do. I am very proud of you for finding this opportunity," she said, and she leaned over and kissed him. "I know you'll be successful."

"Come," Leo said, aroused by her kiss. "We need to try again to make a baby. What do you think?"

"I think that is a good idea," Sophie said as she felt Leo's penis and found it already erect. "I'm not wearing my diaphragm."

They made love very gently with Leo moving slowly in and out of her. Even when Sophie urged him to go faster, harder, he continued the slow movement. Finally when he couldn't wait anymore, he quickened his pace, bringing both of them to climax.

Leo, who often had nightmares about his family, slept peacefully after their lovemaking. Sophie, who took longer to go to sleep, thought about her other baby. She needed a new baby to help her forget. She hoped this time she'd get pregnant.

Chapter Fifty-Eight

In the morning just as Sophie was leaving for work, Leo asked Hannah if he could discuss a business and investment opportunity with her that night at dinner. They agreed the best time to talk was not when Sophie was rushing out the door.

As Sophie closed the backdoor, she said to herself, "He's afraid. That's why he brought it up when he did. I thought we agreed to talk tonight. Oh, well..."

Hannah knew tonight would be important, so not only did she make dinner, but she baked one of her famous plum pies. She loved to bake and wanted Sophie to stop working and take over the cooking. That way, she could return to being a seamstress and selling her knitted items. *Or take care of the grandchildren*, she hoped.

Later in the day, once everyone was settled at the dinner table, Leo started the conversation in German. Leo and Hannah occasionally spoke German to each other because Hannah enjoyed speaking her native language, and Leo felt more self-confident speaking German. Sophie spoke both languages fluently, having grown up in America and Germany.

"Mother," Leo started, using German rather than English. He wanted to sound confident and self-assured. It was easier for him to do this in German. "I have an opportunity to buy a very successful business."

"That's nice, Leo," Hannah said and nodded in encouragement.

"Sophie and I have saved money, and we know we can get a low-interest veteran's loan, but we need additional cash for the down payment." He paused and without being aware that he did it, he switched to English. His accent was prominent. "We were wondering if this is something you would be willing to do. Loan us money for the down payment. I would work out a repayment plan similar to the one I have with the bank. I would pay you an agreed-upon amount each month."

Hannah said nothing. She smiled and looked at Sophie. "And what are your thoughts on this, Sophie?" she asked her daughter in English.

"I think it's a wonderful idea. I know my father left you some money. Maybe he would have liked knowing a portion of that money went to his child and her husband to start a good life," Sophie said, switching the conversation to all English. She searched her mother's face for a reaction, but she knew her mother was an expert at hiding real feelings.

"What kind of business is it? How much money would you need?" Hannah asked, still maintaining a calm demeanor.

"It's a moving and storage company, Mother," Leo replied. "With the end of the war and veterans moving from place to place, people need to move their belongings. South Florida is growing. I think I can pay you back in, hmm, maybe three years. I need approximately $300 more. We have $300 saved, and the bank will loan us the rest," Leo explained, strong confidence showing in his words and voice.

"Let me think about this, Leo. It's a great deal of money. I've got to manage the little money I have to live on and pay my bills," Hannah said, surprising Sophie, who thought her mother would jump at the idea. "I'd like to talk to Sophie alone before I make my decision." She turned to Sophie who was unusually quiet.

"Mother, I'm tired from work. I need a good night's sleep. Can we wait until tomorrow night to talk when I get home?" Sophie responded as she helped her mother clear the table. *What does she want to say to me that she can't say with Leo there? Secrets, always secrets.* She thought as she rinsed the dinner dishes and went to her bedroom.

Leo followed her. "Is something wrong? Did I do something wrong?" he asked tentatively.

"No," Sophie said, truly sounding exhausted. "I just want to go to sleep and deal with it all tomorrow."

Leo accepted Sophie's decision to wait one more day for her discussion with Hannah. He changed into his pajamas, set the alarm clock, and crawled into bed with Sophie. He put his arms around her, and they fell asleep.

Chapter Fifty-Nine

The next day at work, Sophie fretted about what Hannah wanted to say to her in private. Her mother always made things so complicated and secretive. She hated it. She wanted to be honest and forthright, but her mother made it impossible.

At lunch, she used the pay phone to call Leo. She hoped her mother was outside watering the garden or visiting friends. The phone rang three times.

"Hello," Leo said. He'd been in their bedroom reviewing bank documents.

"Hi, dear," Sophie said. "I want to talk to you before I talk to my mother. What are you willing to do to get the loan from Mother? Who knows what conditions she'll place on us? Do you trust me to negotiate with her?"

"Of course I trust you," Leo answered, surprised she even asked the question. "Do the best you can to get her to loan us the full amount we need. I love you," Leo said, knowing Sophie would convince Hannah to agree.

"I love you too," Sophie responded and went back to work. She, who had not experienced love from her mother or father, loved her husband. It wasn't just because he married her when she thought no one would. It was because he treated her with respect; he held her, not just for sex, but also for affection and warmth. He was rarely angry and never criticized her. He was the perfect husband, except for his occasional bouts of depression. *And who wouldn't be depressed if they had gone through what he had gone through?* she thought.

Chapter Sixty

Sophie arrived home from work at 5:00 P.M. Her mother was in the kitchen finishing dinner preparations. "Hello, Mother." Sophie sounded tired. She hadn't slept well worrying about what her mother would say and about the financial risks she and Leo were taking. "Do you want to talk now?"

"Let me get the brisket and potatoes out of the oven, and then we can talk," Hannah said as she wiped her hands on her apron. She opened the oven door and pulled the roasting pan from the top shelf.

"I want to get out of this girdle and stockings," Sophie responded. *For the life of me, I don't understand why we have to wear stockings to work in this Florida heat,* she thought as she went to her bedroom and changed into a sleeveless cotton dress. Leo had left a note for her, saying he was coming home late, at 6:00, so she and her mother had time to talk without him there.

Sophie, in bare feet, walked to the kitchen. She made a glass of iced tea and offered one to her mother. She pulled out one of the red vinyl-cushioned chairs and sat. Hannah took the glass and sat at the kitchen table across from Sophie.

"Sophie, I want to discuss what my conditions are if I lend Leo the money to buy this business. First, do you think it is a good business, one where he can be successful?" Hannah asked, staring into her daughter's eyes, wanting to make sure what Sophie said was the truth. *I can read my daughter's mind and face. She can't lie to me,* she thought while she waited for Sophie to answer.

"Yes, Mother. I believe he researched this very thoroughly," Sophie asserted.

"Here is what I want in return. I want you to continue to live here." Hannah stirred her iced tea while she presented all of her conditions. "If you move into a different house, I want to have a room in that house. I also want grandchildren. I don't know what you and Leo have discussed, but I think the sooner, the better. You are twenty-three years old. Old for starting a family."

Sophie was floored. If she agreed, she'd never be rid of her mother and her dictatorial ways. How dare her mother tell her when to have children and that she would live with them? But Leo said to do whatever she could to get her mother to lend them the money. "I'll ask Leo about your living with us. I think he'll say yes to that. Well, you do help with the cooking. When we have children, you can babysit." She tried to remain logical. "If you continue to live with us, do you expect Leo to support you, too?"

"Supporting me instead of paying me back is a good deal, don't you think? And where would you and your husband be had I not offered you a place to live after you got married?" Hannah's voice quivered with suppressed anger and hostility.

"You asked us to live with you, as I recall. You didn't have to do that. But, yes, it is a good deal," Sophie said, though inside she was screaming, "No! No! No!"

"We have an agreement, then, if Leo agrees to these terms," Hannah concluded. "Please go set the table."

Sophie rose from her chair and headed to the dining room, and then turned to look at Hannah. "I have one demand, Mother. If and when we move to another house, that house is my house and Leo's, not yours. As long as you understand this, we will agree to your terms," Sophie said with a long sigh.

"That's good, because I don't think you want Leo to know about the baby you had less than a year before you married him," Hannah said, ending the conversation.

When Leo got home, he sensed the coldness between Sophie and Hannah. He feared this was because Hannah refused to lend them the money. He often sensed they had a secret between them. Once in a while he would walk into a room, and the mother and daughter would stop talking. Tension filled the room when this happened. He didn't want to get in the middle of his wife and her mother. He wasn't blind to the ways Hannah tried to manipulate Sophie, but as long as she didn't manipulate him, he wasn't going to get involved.

Everyone talked politely to each other as they ate dinner. By the end of the meal, Sophie and Hannah seemed less angry at each other. Leo was glad because he hated being in any environment where there was drama and tension. The rest of the evening proceeded as usual—everyone listening to the radio while Hannah and Sophie knitted.

At 10:00 p.m. Leo and Sophie excused themselves and went to their room. They closed the door and kissed frantically, needing release from the last two days' tension. As Sophie stripped in front of him, Leo slipped out of his clothes and grabbed his penis, rubbing it until it was full-sized. He lay down on the bed, and Sophie slowly lowered herself onto him. He groaned and thrust up. She was so wet and slippery.

"Remember, we are trying to make a baby. Let me be on the bottom, so your sperm will stay inside of me," Sophie said. Reluctantly, he moved and let her get under him.

He was in control now. "Put your legs around me," he whispered to her.

She did as she was told. They were making his child. Faster and faster he went. Harder and harder.

As much as Sophie wanted to scream out her passion and release, she couldn't. They had to be quiet while making love in Hannah's small house.

When they finished, they fell asleep in each other's arms. Both dreamt of a baby.

Chapter Sixty-One

1946

After Sophie explained Hannah's terms to Leo, excluding the ones involving her secret baby, Leo agreed to Hannah's requests. He had enough money for a down payment. As anticipated, Leo secured a loan from the bank and bought his friend's father's business. Once the ink was dry on the loan documents, events cascaded quickly like a waterfall after a soaking rain.

Leo changed the name of the company to *Leo's Moving and Storage.* Sophie quit her job and went to work with Leo, helping out with the financial end of the business. Knowing he had to market the business, Leo joined the Chamber of Commerce and the Lion's Club. With his great personality and sincere warmth, he made friends and contacts easily.

Life was hectic for Leo and Sophie with starting the new business and planning life with children when they finally had them. The couple worked together most of the day, at least until Leo could find the right secretary to help with the business.

"Leo," Sophie said one day in the office as she was straightening her desk. "You can't be so picky about hiring someone. Please try to understand that not everyone can do all the things I do..."

Leo interrupted her, "...and do them so well. What will I do without you here?"

"It will be fine," she tried to reassure him. He wasn't good with bookkeeping and needed Sophie to keep track of their finances and budgets.

"I'll still do the bookkeeping for a while until we find someone. But you have to hire a secretary for everything else. I want to be home with our children when we have them," she said. "I don't want my mother raising our children. She can babysit and watch them when we can't be there, but I want to be the mother to our children."

Leo agreed with Sophie and quickly found a pleasant older woman to take over the secretarial duties. Sophie joined the Temple Sisterhood and Hadassah. She had lunch with her friends, Ruby and Connie, and learned to play Mahjong with a group of women she met at the Temple.

One Thursday evening, several months after Leo took over the business, as Hannah cleaned up the kitchen after dinner, Sophie whispered to Leo, "Let's go to the bedroom. I have something we need to discuss in private."

Leo was preoccupied with business issues. "Sophie, can it wait? I was hoping you'd help me figure out how much we can afford for a new truck. Or should we wait until one of the two large vans we already have breaks down again?"

"Leo, I promise I'll go over that with you later this evening. We have time," she assured him as they walked to their bedroom. Once inside, she blurted out, "I'm pregnant! I saw the doctor today, and he said I am six or seven weeks pregnant." She paused, searching her husband's face for his reaction.

"Sophie... A baby...? A child?" Leo said, and his eyes filled with tears. "I'm going to have a family of my own." He knew that a child wouldn't take the deep pain of his loss away, but it might soften the edges of his silent agony. He hugged Sophie and held her tightly. "Can I tell people?"

"Of course. I wanted to tell you first," Sophie said as she rested her cheek against his short-sleeved cotton shirt that smelled of him—the scent of sweat, cigarettes, and cologne "I can't wait to tell Ruby and Dotty. They both have babies already, so they can help me learn about a newborn." She hesitated for a moment.

Her eyes clouded. "I don't want to be like my mother. I want to be kind to my children and make them feel loved."

"Sophie, you're not your mother," Leo said softly. "Don't worry. We'll be great parents. I want our children to have all the things we didn't." He rested his chin on the top of her head. *A baby. A new life*, he thought. *God is not totally terrible. He let my family die, but he's giving me a baby. I am having a child.* Leo didn't say this out loud to Sophie. The pain of Germany was too great to put into words. Instead, he kissed her and said, "That's wonderful. And I want more, too!"

Chapter Sixty-Two

Hannah sat in a tall-backed chair near the brightest lamp in the living room, knitting, when Sophie and Leo walked out of their room to the main part of the house. "So? What's the secret? You two are beaming," she said as she looked up from the blanket she was making.

"We are going to have a baby, Mother," Sophie said. "You're going to be a grandmother."

Hannah, who rarely smiled, grinned broadly when she rose from her comfortable position and hugged Leo and then Sophie. "Thank, God. I hoped this was it. Oh, my God. We've got so many things to do to prepare for your first child. Especially where the baby will go."

Hannah was right. A baby in the house was going to present a challenge, space-wise. The house had only two bedrooms, Hannah's and Sophie and Leo's, so the baby bassinet would temporary have to go in Sophie and Leo's room. At some point they would need a larger house.

"Leo, do we have enough money for me to start shopping for baby items?" Sophie asked. "I don't want to wait until the last minute."

Before Leo could answer his wife's question, Hannah interrupted. "You know it's bad luck to buy anything for the baby before it is born," she told Sophie and Leo.

Sophie and Leo looked at Hannah quizzically. How had they never heard of this rule? Maybe Hannah made it up.

"Really?" Sophie said to her mother.

"Are you calling me a liar?" Hannah's voice was deep and hard.

"No, Mother, I would feel better about it if I see it myself. We aren't practicing Conservative Judaism. We practice Reform

Judaism." Sophie explained, trying to calm her mother. "I'll stop at the Temple tomorrow and check out what it says in the books there."

Leo, who hadn't uttered a word during the conversation between his wife and mother-in-law, turned to Sophie and said, "It's been a long day. I'm tired. Let's go to bed." He turned to Hannah and said, "Good night, Mother."

Sophie didn't believe her mother. At lunchtime the next day, she went to the Temple's library and looked for a book that might explain the superstition. She found one and read, "In Jewish tradition, buying things for the baby was taboo. Jewish law doesn't forbid gifts for an unborn child, but custom effectively prohibits them. Such gifts once were thought to draw the attention of dark spirits, marking the child for disaster. In addition, many Orthodox Jews will not so much as utter the name of a baby until that baby is born, for fear of inviting the evil eye. In liberal Jewish circles, however, attitudes are more relaxed."

Sophie wrote down the name of the book, the page number, and the exact wording of the explanation she found. When she and Leo got home from work, she found her mother outside in the backyard working in the small garden.

"Mother, I looked up what you told me about buying stuff for the baby. I found a book that explains it. It's just a superstition, not really a law per se," Sophie summarized. "I'm going to buy a few things for the baby. I'm not worried about dark spirits." She tried to make a joke out of the situation.

Without turning to face Sophie, Hannah said, "Do what you want. You do that anyway. I hope nothing bad happens to my grandchild because of your stubbornness."

Sophie was overcome with fear of a different sort. She remembered how horrific it was when she had her first baby. How badly it hurt, how alone and scared she felt. She couldn't shake the feeling that the pain she had before would happen again with this child. She didn't think she could bear it.

At her next doctor's appointment, Sophie talked to her OB/GYN doctor, Dr. Segal, about her fears.

"Doctor, I'm afraid of having this baby." Sophie paused, trying to compose herself, and looked around the room at the metal cabinets, the doctor's cluttered desk, and the diplomas handing on the wall. She continued, "A friend of mine said she had a baby, and they didn't give her anything for the pain. She said the pain was awful, like her body was being torn in half. Can you make sure I get something, please?" Sophie was in tears.

"Of course, Mrs. Rosen," Dr. Segal, a rotund man with kindly brown eyes, said. "We always use medication when a child is born. It's archaic, barbaric; to make women go through the pain of childbirth when they don't need to experience it. No good doctor would force his patient to have a baby without sedation." He reached across the desk to pat Sophie's gloved hand.

Sophie took a deep breath and relaxed, reassured by her doctor that the pain and agony of her first child's birth would not happen again. For a moment she was back in New Jersey, hating her mother and her cousins who tortured her for no reason except to teach Sophie a lesson. Sophie's focus returned to the room where she sat with her doctor.

"Thank you," she told him. "I feel much better.

***

Leo, Sophie, and Hannah settled into a stable period as Sophie's pregnancy progressed. Sophie and Leo bought a bassinet and infant clothes: diapers, rubber pants, shirts, and a pair of tiny pajamas. To avoid arguments with Hannah, they left the items, carefully wrapped and boxed, at the warehouse that served as both a storage facility and an office for *Leo's Moving and Storage*.

It was a hot, humid day in August when Sophie's labor started. Leo, who happened to be home for lunch, rushed her to the hospital.

Once Sophie and Leo reached Sophie's room on the maternity floor, the doctor met them.

"Sophie, dear," the doctor said, "I think you are far enough along that we can take you to the operating room to have your baby. And don't worry. There is enough time to sedate you. Leo, do you want to come with us? You can be in the room until the baby is ready to come out."

Leo, who was terrified of the sight of blood or of anyone being in extreme pain, declined the doctor's invitation. He decided to wait in Sophie's hospital room until they brought her and the infant back. He smoked cigarette after cigarette as he anxiously awaited his wife's return.

As promised, the doctor made sure Sophie had enough sedation so she felt no pain. She was groggy when they lay the infant on her chest for her to see. It was a boy with reddish-blonde hair. She cried with happiness, and then, still under the influence of the sedation, fell back asleep.

Later, when she awoke, she was back in her hospital room. Leo sat in a chair, holding the tiny, sleeping infant.

"Sophie," Leo said as he held his son for the first time. "You have produced a miracle. Our first child is perfect. He represents our future."

Sophie felt a lump in her throat. If she talked, she would cry. She hesitated for a minute and said in a groggy and tearful voice, "Leo, our baby is perfect." She could not say the words "first child" yet. She added, "But where did the reddish-blonde hair come from?"

"My father and his father had hair that color when they were young, so I guess it came from my side of the family. Or did you sleep with the milkman?" Leo said, laughing.

Chapter Sixty-Three

When Leo called Hannah to tell her the news, she was ecstatic. A baby boy! Every Jewish family wanted a boy child first, a child to carry on the family's legacy. When Hannah hung up the phone from talking to Leo, she thought, *So, my Sophie has done something right. She produced a son.*

Leo and Sophie named the boy "Adam" because he was their first child and because he was the beginning of a new family for Leo. Adam was a beautiful child with thick hair and brown eyes. He didn't cry often, and he loved being held and cuddled.

Sophie wanted to nurse Adam, but her friends and her mother tried to convince her that it was an out-of-date practice. Modern babies could get as much or better nutrition from infant formulas and bottle-feeding. It also allowed mothers more flexibility in their lives, not being saddled with a breastfeeding schedule.

Sophie didn't care what her friends or her mother said. She decided to nurse Adam for the first eight weeks of his life. She wanted this baby close to her as much as possible. She didn't want Adam torn from her and given away. She knew her fears were irrational. She nursed her baby anyway.

Leo was uncomfortable watching Sophie put her nipple in Adam's mouth. His association with breasts was sexual, not maternal. He had never seen his sister or any other woman nurse her children. He usually left the room she was in and found some task he "had to" complete in another part of the house.

After Sophie and Adam came home from the hospital, Hannah was very kind to her daughter. She offered to help with the baby as much as she could. She'd always wanted a boy, and now she had one to help raise. Sophie appreciated Hannah's help, because she was always tired from waking up multiple times during the night. If Sophie napped during the day, Hannah was more than willing to keep an eye on her first grandson.

As she fed Adam, Sophie thought about the daughter she gave away, her first child. She could never tell Leo the truth. The fact she lied would break his heart. Although knowing Leo, he would have loved the other child, too.

One day, as Sophie fed Adam and Leo was at work, Hannah said, "Aren't you glad you did what I told you to do when you got into *that situation?*"

With a sneer on her face, Sophie answered, "Yes, Mother. You are right. You're always right."

Sophie's secret, her illegitimate child, weighed heavy on her heart. *Was this why her mother was so mean spirited? What happened to her mother that made her this way?* Sophie thought.

"I think Adam should call me 'Nana,'" Hannah suggested one morning at breakfast, shortly after Adam came home from the hospital. "Is that okay with you?"

"It's fine," Sophie sighed. She didn't care what Adam called her mother.

Leo came home every day from work at 5:30 sharp to eat dinner. After they finished and the women washed the dishes, he would play with Adam. He'd take Adam outside to look at the world beyond their small house. He would bring him back into the house and sit on the floor, watching his son lay on a blanket. He felt whole and happy when he was with his son. This tiny human filled part of the hole in his heart.

Adam alleviated Leo's sadness, at least for a while. Leo had heard nothing from or about his family and what happened to them in Germany. After all this time, he decided to just not talk about it anymore, not even to Sophie. *I will focus on my son. He and Sophie are my family now,* he would say to himself when pictures of what might have happened to his family encroached on his thoughts.

He did focus on his son to the extent that Adam was worshipped as if he were a god. Hannah and Sophie treated Adam this way too, setting up a lifelong pattern for Adam: needing to be worshipped by everyone, all the time.

Chapter Sixty-Four

1947

"Leo." Sophie approached her husband one night after dinner as he played with Adam on the small living room floor. Stuffed animals, small balls, and wooden blocks covered the rug as if a high tide had flooded the city and a toy store's inventory had been deposited on the Rosen's rug. Sophie surveyed the mess at her feet and began, "I think we need a bigger house. Adam is getting older and needs his own room. He can't stay in our room much longer. And, as you can see," she waved her hand across the living room, "we have no room to move around."

"I agree," Leo told her as he surveyed the room, and then smiling, glanced at his wife's face. "For many reasons, he needs to be in his own room. We've not had sex since you had Adam, even when we know he's asleep. I miss it. Don't you?"

"You're right. Tonight when he is asleep, we can do something about that," Sophie teased, smiling at her husband as he held their small child. She felt a warm pool of happiness fill her heart.

Hannah's living with them was a blessing after all. She loved her grandchild and babysat for them when they went out. One weekend, Leo and Sophie went to Miami Beach for a short vacation and left Adam with his adoring grandmother.

"Maybe you'll make another child while you are gone." Hannah smiled as Sophie and Leo finished packing the car.

They spent the weekend going to fancy restaurants, sitting in the sun on the beach, and having sex. Even when Leo slept, worn out from the last time, Sophie would suck his penis until he was hard again. She slid onto him and rocked back and forth until they were both coming. They had sex in the shower, on the couch, and on a chair on the small deck overlooking the ocean, turned on by the fact people might see them. Sophie often wondered why she had such a strong sex drive, but there was no one for her to ask. She would die of embarrassment if she had to discuss this with her doctor or even her best friends.

On Sunday, they drove home, satiated and happy, ready for work on Monday. If another baby was on the way, Leo wanted to make sure he could provide for his growing family's basic needs as well as the luxuries he never had. Automobiles, clothes, toys, fancy vacations, and a spacious home. He knew if he earned enough money and was successful enough, his occasional sadness would go away. At least, this is what he told himself.

Leo's business continued to thrive and grow. Leo understood what his customers wanted and strived to satisfy even their most demanding needs. He was well liked by everyone he met. People sensed his warm heart and the truthful way he handled business and social situations. Sophie was very proud of him. Initially, she worried about his lack of formal education and exposure to the finer things in life. She was pleasantly surprised that even though he came to this country at seventeen, only speaking German, Leo had managed to make a name for himself.

However, no matter how successful Leo was or how many gifts he bought his wife and son, he still had bleak, dark days. It was a pleasant, tropical Saturday morning when, Sophie came home from the grocery store to find Leo in the bedroom.

After putting the groceries away, she tiptoed to the door and cracked it open. "Leo, are you okay? What are you doing in here, in the dark? It's a beautiful day. I thought we might go to the beach later."

"Oh," he moaned. "I have a headache. The light and noise bother me. I feel nauseas. Just let me rest," he said and withdrew from any interaction, making it very clear he didn't want Sophie in the room or to help him. "Please close the door when you go."

Later, when she went to bed after getting Adam to sleep, she asked as neutral as possible, "Leo, is there anything I can do to help?" She gently brushed his hair back into place, letting her fingers linger on the side of his neck.

"No," he replied. "I've had these headaches on and off my whole life. They appear. They go away. They reappear."

"So the headaches aren't new," Sophie paused as she attempted to ask her question in a way that wouldn't upset Leo. "Is there anything else wrong, Leo, besides your headache?"

"I failed them, Sophie," he murmured. "I might as well have killed them myself."

Sophie moved over to be closer to Leo. She knew whom he felt he failed: his parents, sister, brother, and nephews. "Honey, there was nothing more you could have done. You were a child. The situation was not under your control. You didn't kill them. You tried everything in your power to save them. It just wasn't possible. Please try and let it go. Focus on us, your new family."

Leo who had been crying softly, wiped his eyes and looked at his wife, a woman he cherished. "I am trying, Sophie. I am trying."

A few days later he was fine, back to his other, more happy self.

Once his black mood had lifted, he said to Sophie, "I will never speak of my family again. It's too painful. Maybe it's best to bury them. They're dead."

"Leo, are you sure that is what you want to do? Just bury them and never talk about them?" Sophie asked, although she wasn't surprised this was the route Leo wanted to take. Her mother had chosen the same coping mechanism about the members of her family who were lost during the Holocaust. Many of the Holocaust survivors Sophie met were the same way: never speaking of what happened as if silence made the pain and anguish any less.

Leo kept his word. He didn't speak of his family again even when his children were old enough to ask, "Where is our other grandmother? And our grandfather? Is he dead like our other grandfather, Nana's husband?" At least he kept his word until many years later when he placed that burden on one person, someone not mature enough to handle the emotional fallout of such knowledge.

Chapter Sixty-Five

1947

Adam was just over a year old when Sophie discovered she was pregnant again. She hoped having another child would help Leo feel more like he was part of a family. Although he didn't mention it anymore, Sophie knew he was still deeply pained by the loss of his family in Germany.

"Sophie," Leo said when she told him the news. "Another child? We're truly blessed." He hugged Sophie so tightly she could barely breathe.

"Yes. A second child," she answered. "But, Leo, I am worried about Adam." She shook her head and thought about the fuss they had all made over Adam.

"Sophie, you worry too much. Adam will be fine," Leo told her. "Why wouldn't he?"

"Never mind, Leo," Sophie said. She didn't want to upset Leo with her fears. He had enough on his plate. She worried anyway.

Adam was the center of the family's universe. He was treated like a god, the family's savior. He held a different significance for each family member: a new family for Leo, a replacement for the baby Sophie had given away, and proof of the correctness of all Hannah's actions up to this point.

Even at an early age, Adam knew how to manipulate adults and to get what he wanted. Adam's needs, desires, and whims dictated all family life.

Only now, as she contemplated the new baby's arrival did Sophie worry. *How would Adam adjust to a new baby and sharing the spotlight? Had they been too effective in making Adam feel special?*

***

"Mother," Sophie said at dinner one night. "I'm going to have another baby. Probably in the spring." She turned to Adam whose highchair was next to her seat at the table. "Adam, you are going to have a brother or a sister. Isn't that exciting?"

Adam was precocious and could say a few words. "No. Adam baby. No baby." He threw his bowl of food on the floor.

Sophie pushed her chair back, stood, and cleaned up the mess on the floor. "Adam, you'll love having someone to play with. We'll love you just as much," she said as she took Adam from his high chair and hugged him.

Adam squirmed and repeated, "No baby. Adam baby."

***

Two weeks after Sophie's announcement about a second child, Leo came home with a surprise, one he hoped would distract Sophie from her fears about Adam. "You said we're going to need more space. I found the perfect house for us. It's on Flagler Drive and on the water near the bridge to Palm Beach."

"On the water?" Sophie cried. "You must be joking. How can we afford a house in those neighborhoods?" Wealthy people who couldn't live in Palm Beach lived in the mansions on the West Palm Beach side of the intercostal waterway called Lake Worth.

"I found out about it because the family who owns it wants to get rid of it quickly," Leo explained. "They called me to move the furniture out of the house and into storage. It belonged to their great-aunt who died last year, and they don't want the house. They live in New York and see no reason to hold on to it. They haven't put it on the market, so there will be no commission for a real estate agent."

"Okay," Sophie said. "But I'm not getting my hopes up about it."

199

Leo answered, "We can go look at it tomorrow. I know you'll like it."

The next day, Hannah, Sophie, Adam, and Leo toured the white stucco house with an ivy-covered wall surrounding it. The back of the house faced Palm Beach. The house was built before the Depression and had five bedrooms and three bathrooms. It was two stories with one master bedroom on the first floor and one on the second floor. A balcony surrounded the second floor. The floors in the house were either expensive hardwood or tile, both of which had to have been imported. Large windows faced the backyard and the water. Palm and fruit trees dotted the property.

Sophie loved the second-floor master bedroom with the iron balcony and thought they could give Hannah the downstairs one. In the backyard, there was a boat dock, pool, and pool house. There was plenty of sunshine in the yard for Hannah to grow roses. Mature lemon, lime, orange, and grapefruit trees dotted the property.

Although the price of the house was at the top end of what they could afford, they bought it. Hannah sold the small house on Flamingo Drive. She agreed to let them use part of the money she received from the sale to help with a down payment for the new house. All of them were excited about moving into their new, bigger, and more prestigious home.

Chapter Sixty-Six

1948

They moved into the house on a sunny day one month after Sophie gave birth to her second child, Joseph. Joey for short. Joey was the opposite of Adam in coloring and personality. He had dark hair and eyes and came out screaming. As happy a baby as Adam was, Joey was more demanding. He had to be held or carried for most of the day or he would wail uncontrollably, which would upset Adam.

"Baby loud. No baby. Go away baby!" Adam said to his mother one afternoon that seemed to go on forever with Joey's crying.

"No, Adam, we can't get rid of Joey. He is your brother," Sophie said, growing tired of Adam's demands and blatant jealousy of the new baby.

"I don't want him!" Adam screamed and stomped his feet. He began to wail as loud as the baby. The sound was unbearable to Sophie.

The only person who could calm Joey was Hannah. He appeared to sense a strong connection to her when she held him. Hannah took great delight in Joey's adoration. She enjoyed it when Sophie, in desperation, handed a screaming Joey to her, and the baby stopped crying.

Sophie was aware of her mother's triumphant looks but decided not to say anything. If it kept Joey quiet, she wasn't going to make a big fuss about Joey's apparent affinity for Hannah.

One afternoon while the two women played with the boys in the backyard, Sophie said, "Mother, we are going to have to try and not play favorites with the boys."

Confused and becoming defensive, Hannah asked, "Why? Am I doing something wrong? Do you disapprove of the way I help with the children?"

"No, mother, that's not it," Sophie said as she handed Adam to Hannah and she took Joey from her mother. "We are expecting another baby soon."

"Another baby? Why didn't you tell me? Three children is a good number. Maybe it will be a girl this time." Hannah envisioned the granddaughter she would have. A perfect young lady—smart, talented, obedient, and the most sought-after girl in the Jewish community. Maybe she would marry a doctor.

Later, after the women put the children down for their naps, Sophie went to her room to rest too. She wasn't just concerned about her mother's handling a third child. Sophie was worried about another baby in the house because of Adam. Although he and Joey played together every day, Adam still exhibited hostile behavior to his brother. Several times she witnessed Adam sock his baby brother very hard on the side of the head. Another time, Adam pushed Joey down the four steps to the backyard. When she confronted Adam about these incidents, he answered, "I don't want Joey. I want to be the only boy. First boy is special."

Sophie explained to Adam, "You are our firstborn and that will always make you most special. But Joey is special too, because he is our son and your brother. You need to get used to having a brother because you are going to have another brother or sister very soon."

Adam's response to this was to scowl at his mother and turn away. He stomped out of the room, muttering, "I don't want another baby. I don't want Joey!"

Chapter Sixty-Seven

1949

Leo and Sophie were thrilled to be expecting a third child. Although Sophie had no concerns about giving birth to another child, she worried about how much weight she had gained with each of her previous pregnancies. She hoped that after this child, she would lose all of the weight she had gained. She didn't like her body when she looked in the mirror, although Leo didn't seem to mind her Rubenesque figure. He still reached out for her when they were alone in bed at night. Leo's appetite for sex with Sophie didn't diminish. It was one of the threads that held them together.

"Leo," Sophie said one night as they talked quietly in their room just before they fell asleep. "I hope the new baby will be a little girl. I can dress her up in frilly dresses. How nice it will be to have a child who doesn't wear shorts and t-shirts all the time, who isn't constantly fighting, skinning a knee, and coming home filthy dirty." She didn't tell Leo the other reason she hoped for a girl. She wanted a girl to take the place of the daughter she gave away. It was still painful for her to think about the child she gave to her cousins whoever they were.

"Me, too," said Leo. He wanted a girl so he could name her after his mother, the mother he lost and never found. He loved his boys, but he knew a daughter would help him feel less sad. "I do too, Sophie," he said and turned away from Sophie so he could fall asleep.

The subject of having a daughter came up another evening, after the boys were asleep and Hannah was in her room, Sophie said to Leo, "I'm so glad we bought this house. With a third child on the way, I'm glad we have all this space. If we have a girl, she'll need her own room one day."

Leo agreed that the house was a great investment. And that they needed the additional room for their growing family. *Sure*, he thought, *the property taxes for it had increased, but so did the value of the house.* He was able to refinance the house to get enough money to start a second business, a window-cleaning service.

Windows in the shops and houses in Palm Beach were coated with a fine layer of sea salt because they were so close to the ocean. The air was full of salt and it drifted across the elite island. The millionaires paid for services to remove the salt from their cars, homes, and businesses. Leo knew he could build a successful business because many of his clients asked if he knew anyone who could keep their windows clean.

Even though financially, Leo was doing well, he still had dark days. Days that he sat in a chair in their bedroom staring at the wall and crying quietly about the family he lost. His headaches were more severe, and none of his doctors could rid him of the relentless pain and throbbing. On the days when Leo was closeted in the bedroom with the blinds drawn and the lights off, Sophie knew to just leave him alone and to keep the boys away. Leo would come out of his stupor in a day or two, so she wasn't too worried.

***

The third baby was a girl. She was the smallest of Sophie's babies. Sophie despaired that her new baby girl wasn't the best looking of her children when they were born. She had very little hair and what was there was so fine, you couldn't see it. Her face was scrunched up and wrinkled and looked nothing like her first daughter had. She thought about her first daughter and how pretty she was as a newborn with apple red cheeks, dark black curls, and penetrating black eyes. Her first little girl looked beautiful, and this new baby was small and crinkled.

Leo, however, thought his daughter was the most beautiful baby he had ever seen. He didn't care if she looked bald. He loved her eyes that reminded him of his mother's eyes. Leo swore she looked directly into his eyes, showing an unexpected sense of recognition. Leo loved his sons, but this small girl stole his heart from the moment he saw her.

They decided to call her, Madeleine Gerry. Goldie was Leo's mother's name, so they used the "G" in memory of her. Sophie looked forward to being able to dress Madeleine in lace, bows, and frills. She envisioned mother-daughter outfits and matching gloves and bags. After four years of only boys' clothes and toys, Sophie was ready for a change. She wanted to buy Madeleine gold bracelets and Madame Alexander dolls in fancy outfits. Sophie finally had a daughter to take the place of the one she gave away. This child would take away the pain of giving up her first daughter, or so she hoped.

Chapter Sixty-Eight

1950

Sophie and Leo had dreams and expectations, overt and covert, for all of their children. They never named them all, but if asked about it, their list would be long. Smart, talented, open-minded, attractive, competitive, good leaders, kindhearted, obedient, loving, well behaved, active in their community, religious, not prejudiced, and thoughtful of others. But most of all, they wanted their children to not suffer the losses they had suffered or to know about the horrid things the Nazis had done to the Jews in Europe.

"Leo, we have lost so many family members," Sophie brought up one afternoon, when Hannah had the children outside and it was quiet in the house. "I never had a father, and you lost yours and so many more loved ones in such a traumatic way. I want our children to feel secure and loved,"

"I agree. I also want our children to have the things we didn't have," Leo said. "I will do whatever I need to do. I don't want them to experience the hardships and horrors I did." He stopped for a moment, his eyes filling with tears, and continued. "I want you to promise me you won't tell them anything about how my family died. Can you do that? And, please, tell your mother not to tell them, either."

Sophie sighed and held Leo's hand tightly.

***

Sophie and Leo vowed to provide their children a more stable life than each of them had experienced. Other than Hannah and Hannah's sister-in-law and family, no relatives lived near them. Hannah's husband's cousins lived in New York and New Jersey. Leo's cousins lived in Atlanta and New Jersey.

Although it was hard to keep up with their distant relatives, Hannah and Sophie tried, primarily through letter writing. Hannah had been trained at an early age to write letters as a way to keep up with family and friends. She passed this practice on to Sophie. Leo who wasn't an accomplished writer in German or English tended to use occasional phone calls as a way to communicate with his cousins.

None of these practices were the same as having immediate family close by them. Even if they wanted to drive or take the train to visit relatives, it was difficult for Sophie and Leo to travel with three young children. Their relatives rarely traveled to Florida. They complained about the heat and humidity and the backwardness of the small Florida town Hannah and Sophie chose as home.

In spite of these obstacles, Sophie and Leo were determined to create an extended family for them and their children even if the people weren't blood relatives. It helped that Sophie and Leo were outgoing and very community and service-oriented. They became active in their Temple. Sophie was the president of the Sisterhood and Hadassah, and Leo was president of the Brotherhood and the Temple Board. Leo remained active in the Lions Club serving as President when nominated by a friend in the club.

Sophie and Leo gave memorable parties at their house and maintained relationships with couples and families they met through their community activities. These were the people who became the children's aunts and uncles, the people who became the Rosens' extended family.

Chapter Sixty-Nine

1950 - 1952

One day, Hannah was babysitting the two boys, and Sophie had taken Madeleine to the doctor for the second time in two weeks. The boys were rolling on the floor in the dining room, where all of the good dishes and collectibles were housed in glass cabinets. Their tiny, yet powerful, legs banged into the furniture. Hannah screamed at the boys, "Stop it, you two. I mean it. I'll go in the backyard and get a switch if you don't behave."

The boys had never been hit even when they acted up. Normally, Sophie put each of them in his room for five to ten minutes. The next time, when Hannah was babysitting, the boys threw a ball in the living room and broke a lamp. Hannah went in the backyard and retrieved a small limb off a tall bush.

"The two of you come over here!" she yelled. "Now."

She hit each boy twice on the bottom. Both boys started crying and were still crying when Sophie got home from the pediatrician.

"Mommy, Mommy!" Adam cried. "Nana hit us. She hit us with a switch. It hurt. She hurt me and my brother."

Sophie was furious. She wanted her mother to help her with the boys, but she didn't want her to hit them. Leo would have a fit when he heard that Hannah hit the boys. Sophie pulled the boys close and hugged them. "Go to your rooms. I'll talk to Nana."

"Mother," Sophie said as calmly as she could. "Please don't hit them. I know they need discipline, but don't hit them. You can send them to their rooms. You can tell them what they did wrong, but please don't hit them."

"Sophie, how exactly do you think we can punish them if we don't spank them once in a while?" Hannah demanded. "I know what I am doing. I didn't really hurt them. I just hurt their feelings. If I can't punish them when I babysit, how do you think I can handle them? I just won't babysit them," she said defiantly.

"You'll have to learn new ways of punishing them. And don't start with the 'I won't babysit them.' I know you don't want a babysitter here," Sophie said. "If you want to continue to live with us, per our deal, you do not control this house and my children."

Sophie was proud of herself for standing up to her mother. She knew Hannah was a big help with the children, but she also knew Leo wouldn't tolerate his mother-in-law beating his children.

That evening, when Sophie and Leo were in their room with the door closed, Sophie felt she had to tell Leo about what happened with the boys and her mother.

Leo, who rarely raised his voice, did, and told Sophie, "You tell your mother these are our children, not hers, and I don't want her hitting them for any reason. And if she can't obey my wishes, she won't live here any longer."

Sophie, knowing she had to calm Leo and make her mother follow her husband's wishes, said, "Leo, you are right. I've already told her that. She understands. It won't happen again. She promised."

Sophie paused and watched Leo's face carefully to see if he looked reassured. "Leo, she is a big help. She has done so much for us. I hope you can forgive her. It won't happen again."

Leo didn't like showing anger. He suppressed those feelings like he did his crushing feelings of loss. "I know your mother has helped us out, but I am supporting her now. I hope she obeys my wishes."

"Leo, I'm glad you acknowledge that she helped us," Sophie said, relieved Leo was willing to give her mother another chance. "Remember, she gave us money for your business. We owe her for that. As you know, she can be very difficult, and she never feels we have done enough for us." Sophie stopped talking and stared at the shadows, caused by the lamp's light, on the wall. She continued. "She holds it over me all the time that if she weren't here to help with the kids, we'd have to hire someone. On the other hand, she couldn't live the life she does if she didn't live with us."

"What if we set her up in her own place? Would she be happy with that arrangement, as opposed to living with us?" Leo asked hopefully. He loved his mother-in-law but would rather she live some place besides with them. Hannah's power over Sophie puzzled him, yet he didn't ask for an explanation. He didn't want to cause a rift in the family.

Sophie hesitated before she answered. She remembered her promise to her mother. She had to let Hannah live with them, or Hannah would tell Leo about the baby Sophie had. "No, Leo, I think she should stay here with us. I need her help with the children," she lied. She felt like she had made a bargain with the devil when she let her mother manipulate her many years ago.

"All right, it is settled. She lives with us. Just remind her that the kids are our children. We decide how they are disciplined," Leo said as he moved closer to Sophie and began kissing her neck.

Chapter Seventy

1953

When Madeleine was four and the other children five and seven, Sophie unexpectedly became pregnant with another child. They had not planned for another child, but birth control was not 100% reliable. Hannah thought it unseemly for her daughter to have a fourth baby. They weren't in rural Germany and didn't need to have a household of children like the peasants in the fields.

Madeleine wanted a sister. Then it would be even: two boys and two girls. Sophie wanted another daughter. She loved her sons and daughter but wanted another girl, one who allowed her mother to treat her like the frilly girl Sophie so desperately desired. Madeleine resisted all efforts to dress or behave like a girl. She wanted to be like her brothers and not be made to wear the *stupid clothes* Sophie and Hannah bought or made for her.

The fourth baby turned out to be another boy. Although disappointed the baby wasn't a girl, everyone was happy with him. He was born a happy baby and was an easy child to manage. They named him Jeffery, but called him Jeff most of the time.

Sophie knew Madeleine was disappointed the baby was a boy. Furthermore, Madeleine had to give up her room and the crib she still liked to sleep in once in a while. Madeleine had a full-blown tantrum and wouldn't get out of the crib when Sophie and Leo brought the baby home. In desperation, Sophie told Madeleine that the baby was her baby too. Madeleine believed it. Madeleine stood by his crib and watched him sleep. When he woke up, she would be there by his crib, talking to him. "Hi, Jeffie." She would point at herself and say in her baby voice, "Big sister take care of you."

Chapter Seventy-One

1953 - 1954

Adam didn't like having siblings. During his most critical developmental period, for almost two years, he was the family's only child, a boy, and a "savior," of sorts. He'd been bathed in attention and adoration before Joey arrived. First when Joey was born, Adam experienced his first feelings of resentment, although he was too young to understand what he felt. He noticed people weren't as quick to respond to his demands. The baby seemed to come first.

Luckily for Adam, Joey seemed to prefer Hannah's attention, and she gladly responded to Joey's every cry or whimper. Within a few months, Adam felt secure with his parent's attention. Once again he was their special child. Their first born.

But, then, there was Madeleine. She demanded so much attention from all the adults. From the time Madeleine was born, she was a difficult child. She was allergic to milk, dust, feathers, grass, and trees. She sneezed and wheezed and went to the doctor's more than all the boys put together. Adam could feel his parent's attention being drawn away from him when Madeleine couldn't breathe and his father worried about her. Or when his mother wanted to be with the baby girl, to dress her up or show her off rather than be with him.

When Jeff was born, Adam barely concealed his disdain for his youngest brother. They didn't need another baby as far as he was concerned. He basically ignored him or pinched him when he thought no one was looking. Madeleine, though, was looking and would defend her baby brother.

"Mommy, Adam hurt the baby," Madeleine said, crying, as she ran to tattle on Adam.

Adam, close in pursuit, said, "She's lying. I didn't do anything. She's just a tattletale."

Sophie, who was in her room dressing to leave for a meeting at the Temple, turned to her two children and said, "Can't you see I am busy? Madeleine, I want you to stop this always bursting in to tell on someone. And Adam, haven't I told you to stop picking on your brothers? Now, leave, I am running late." She shooed them from her room and continued fastening her gold charm bracelets.

Madeleine left the room in tears. "Mommy doesn't believe me. She doesn't love me," she said.

Adam turned and hit Madeleine on the arm. "Don't you do that again. I will hit you harder next time. You're right, she doesn't love you," he said, sneering at his sister.

Chapter Seventy-Two

1954 - 1956

To Sophie and Hannah's chagrin, Madeleine wanted to be a boy. "Mommy, I don't want to wear that dress. It's itchy. I want to wear clothes like Adam and Joey's. They don't wear itchy clothes with frilly things on them," Madeleine explained one day as her mother struggled to get a new dress on her.

Besides the clothes she was forced to wear, Madeleine resented other differences between her brothers and her. Like the fact that her brothers could stand up and pee while she was supposed to sit down on the toilet. When the children were playing outside in the backyard and Madeleine had to go the bathroom, she had to stop and run in the house. The boys could go over to the closest bush to urinate. *This was so unfair*, she thought.

She decided to try and pee like her brothers did. One day Hannah found her standing next to the toilet with her brothers, urine running down her legs.

"Madeleine!" Hannah shrieked at her. "Young ladies do not go to the bathroom that way. Why in the world would you stand there and get everything all wet? You need to clean up that mess now."

Madeleine ran to her room and slammed the door. "Maybe I am not trying hard enough to do it right. Maybe I need to practice." She went to her parents' bathroom and tried again, this time with her shoes, pants, and underpants off. She only got the floor wet this time. Reluctantly, she accepted that she had to sit on the toilet no matter how much she tried to be like her brothers.

In spite of Sophie and Hannah's distress about her behavior, Madeleine determined that if she couldn't be a boy, she'd at least act like one. Being a girl wasn't going to stop her from playing all the games they played. She played football and baseball with them, raced them around the block, and rode her bicycle with them. They were allowed to ride their bikes up and down their flat, paved street as long as no cars were coming.

One day when Madeleine was seven, Hannah pulled Sophie aside. "Sophie, you need to speak to your daughter. She rides her bike around without a shirt on. Have you noticed her breasts lately?"

"Mother, she is seven," Sophie replied, bothered by her mother's interference with how Sophie and Leo raised their children. Worried about how Leo hated it when Hannah ordered Sophie to discipline the children.

"I ask again: have you noticed her breasts?" Hannah said more firmly.

"I will look into this and take care of it, Mother," Sophie said, her voice going up an octave.

That evening when Sophie watched Madeleine in the bathtub with Jeff, she looked at her daughter and noticed that her breasts were budding. *How could this happen? Madeleine was only seven. Isn't that too young to start developing?*

As Sophie tucked Madeleine in bed, she told her, "Madeleine, when you go outside and play, you have to wear a shirt or a bathing suit top. You are growing up, becoming a young lady."

"What does that mean? Why do I have to wear a shirt?" Madeleine asked, confused that her mother was telling her this.

"You are starting to develop breasts like mine and Nana's," Sophie said.

"Mine aren't big like yours. Mine are tiny. Not much bigger than my brothers'," Madeleine replied.

"Well, they are developing. You need to wear a shirt. Don't argue with me," Sophie said, beginning to get anxious. *Was Madeleine always going to be difficult? Would everything between them be a struggle?*

"Okay, Mommy. But I don't like it," Madeleine said and cried herself to sleep after her mother left the room.

***

Besides being born with asthma and allergies and developing breast at a very young age, Madeleine was born with another burden: she was very attuned to other people's feelings, an *empath*. Not that she knew what to call it. She believed she could sense other people's feelings. Madeleine thought everyone was this way. Therefore, other people read her feelings too.

One day, when Madeleine was eight, she told Sophie, "Mommy, I feel sad today."

"Why in the world would you be sad? What is it you want that we don't give you?" her mother said impatiently, not really wanting to talk with Madeleine right now.

"I think it's coming from Daddy," Madeleine explained. "I feel it in the air when I sit in the room with him. I try to make us both un-sad, but it isn't working."

"Madeleine, I have told you over and over that you can't feel other people's feelings." Sophie was more impatient. "Go play outside. I don't know where you get these weird ideas. Surely not from me."

***

Madeleine found a way to compensate for her allergies, her not really being a boy, and her hurt feelings. She ate. Foods that made her feel good, candy and ice cream, cookies and cakes. Sugar made her feel best but so did bread, rolls and butter, and fried food.

She gained weight, and everyone noticed it. Adam and Joey teased her through dinner calling her "fatty." When no one defended her, even Leo, she ran to her room crying. *"No one loves me,* she thought. *If they did, they'd tell my awful brothers to not tease me. But, no one cares. My daddy didn't even come upstairs to see if I am okay.* Eventually, after crying for ten minutes, she wiped her face and went back to the living room where the rest of her family was.

Sophie looked up and said, "I see Sarah Berhnardt has returned."

Madeleine crawled into her father's lap and remained there until it was bedtime.

Chapter Seventy-Three

1953 - 1959

Adam, as the first born, became his siblings' leader and dictator. He took every opportunity to tell them what to do, and he made sure the other children knew their place, telling them, "You know Mom and Dad trust me most. I was their firstborn child. I'm more important to them than all of you."

One rainy afternoon, when the four children played together on the living room floor, he told them once again, "Here are the rules. I'm in charge and what I say goes. Do you understand?"

Joey, fed up with Adam's taunting and never-ending need to be in charge, told Adam, "No. You can't always win. You aren't the best at everything."

Adam slugged Joey on the arm. A fistfight ensued. Madeleine and Jeff left the room, retreating to the sun porch, to play another game by themselves. They let their older brothers fight it out.

Joey, Jeff, and Madeleine grew to dislike playing with Adam. If Adam lost, he would start a fight, or he'd berate his younger brothers and sister, calling them names. He knew exactly what to say to each of his brothers and his sister, what would provoke each child's feeling or provoke a fight.

"Jeff, you are a real crybaby. Grow up. Nobody likes a crybaby."

"Joey, you may be able to throw a ball, but you are as dumb as a rock."

"Madeleine, you are just a girl so you don't count."

Generally, Hannah intervened. She was left in charge of the children when Sophie and Leo were tied up with work or their growing responsibilities in various religious and community organizations.

Hannah had her ways of controlling her grandchildren. Much of what she did was based on what she experienced in her own home growing up. The boys were kept in line by the threat of being switched, and Madeleine was punished with words.

"You ungrateful child."

"You will end up being no good."

"You won't be accepted if you continue to do that."

The four children dared not tell their parents about how their grandmother treated them because they were afraid of what Hannah would do if she found out they had complained.

***

Madeleine felt verbally abused by everyone in her family except her father and baby brother. When she read books to Jeff, he sat in her lap, leaning back into her body. She loved the feel of his small, warm body next to her and the way he laughed with her at the funny parts of the stories she read.

She loved it when her father held her in his lap. Her very favorite thing was to do "butterfly kisses" with her father when everyone was on their parents' bed to watch TV. He would lean over and flutter his eyelashes against hers. He had nicknamed Madeleine, "Butterfly." It drove Sophie crazy that Leo refused to call Madeleine by her real name.

He sometimes looked at her and said, "Butterfly, you remind me of my mother." If Madeleine asked where was his mother, he'd only say, "She's dead," and not answer any more questions.

Other than her father's occasional touch, no one in her family comforted Madeleine except one of their cleaning ladies. One day, Lottie, their maid, found Madeleine crying. "Honey, child, come here. No one hugging you? Come sit in my lap for a while." She brushed

Madeleine's blonde curls away from her face and patted her gently on her back. "It's gonna be okay. It's gonna be okay."

She hated her mother when Lottie was fired over an incident Madeleine didn't understand. All Madeleine saw was that her mother had taken away the only person besides her father who ever comforted and hugged her.

Chapter Seventy-Four

1959 - 1964

Adam was a model child at school and in front of his parents. His teachers wrote glowing reports about Adam.

"Adam has demonstrated exceptional leadership qualities with the other children in his class." "Adam's reading, writing, and arithmetic skills far exceed the average child's." "Adam is a pleasure to have in my class."

He was a very different child with his brothers and sister. One day Joey looked out the window and saw Adam holding Madeleine's head under the water in the swimming pool in backyard. He ran outside and screamed. "Adam, stop that. Let her up. She can't breathe."

Adam let go of his sister's head and said, "I was just playing with her. I wasn't hurting her. Was I, Madeleine?"

Madeleine, not wanting to make Adam angry, said, "I'm okay. We were playing." She got out of the pool and went back into the house with Joey.

Another day, the neighborhood children were in the Rosen's front yard playing baseball. Adam hit Joey in the head with a bat when he swung the bat around for practice.

Joey began screaming and blood ran down his face.

"I didn't mean to do it," Adam said. "I didn't know you were behind me. I promise."

Madeleine, who had been watching the game and had a different opinion about what she saw, ran home, screaming, "Adam killed Joey!"

Sophie and Leo came running out the front door. They had a handful of kitchen towels and ice for Joey's bleeding head. They decided it would be best if they took Joey to the Emergency Room, as he probably needed stitches.

While Sophie and Leo were at the emergency room with Joey, Adam sat on the front steps with Madeleine and Jeff.

"Do you really think I killed him?" Adam asked Madeleine.

"I think you tried to," Madeleine replied. "I don't think you care if you did or not."

"Madeleine, no, you are wrong," he replied. "I'd never do something like that."

Madeleine didn't believe him. The look on Adam's face didn't match the words he said. "Hmm, that's what you say," she replied. "Come on, Jeff, let's go play cowboys and Indians and leave Adam here."

Jeff was the youngest and was used to his older siblings telling him what to do. After watching a show on television where a stuntman threw knives at a wall around another stuntman, Adam convinced Jeff to stand against a wall in the boys' playroom. Adam planned to throw three kitchen knives around Jeff. The other children, who thought Adam was just kidding around, were startled when Adam threw the first knife and narrowly missed Jeff's head.

"I'm telling Mommy!" Madeleine said as she ran from the room pulling a screaming Jeff with her. "She is going to get you!"

Sophie, who was in the laundry room folding the towels the maid had left out to finish drying, heard the crying and screaming. She met Madeleine and Jeff in the hallway coming to get her. "What is going on in there? Why is Jeff crying?"

"Mommy, Adam threw a knife at me!" Jeff howled, more scared than hurt.

"Madeleine, is this true?" Sophie asked as she folded the last washcloth.

"Yes, he did! I swear he did," Madeleine answered.

Sophie adored her firstborn son and found it hard to believe Adam meant to hurt Jeff. "Jeff, I don't think he meant to hurt you. He saw it on TV and wanted to try it. Now, go play someplace else and I will talk to Adam."

While Jeff and Madeleine talked to their mother, Adam twisted Joey's arm behind his back. "Don't you dare tell Mommy what I did? I'll really hurt you if you do. Just keep your mouth shut. Just leave so she doesn't see you at all," he told Joey.

Adam was alone by the time Sophie entered the room. "Mommy, I promise it was an accident. I didn't mean to throw it. I was just pretending I would and the knife slipped," he said.

Sophie paused a moment and said, "Adam, you could have hurt Jeff. He's just a baby, and you are a big boy. No more stunts like that. No more knives. Accidents can still hurt people."

Adam's eyes filled with tears and he replied, "I promise it will never happen again. I'm sorry." He dropped his head and left the room.

As Adam got older, he fought with his siblings less. One of the last times Sophie had to intervene in a dispute, she resorted to yelling at Adam. She loved her oldest child, but he could make her so angry. When she corrected Adam, he said to her, "You can't tell me what to do. I don't care if you are my mother. I can do what I want."

She slapped him. "You do not speak to me this way. I'm telling your father about this when he gets home. He will not like it," she threatened. She didn't like involving Leo in the children's discipline, but Adam needed to know his father didn't approve of this behavior either.

That evening, after dinner, Sophie pulled Leo aside and told him about the day's events. Leo, who hated violence, was infuriated with his oldest son. Adam had the potential to excel in academics and leadership, to become a great man. Leo believed it was his responsibility to teach his son a critical lesson: you do not disrespect your mother.

"Adam," he called. "Please come to our bedroom."

Adam knew his father was upset, but he had no idea what his father would do. "Daddy, I am sorry I said that to Mommy."

"Sorry is not enough," Leo said as he pulled out his belt and hit Adam twice, hard, on his butt. "You do not talk to your mother that way."

Through tears, he said, "She hit me and now you hit me. You never hit anyone else." He left the room knowing he would never forget his father's beating him.

Chapter Seventy-Five

The family attended Temple every Friday night, and the children were expected to go to Sunday school at the Temple every Sunday. Sophie and Leo were members of local nonprofit organizations. Sophie volunteered for her children's PTA and was PTA president at each school—grammar, middle, and high school—at least once. Leo successfully developed his two businesses, enough that the local Democratic Party noticed his business acumen and skills.

Beginning when the children were young, Leo was involved in community affairs. Leo, whose past compelled him to hate any form of prejudice, became involved in local politics, pushing for reforms that supported minority rights. In the early '60s, Leo was one of the few white residents to sit at Woolworth's counter with the black members of the community, effectively closing down the store.

Leo and Sophie wanted their children educated through travel. Every summer, they took car trips throughout the East Coast particularly the North Carolina mountains and the Florida Keys. There were occasional trips to Atlanta, New York and New Jersey to see distant relatives and the people who housed Leo when he first arrived in America.

Leo and Sophie believed education was the key for their children's success. Although Leo didn't graduate from high school, he continued his informal education through reading and private instruction. Sophie, who never graduated from college, wanted all her children to finish college. The children did well in school. Adam and Madeleine were generally in advanced classes and received all A's and B's. Joey and Jeff struggled in school more. Jeff had dyslexia, and Joey had a short attention span, but they still received grades of B's and B+'s.

The children were encouraged to pursue interests of their own. Joey was affable, gregarious, and loved sports. His eye-hand coordination and athletic ability appeared early in his life. Sophie and Leo enrolled him in activities to develop his innate capabilities. He played football and baseball. Starting when he was twelve, Joey attracted girls.

The Rosens' neighborhood was filled with children, all close to the same age, who gathered each day after school or during the summer to play Kick the Can, football, and baseball in the streets. After WWII was over, the husbands and wives who had postponed having babies started having them in great numbers. Children rode bikes and roller-skated, and swam in the pools and the ocean all summer.

Adam found activities where he could be the leader, such as Student Patrol, school clubs, and anything political like the student council. He knew how to talk to his peers and rally support for whatever cause he thought his peers favored. Outside of his home, his fellow students and teachers found Adam likeable, charismatic, and a good leader. He showed empathy and support to other children and adults. His favorite sport was basketball, so he wouldn't have to compete with Joey at baseball. He was shy around girls and didn't date much when all his friends paired off in middle school with girlfriends.

At home, it appeared to his brothers and sister that most of the choices Adam made reflected his need to be recognized. He would come home and tell everyone, "I won the election" or "I came in first." He was clumsy at sports, which was good for him, as he didn't have to compete with Joey, who was gifted in almost every sport he tried.

Hannah, in addition to helping raise the children and cooking dinner, played canasta with her friends and traveled to New Jersey each summer to visit her relatives with whom she stayed in touch with through letters. She encouraged the children to write letters to their distant cousin even though they hardly knew these people.

On the surface, it looked like the Rosen family and Hannah had a perfect life.

Chapter Seventy-Six

No matter how honorable Leo and Sophie's intentions were or how hard they worked to create and maintain a healthy, loving family, reality intervened. Strong, disruptive currents ran beneath the calm water on the surface. Cracks created by past truths and secrets waited to break through the surface, causing chaos. If anyone was going to see the cracks, it would be Madeleine, who had a sixth sense, who could see and feel things the rest of her family did not.

Madeleine listened carefully to what people around her said even if she wasn't supposed to hear it. One time, she heard Sophie and Hannah brag to their friends about how proud they were of the three boys. Adam was a great leader, Joey a great athlete, and Jeff such a funny and lovable child. The only positive comments that Madeleine overheard being said about her were how smart she was and how much weight she had lost, or gained.

She knew, based on subtle and not-so-subtle signs, that boy children were more important than girls in her family. When Adam and Joey had their Bar Mitzvahs, they were praised and given parties and gifts. When Madeleine turned twelve, she had to beg her parents to let her have a Bat Mitzvah the next year when she turned thirteen. Their temple and rabbi didn't encourage girls to have Bat Mitzvahs yet, but Madeleine knew some girls who had them.

Sophie told her, "Girls don't need to do it."

"But I really want to do it. I'm just as smart as my brothers. Why wouldn't I have a Bat Mitzvah?" she insisted.

Sophie hesitated while she considered Madeleine's argument. *None of my friends had a Bat Mitzvah, and they had turned out fine. They found husbands to support them and are good wives and mothers. God forbid any of my friends having to work while her husband is alive like Ruby has to work. It just doesn't look right.*

"Well?" Madeleine prompted Sophie for an answer.

"I guess there is no harm in it. The party after the Bat Mitzvah will serve as your thirteenth birthday party," Sophie answered. "Now go ride your bike or something active. You are putting on weight."

***

Madeleine, who wanted to understand everything, was puzzled about the mixed messages she received about physical touch. She couldn't remember being held by her mother or grandmother. Hannah and Sophie had not grown up in families that displayed physical affection. Hugging and kissing were reserved for special occasions such as when you hadn't seen someone in a long time. Leo's family had been more demonstrative, so Leo was more comfortable with holding Madeleine on his lap or hugging her.

"Where is your mother, Daddy?" Madeleine asked.

"She's dead, Butterfly," Leo answered quietly.

"How did she die?" Madeleine wanted to know.

"She died in Germany," Leo said even softer.

"But how did she die?" Madeleine continued to probe, not knowing the pain it caused her father to discuss this topic.

"That's enough questions, Madeleine," her mother interrupted. "Leave your father alone."

When Sophie left the room, Leo said to Madeleine who was still sitting in his lap, "I haven't told anyone else about this except your mother. But I think I can confide in you. You can't tell your brothers. Okay?"

"Okay, Daddy," Madeleine said feeling slightly uncomfortable about his sharing this with just her.

"When I was seventeen, my parents sent me away, on a ship to America. The Germans were beating and killing the Jews in my town and all over Germany. I was the only one to get out. So, my mother and father and all my brothers and sister and cousins and

229

everyone else Jewish was killed," he whispered to Madeleine. His eyes filled with tears.

Madeleine had never seen her father cry before, so she was scared. She hugged his neck and said, "Daddy, don't cry. Why did these people kill your family?"

"Just because they were Jewish. So, don't tell anyone what I told you," Leo said as he sat with Madeleine in his lap.

"I won't, Daddy. I won't," Madeleine whispered.

Chapter Seventy-Seven

1959 - 1964

"Being a girl is confusing," Madeleine said one day to herself. She tried to make sense of the mixed messages she got from her mother and her grandmother. There were rules she didn't find out about until she broke them. In the diary that she began at age nine, she wrote:

1. *Always wear a shirt except if you have a two-piece bathing suit, and then you can wear a top that looks like your bra and only covers part of you.*
2. *Dress to make boys look at you and think you are pretty, but don't dress too sexy (I need to look that one up. I am not sure what sexy is.).*
3. *Don't show men your underclothes except you can wear bathing suits that show more than your underclothes do.*
4. *Boys shouldn't see you in anything see-through, but it's okay to wear sheer pajamas around your brothers.*

Madeleine, who sensed there was no one in her family in whom to confide, wrote almost every day. She hid her diary in her underwear drawer. Years later, she found out that her mother, grandmother, and Adam knew where it was and read it on a regular basis. Although the household was rife with secrets, she was allowed very few.

Chapter Seventy-Eight

Madeleine's room had, at one point, been an anteroom of her parents' room. It had served as the baby's room. When Jeff was five and he moved into Joey's room, the baby's room became Madeleine's again. Madeleine spent hours in her room, her refuge. Besides having a room to herself, she had a phone in it. Her parents gave up on having just one phone line for the house when Madeleine was an early teenager. They put an extra line and phone into her room. She spent hours talking to her friends without her brothers or parents bothering her.

When Sophie and Leo let Madeleine move back into the anteroom, they didn't foresee the unintended consequences of their decision. Madeleine could eavesdrop on her mother and father. This was how she picked up information and heard remarks not intended for her to hear.

"Did you hear about Geraldine's oldest daughter? She is going to marry the father. They are so young. I hope it works," Sophie said to a friend she was talking to on the phone.

"Don't you think Paula's daughter is heavy? I know Madeleine struggles with this, but we're sending her to a camp where she will sit at a table with other girls who need to lose weight," Sophie told a different friend.

"Our Adam is going to be president of his club. He is such a great leader. It's too bad Joey is so rebellious. His father and I just don't know what to do with him."

Madeleine's room, being so close to her parents', afforded her entry into her parents' sex life. She heard noises from her parents' room that she didn't understand.

"That feels so good! I'm gonna come quick," her father said, sounding like he was in pain.

"Oh, oh, yes, yes," she heard her mother moan.

"I'm coming, I'm coming. Oh, God," her father screamed.

She knew the noises were private ones because she never heard these noises at any other time. Once, she walked through her parents' room on her way to the bathroom, and she saw her father's hand on her mother's breast. After that incident happened, her parents moved Madeleine to the guest room and expanded their bedroom to include the anteroom.

Chapter Seventy-Nine

1964 - 1966

Although Adam didn't date much in high school, it wasn't because girls weren't attracted to him. Several of Madeleine's friends had crushes on him. Girls asked Adam to go on dates with them, and occasionally, he would acquiesce. He went to all of the high school sporting events and dances and brought a date if he absolutely had to bring one. He was just more comfortable hanging out with his male friends.

Joey, as opposed to Adam, had girls hanging on to him. He was a jock and a flirt, and he broke girls' hearts through middle and high school. Girls called him at home, and Hannah told the girls, "It isn't polite to call boys. You should be ashamed. If Joey wants to talk to you, he'll call you. No, I won't give him a message for you."

Madeleine, too, was a flirt. Many a time, Adam would bring his friends to the house, only to have Madeleine parade in and out of whatever room the boys were in. Joey tended to spend more time at his friends' houses than his own. He didn't want Adam or Madeleine interrupting his time with his friends. He saw enough of his brother and sister when they were all home.

Madeleine's group of friends began pairing off when they were twelve. There was a group of boys and a group of girls that went to the movies together on Saturdays, had dancing parties, and occasionally played kissing games like spin-the-bottle. Sophie and Leo didn't mind that Madeleine went to the parties, because they knew most of the other kids and many of their parents. Her parents didn't know exactly what she was doing at the parties.

One day, when Madeleine was twelve, she got home from school and heard her grandmother berating her mother. "Sophie, you shouldn't be letting Madeleine go to the movies with a boy. You know where that will lead. You are giving her way too much freedom. I warn you, you need to stop it now."

"Mother, please, do not tell me how to raise my child. I don't mind that she goes to movies with her friends. Even a boy. It's harmless," Sophie said, weariness in her voice.

"Don't say I didn't warn you," Hannah replied loudly as she walked out of the kitchen to the laundry room.

Madeleine had no idea why her grandmother was yelling at her mother about her. She hadn't done anything wrong. Neither had her mother.

Chapter Eighty

Madeleine was thirteen when her first boyfriend, Todd, a fourteen-year-old, asked her to go steady. They met at the movies, sat close together, and kissed. Madeleine felt light-headed from kissing. They saw each other every day at school. They passed notes in the hallway during breaks from classes like the other couples did.

Madeleine was breathless from all the physical contact. She never felt such strong positive emotions before. No one had held her for such a long period of time. Not one of her parents or her grandmother had hugged her and held her much at all after she was eleven years old.

Sometimes, Todd came over to her house in the afternoon after school. They'd sneak behind the pool house to make out. She allowed him to touch her breasts which by then, were large for her age. They French-kissed and fondled each other until she was weak at the knees.

She heard her grandmother calling to her. "Madeleine, where are you? I don't see you. What are you doing?"

Madeleine and her boyfriend were very quiet. They knew Hannah wouldn't come looking for them where they were. When Hannah moved to the front of the house to look for her, she and her boyfriend moved around the house and walked in the back door. When her grandmother found them, they were innocently playing pool in the playroom.

That night, Madeleine heard her grandmother yelling at her mother, "Sophie, I am not joking about this. I know she and that boy are kissing and doing other things she shouldn't be doing. Do you want to have a slut for a daughter? Like you?"

"Mother, I will address this with Madeleine. You don't need to yell at me about it. Just stop," Sophie replied. "I will take care of it."

Sophie asked Madeleine to come to her room to talk. "Sophie, your grandmother and I are concerned about your suggestive behavior. It seems you are getting too involved with your boyfriend. I am afraid that this behavior will get you in trouble."

"My suggestive behavior?" Madeleine yelled at her mother. "Who buys me all the sexy clothes with the back cut out of them? Who wants me to dress older than I am? You! You're a hypocrite, and I hate you!" Madeleine screamed and slammed the door.

Madeleine, once again, thought about how unfair it was being a girl. Her brothers were allowed to do what they wanted. The older boys each got cars when they were sixteen, so no one knew what each was doing. Joey had girls calling him all the time. Adam dated infrequently, but the girls still asked him out. No one called them names. Hannah never yelled at Sophie about what the boys were doing.

Hannah wasn't the only one upset about Madeleine's dating. Joey found it difficult when Madeleine started dating—because she dated some of his friends. The two siblings were so close in age that they had friends in common. He hated hearing the boys talk about his sister.

"Hey, Joey, your sister is really hot. I heard she went to second base with Bobby. What do you think?" one friend asked him at lunch.

He came home and yelled at Madeleine, "Don't you realize they think you are easy? Too fast? You have to stop dating people I know."

Another time, he told her, "Maddie, you know that guy is a jerk. You're going to get a bad reputation hanging out with him. He only dates you because you are my sister."

These comments only added to the confusing messages and emotional abuse she got from her mother and grandmother. Her father never made hurtful comments to her. But, he didn't stand up for her. He didn't stop Hannah and Sophie from making mean comments to her. That hurt Madeleine as much as the hateful comments her grandmother and mother made to her.

Chapter Eighty-One

1964 - 1966

By 1964, when Adam went to college at the University of Florida, Leo's businesses were profitable, and the family was prosperous. He owned three businesses with a new branch of his moving and transfer company in Boca Raton where IBM was moving their new computer division. He had been a city commissioner for eight years. His family had every material item they wanted.

Sophie and Leo had a built-in babysitter. Hannah took care of Joey, Madeleine, and Jeff whenever Leo and Sophie wanted to go out for the evening or away for a vacation to New York or Cuba. A maid came to the house five days a week to clean the house. Sophie was free to socialize during the week or spend time with her various Temple and community activities.

Leo and Sophie's lives were good. Their children were smart and didn't get into trouble at school. They all had active social lives, and the Rosen's home was a welcoming place for parties for them and their children. Adam was settled into college, and Joey was sure to get a scholarship to a good university.

***

As predicted, Joey got a baseball scholarship for the fall semester at the University of Florida. Everyone except Adam was happy for Joey. Adam had blossomed at college. He was president of his fraternity and planned to run for president of the student body the following year. He didn't want his brother stealing any of his limelight. He was jealous of the attention Joey received for being a good athlete at "his," Adam's, school.

He resented the attention any of his siblings received for achievements. It drove him crazy to know he couldn't be number one in everything. Joey was more athletic and could get any girl he wanted. Madeleine was smarter and more social. Jeff was better at building and fixing items and at entertaining people by making them laugh. Adam took solace in the fact he was the oldest, the first-born male. *Everyone* knew that the first-born child was more loved, was a natural leader, and usually was more successful than children who came after the oldest.

With Joey and Adam in college, and with only two children were home, Sophie thought she and Leo would be able to spend more time together. She hoped that Leo would be happy at his childrens' success and not have as many days when he was sad and depressed. The opposite happened. He began to have more days where he felt he couldn't get out of bed. His head hurt. His back hurt. He stopped having sex with Sophie.

Even Madeleine noticed a difference in her father. One evening, when Madeleine got home from her job at *Burdines Department Store*, she found her father in tears sitting in a chair in the dark living room.

"Daddy, what's wrong?" She asked, terrified by the sight of her beloved father in tears. She knelt by his chair.

"Nothing, Butterfly," he said so softly she could barely make out what he said.

"Why are you crying? Is it about your family? Your mother?" She asked.

"Yes, a little bit. But, I'm just sad," he said. "I think I'll go upstairs now." He shuffled out of the room, walking as if it took too much energy to lift his feet when he walked.

Madeleine didn't know what to do. She thought she knew what was making her father so sad, but she couldn't tell anyone. Not even her mother. It was her father's and her secret.

She found her mother in the dining room with a pile of paper in front of her.

"Mom," Madeleine said. "What is wrong with Daddy? He seems sadder than usual."

Sophie looked up and said, "Madeleine, I don't know. I have taken him to several doctors and other than his headaches, none of them know what's wrong. He takes pain pills but they don't seem to help."

"So, what are you doing with the businesses, if he isn't going to work?" Madeleine asked.

"What do you think I am doing right now? I am going over the finances for the three businesses. I am doing the work your father can't do," Sophie said sounding exasperated and overwhelmed. "Now leave me alone. I have all this to finish by tomorrow." She pointed to the stack in front of her and grabbed a cookie from the open bag of Oreos that sat next to the folders and envelops.

Madeleine left her mother at the dining room table and went to her room and closed the door. Subconsciously, Madeleine absorbed the ideas that *my father takes pills for his sadness and pain, and my mother eats to relieve her anxiety.*

Chapter Eighty-Two

"My God, what will I do if Leo doesn't snap out of this? Two more children to go to college? Three businesses to run? A mother to support? A house on the water? There is no way I can do this alone," Sophie said to her best friend, Ruby, on the telephone one night when everyone was gone or in another room in the house.

"He'll snap out of it. He always does. Just hang in there. He's lucky to have you," Ruby replied, trying to reassure her friend.

"I am thinking of selling the house and getting a smaller place. The kids will have farther to go to school, but they can do it," Sophie thought out loud. "And my mother is driving me crazy. She never stops criticizing Madeleine. No wonder Madeleine never wants to be at home," she added. Her voice changed, sounding more like a proud mother. "It's one boyfriend after another. The last one broke her heart. She's young, too young to be in a serious relationship anyway."

After talking to Ruby, Sophie waited a week to approach Leo when he was in one of his better moods. "You know, with the two oldest boys gone, we don't need a house this big. We could sell this house and find a smaller one. I'll take care of it, if it's okay with you," she said one night after Leo had a day with no pain and no depression.

"You're probably right. We have four children we have to send to college. The kids rarely use the pool anymore. Let's go ahead and see what we can do," Leo agreed.

Their house sold quickly. They owed very little to the bank on the house. With the proceeds from selling it, they had enough money to buy a smaller house two blocks away from their current house, one that wasn't on the water. The new house had four bedrooms, two baths, and a large lawn in front and in back. No one seemed to mind moving as long as the remaining two children didn't have to change schools.

Once the family settled into the new house, and there was less financial pressure, Leo seemed better. He had fewer headaches and worked full-time, taking the burden off of Sophie who had to manage the home and the businesses.

***

Adam and Joey continued to do well at college. Leo and Sophie drove to Gainesville several times to see Joey play ball and see Adam, who was running for president of the student body. In spite of Adam's own success, he found it hard to share the spotlight with his brother. Dinners as a family, when everyone was in Gainesville, were difficult.

"Joey," Leo said, "I am so happy to have a son who is such an outstanding athlete. We're so proud of you."

"Thanks, Dad. I really appreciate you coming to see my games. It's a long drive, and with you being so busy, it's great you can take the time to come," Joey said as he shoveled food into his mouth. He burned hundreds of calories each day practicing or playing baseball.

"Of course we come. I wish we could come more," Sophie added.

"Well, he may be an athlete, but he isn't very smart. He has to take special courses for dumb jocks," Adam inserted.

"That's not true, Adam, and you know it. You couldn't hit a ball with a stick a mile wide," Joey responded.

"Well, you are just a dumb jock who can't do anything but play ball—" Adam continued.

"Boys, you will upset your father. Stop arguing. We love all our children equally," Sophie interrupted.

"Boys, I love you both," Leo added. "I love all of you more than you know. Please don't fight."

Chapter Eighty-Three

By September 1966, it was evident to Sophie that Leo's depression was worsening. He wouldn't go to work or change out of his pajamas. He complained of headaches and retreated to the bedroom with the drapes drawn. He cried and moaned, but wouldn't talk to her. She had run out of options for what to do. She yelled at him, coaxed him, bribed him, and took him to doctor after doctor. It was affecting the family and the business. Finally, Sophie knew she had to admit Leo to a local in-patient facility to deal with his severe depression.

The psychiatrists tried the few drugs available for depression, but none provided Leo with relief. His headaches were unrelenting. He spent days catatonic in a chair, tears running down his face. His doctors put him in a full treatment program involving individual, couple, family, and group therapy. Leo said little in any of these sessions.

"Sophie, why do you think Leo is so depressed?" asked Dr. Weiner in one of Sophie's individual sessions.

"I think he carries so much guilt for not being able to save his family in Germany," Sophie answered. "He wouldn't talk to anyone about the whole thing. He never told the kids what happened to his family until the movie *Judgment at Nuremberg* came out, and Adam, Joey, and Madeleine saw it while at camp." She twisted in her chair and shredded the tissue in her hands. "The boys came home very upset that no one told them how their grandparents had died. Madeleine acted like she knew already, but I know Leo would never share that with his daughter. He's only talked to me about it."

"That would be upsetting for the children to find out that way. Did he talk about it to them after they found out?" Dr. Weiner continued to probe.

"No. He'd tell them he didn't want to think about it," Sophie answered.

"So in some way, it was a family secret?" Dr. Weiner pushed.

"I guess you could say that," she answered but volunteered no more.

"Were there any other family secrets he might have been keeping? Or did you have any secrets he or the children didn't know about?" He sensed that Sophie was holding back bits of information that might help him understand this troubled family.

"Of course not. Other than Leo's family being killed by the Nazis, we are a very normal family. We are very open and honest. Sometimes too much. Too frequently, people yell what they think at each other," Sophie admitted.

***

When Leo didn't improve in the local facility, even after electric shock treatment, Sophie moved him to a teaching hospital in Gainesville, Florida. Once a month, she drove from West Palm Beach to Gainesville to spend the weekend with Leo and do couples and individual therapy.

"Sophie, how are the children handling their father's institutionalization?" Leo's new psychiatrist asked. "I'd imagine they are taking this hard."

"Actually, they are doing fine. You know, my two oldest boys are in school here. Adam is active in politics, and Joey is on the baseball team," she bragged. "My mother takes care of the younger two, Madeleine and Jeff. Madeleine is a senior. She's already been accepted to college. Jeff, the youngest, is doing okay in middle school." Sophie didn't acknowledge any problems with the children. She had no idea what either of her youngest children did during the weekends when she was gone.

"Do you think it would be beneficial to at least involve the two boys here in Leo's treatment? That might be good for Leo and for them to talk about what is happening," the psychiatrist gently suggested. He knew Sophie avoided facing any problems she or the children had with the current situation: their father hospitalized in a psychiatric ward and their mother managing the businesses and driving back and forth to Gainesville.

Only Leo had problems. There is nothing wrong with me. I have to be strong to support this family. It's Leo who needs to get well. Sophie thought.

"No, I'd rather not do that," Sophie added quickly. "It wouldn't be fair to the other two kids to have their older brothers be involved and not them. I think I'd rather leave all of them out." She paused and quickly added, "The older boys can visit, of course, but I don't think they would do well in a group therapy situation like you have here."

"Sophie, are you sure? I am wondering if there is another reason you don't want the children involved. Is there something you don't want to discuss? To have out in the open in front of the children and Leo??" he asked.

"Absolutely not. It's not me." Sophie's nostrils flared. "I just want to protect the children from seeing their father like this. I know how hard this is on me. I can't imagine asking them to see how awful their father is doing." Her eyes filled with tears. "Are you trying to distract me from my being upset with how little progress we've made? I would have thought a teaching hospital would be able to do more than it has," she said, turning on the psychiatrist. "I really don't think he is getting better, and my driving here every month is very difficult and hard on the family. You know I had to take over running the businesses so my family can survive and so that I can put my children through college. This is a terrible hardship on us all."

"Sophie, it must be very difficult for you. I'd like you to talk to me about the hardships you are facing. I think you need someone to talk to about how you are handling all of this." He sensed that Sophie needed more support than she was getting. Over the time he had worked with Leo and got to know Sophie, he had developed a nagging feeling that Sophie was hiding something from him.

"I just told you. There is nothing more to say. I want Leo well and home so we can go back to being a family," Sophie replied, ending the conversation.

Chapter Eighty-Four

With her father away in a psychiatric hospital, there was a huge hole in Madeleine's heart that she tried to fill with male attention. She knew how to dress and act to attract boys, so she generally had one boy or another in her life. She spent her weekends drinking to hide her feelings ---- shame, sadness, and fear. She only told her best girl friend, June, where her father really was. In a psychiatric hospital. She kept this secret from everyone else, including her teachers who noticed how out of control Madeleine was at times.

Luckily, she was part of a large circle of girl friends. Madeleine was part of the "in-crowd" in her high school although just at the fringe. Most of her friends were not Jewish. She was bright and flew through her courses, in spite of the fact that she spent most of her weekends partying.

All her life, she felt different from other kids at school. No one else seemed to have a family like she did. She didn't know her father's family because they all died in Germany. He had only talked about them that one time and never would answer any other questions she asked. She also never knew her other grandfather, Nana's husband, either. He died before her mother was even born.

No one else she knew had a grandmother who lived in his or her house. Most people had grandmothers who acted like grandmothers, not like a parent. Madeleine often thought her mother acted more like a jealous sister than like a mother to Madeleine. Worst of all, she didn't know of anyone's father having serious psychological problems or a father who tried to kill himself. Leo had made a feeble attempt to kill himself when he was first hospitalized. Madeleine learned of it when she heard her mother on the phone with one of her friends.

Chapter Eighty-Five

1967

Growing up Madeleine had heard the message that a girl went to college for one reason: to find a man to marry. Her mother repeatedly told her, "I got married at nineteen. I had to drop out of college." Madeleine wondered which part of the message she should pay attention to, the regret of dropping out of college or the part where her mother married at nineteen.

Madeleine knew she was meant to go to college, to be something besides a wife and mother. Even Adam didn't change her mind. One day, the summer before Madeleine was scheduled to start college Adam told her, "There's not enough money for you to go to college. It's more important that boys go. The money should go for me to finish college and law school."

She told him, "That's bullshit, and I am going to college no matter what." How could she not go to college? She knew there was so much more to learn. All her life, books had been her lifelines. She read everything people told her to read and books they told her not to read. The more she read, the more she knew she would never settle for a life without a profession. Of course, she wanted to be a mother and wife too.

She wasn't sure what she wanted to be. When Leo was released from the hospital in Gainesville and came home, he said to her, "Butterfly, be a psychologist so you can help me." If her father wanted her to be a psychologist, then she would be one.

Madeleine also wanted to get away from West Palm Beach and start over. Because of her crazy and wild behavior in high school, people accused her of not being a "good girl." Of doing things with boys she wasn't supposed to do. Of having sex with boys. Just because she and her best friend June drank and hung out with the guys, many of whom drank, it was assumed they had slept with the boys. The reality was, Madeleine was a virgin when she went away to college. A fact few of her high school friends believed.

She went to college in Georgia to be in a different place than where her two brothers were in school. She didn't want to be simply known as Adam and Joey's younger sister. She wanted her own identity. She also chose the University of Georgia because it was known as one of the top ten party schools in America. She saw this in *Playboy* magazine. Something she had been reading since she was ten when she discovered it in the cabinet by her father's bed. The cabinet where her father kept books like *Fanny Hill* and *Tropic of Cancer.* Books he told Madeleine not to read, which only made Madeleine more determined to read them.

Within a month of being at The University of Georgia, she met a man, Barry Levine, at a fraternity party. Although not conscious of what she was doing, she picked a man who her parents and grandmother would think was perfect. He was from a strict Conservative Jewish family, had great professional potential, and was good-looking. He was a few years older than she, had a car, and had blondish hair.

They met in the fall of her freshman year and were going steady by the end of the next semester. He was from a small town not far from the university. After dating for three months, he took her home to meet his family. They seemed to approve of her and made her feel welcome. Barry's family seemed like such a normal family after having grown up in hers.

One weekend after she met Barry's family, Madeleine and Barry flew to West Palm Beach for Madeleine to introduce Barry to her family. As if too good to be true, everyone liked him. When he was around, her family acted normal with no fighting or yelling. Even Hannah, who was critical of every boy Madeleine dated, approved of Barry. Madeleine felt her parents' and grandmother's pressure to get married soon, to not wait until she finished school.

"Madeleine, it's okay to get married, you know. I did when I was nineteen," Sophie told her on the phone after she and Barry returned to school from their break.

"I know. You've told me hundreds of times, 'I was married by the time I was nineteen.' How could I possibly forget?" Madeleine said with a sarcastic tone that she knew her mother would recognize.

Chapter Eighty-Six

1967

"Did you ever have sex with anyone?" Madeleine asked Barry six months after they began dating. They had been through the normal sequence of sexual exploration, except for oral sex and intercourse. It was time for them to decide if they would go "all the way" or not.

"Once with my first real girlfriend, and then, several times with another girl," he said. "The first time was a fiasco. She panicked, so we stopped. We finally finished later when she calmed down. After that night, she didn't want to try again. We broke up shortly after that." He paused and checked Madeleine's reaction. "The other times were with a girl I dated my freshman year. She wanted to get married, but I wasn't interested in that yet. So we broke up."

"I'm glad you aren't a virgin. I wouldn't want us both to be virgins," she explained. "I'm a virgin. I dated a lot in high school but never had intercourse. It was drummed into me I had to really love the man and plan to be married if I was going to go all the way with him." Madeleine added. Her family wanted her to be a virgin until she was married, not just planning to marry.

Barry gave Madeleine his fraternity pin shortly after this conversation. Being pinned meant that their relationship was moving to the next level: engagement and then marriage. To celebrate getting pinned, they drove to Myrtle Beach with three other couples, where they rented a large four-bedroom house overlooking the beach and the Atlantic Ocean.

The first evening, after dinner, when they were alone in their room, Madeleine sat on the edge of the bed and said, "I'm ready to have sex. We're pinned, which means we'll probably get married soon." She waited to see if Barry reacted negatively to her saying "married." He had been the one to explain what getting pinned meant. She added, "It's okay to go all the way now."

Having anticipated that they might have sex on this trip, Barry said, "I love you. This is a serious relationship. I don't know when we'll get married, but we will. And, well, I brought rubbers, just in case."

They could hardly wait. The tension had been building up since they drove to the beach. They hurriedly undressed and turned off all the lights in the bedroom. The room and bed glowed pale yellow from the light in the bathroom. Madeleine and Barry barely saw each other.

After kissing and progressing through their usual foreplay, Barry put on a rubber and pushed to enter her. Madeleine felt a tinge of pain. "Ouch," she said involuntarily.

"Does it hurt?" Barry asked. "Should I stop?"

"No. Keep going. I am ready," Madeleine responded. She thought about how everyone had assumed she had sex years ago. About how wrong people were.

He entered her again and almost immediately said, "Oh, my God, I am going to come. I can't stop." He convulsed and lay on top of her. "I came too fast I know." She couldn't see the blush on his face.

"It's okay," Madeleine assured him, kissing him on the lips. "We have all weekend."

They stayed on top of the sheets, exploring each other's naked bodies. *This is what I have been waiting for*, Madeleine thought. *This closeness feels better than what I imagined. Sex with Barry may be the way I get the closeness I want.* She couldn't say this out loud to Barry. He might not understand, and she didn't want to ruin this evening.

An hour later, Madeleine reached out for Barry's penis. She rubbed it until it became hard. "I think I am ready to try again," she said to him.

"Evidently, I am, too," Barry said as he put on another rubber.

This time, Barry took his time kissing her, rubbing her nipples, which were hard as rocks, plunging his fingers in and out of her vagina, and rubbing her clitoris until she said, "Barry, quick, get inside me. I think I can come, and I want to feel you in me."

He had been holding back, concentrating on her pleasure. He was amazed at how hard he felt, how potent. He started moving slowly inside her, but within seconds was ramming into her with a power he had never felt before. When he couldn't wait any longer, he said quickly, "I'm going to come! I'm going to come!"

He did, but didn't pull out. He continued to grind his pelvis into hers, hoping she would come, too. It worked, and she did.

"Oh, Barry, I love you so much," Madeleine whispered in a sultry tone. "I have never had an orgasm by intercourse before, only through dry humping and masterbating. I could get used to this." She said as they faced each other.

"I love you too," he said. "I think we are going to have to get married because I don't see us going back to how we used to be. I know I want to keep doing this, and I know you do too."

"Married? Really?" Madeleine asked.

"Yes, married. But I don't know when we can," Barry said as gently rubbed her nipples. He knew she loved being touched anywhere, everywhere. He loved to hear her moan and scream when she came. Madeleine's passion and sensuality was contagious, and he, too, starting moaning and screaming when they had sex.

Chapter Eighty-Seven

Barry was serious about getting married. He'd been raised to believe that sex outside of marriage was wrong, immoral. They needed to get married if they were in love and having sex regularly. But, how could they afford to get married? Neither Madeleine nor Barry made enough money to get married and graduate from school unless their parents still supported them. Madeleine needed three years to complete her Undergraduate and Masters Degrees in Psychology, and Barry had three years left to finish law school.

Barry drove home two weekends after they returned from Myrtle Beach. He didn't take Madeleine with him because he didn't want her to hear anything negative his parents might say. They were deeply religious people who could be very judgmental about people or actions they believed were against their prescribed rules. *No sex before marriage. Go to Temple Friday nights or Saturday during the day. Keep a kosher home. Say prayers in Hebrew before every meal.*

Barry was the only boy in the family. He had three older sisters who married right after college and each sister had two children. His mother, Jane, and sisters had treated him like a prince from the moment he was born. His father was a silent, gruff man, who let his wife make the decisions about their home and family life. He was a successful businessman who didn't need to be the complete master of the house like he was at work. Barry found it very difficult to talk with his father, so he chose to talk to his mother when his father was not in the house.

Initially, the conversation between Barry and his mother didn't go well. Although Madeleine was Jewish, she was a Reform Jew. She dressed too provocatively for his mother's taste. It was 1967 and women weren't wearing bras all the time. When

Madeleine went home to Barry's house one weekend, she didn't have a bra on, and Barry's mother could tell. Barry's father noticed it too and just chuckled when his wife pointed out how unladylike Madeleine's wardrobe was.

Furthermore, Madeleine wouldn't go to Saturday morning synagogue services. She couldn't understand the service because it was all in Hebrew. She found it odd and disconcerting that people walked in and out of the service all morning. If they could do that, she could stay at Barry's house and catch up on her sleep. It was evident to Jane that Madeleine was possibly a wild child, and how could Barry handle that?

After hours of discussion, and Barry being more assertive than he's ever been with his mother, she relented. She and Barry's father, Morris, would help send Barry to law school and provide one half of their living expenses. They expected Barry and Madeleine to work when they could to pay for their own entertainment and incidentals.

Unbeknownst to Madeleine, Barry's parents contacted Sophie and Leo to discuss the situation. Sophie and Leo were delighted that Barry was going to propose to Madeleine. Jane explained what she and Morris had decided to do to support Barry so he could finish law school and be married. Sophie and Leo could hardly say "no," that they wouldn't help Madeleine with money for schooling and living expenses like the Levines were doing for Barry.

Barry's parents talked with Barry to explain the parents' agreement. Two months after the Myrtle Beach trip, Barry asked Madeleine to marry him. Of course, Madeleine said, "Yes," and assumed they would have to wait to get married until they had jobs.

When Madeleine called home to tell her parents that she was engaged, Sophie got the shock of her life.

"Congratulations!" Sophie gushed into the phone.

"I'm happy for you," her father said.

"I assume we'll have to wait until I graduate," Madeleine added.

"Not exactly," Sophie interrupted. "We have been in touch with Barry's parents and talked through how we can make it work so you can get married this summer."

Madeleine was speechless. *Her parents knew Barry was going to ask her to marry him? His parents knew?* "So, what have you worked out? And why wasn't I involved in the conversation?" Madeleine said. She knew one fear her parents had, that she would get pregnant and have a baby out of wedlock, or worse, have a backstreet abortion.

"Barry was involved, and you didn't need to be. We all want you two to get married sooner rather than later for several reasons, one being he'd have to go right into the Army after graduation, before Law School. Married men are less likely to have to go on active duty. Another being that we'd like you to have children, but not until you are married." Sophie paused. Madeleine said nothing.

"Your father and I discussed it. We will still pay for you to go to school. Once you are married and live in Athens, you can get in-state tuition fees," Sophie told her.

"What about paying for rent, utilities, living expenses, and clothes? I can probably get a teaching assistant position, but it doesn't pay enough to live on," Madeleine said to Sophie.

Sophie hesitated while she composed her reply. "His parents will help him out like we will. Your father and I will help with your part of the living expenses. What do you think of an August wedding?"

Madeleine processed what her parents told her. *They agreed to pay for a huge formal wedding and to continue paying for her to go to school because she brought the "right" man home.*

While her mother rattled off a list of tasks that had to be completed: pick a date, find a dress, and order invitations. Madeleine stopped listening and thought. *They think he can make me be the woman they want me to be. Just by marrying the right guy I can live off campus, drink, and do drugs. I won't have this much freedom if I stay single. So why not marry? Why not make my mother and father happy? And I love Barry. This feminist movement I read about may be the best thing that ever happened to me. I can have it all.*

She tuned back into her mother's voice. "Mom, that's great. We can get married in August." Engaged by nineteen and scheduled to be married by twenty—almost on the same schedule as that of her mother's.

Many years later Madeleine joked with people that her parents paid for her to get married. It was true.

Chapter Eighty-Eight

1968 - 1970

Madeleine and Barry married in 1968. The wedding weekend, planned by their parents, was magnificent. Eight bridesmaids and groomsmen. Fancy reception in Palm Beach. Just the way it was "supposed to be."

As Madeleine walked down the aisle in the Temple, holding onto her father's shaking elbow, all she wanted was for him to say, "It's okay, Butterfly. You don't have to get married." She was terrified she had made the wrong decision to get married so soon. She'd been swept up into the idea of having a wedding and being the center of attention. Everyone was so happy about it, even her father. She desperately wanted to make him happy. She was supposed to save him.

Instead, he squeezed her arm and whispered, "It would be okay with me if you had a baby tomorrow."

***

Nineteen hundred and sixty-eight. The summer of free love, LSD, pot, boys with long hair, and girls who didn't shave under their arms. This was the summer Madeleine and Barry married. Just when women were burning their bras and questioning their traditional roles, Madeleine was married. Just when Madeleine discovered there were women all over the United States who felt like she did, she was stuck in a small apartment in Athens, Georgia, learning to cook and entertain using the perfect china and silverware.

Madeleine had chosen Barry for his stability and their sexual compatibility. She'd spent her last two years of high school with her father in and out of psychiatric units. She craved someone who could be there for her, so she could feel secure. She married him for all the wrong reasons. She married the man her mother, father, and grandmother wanted for a son-in-law. She married a man so her parents and grandmother would approve of her. Not a man who could let Madeleine be the person she wanted to be. He had married one woman in 1968, and by 1969, he had a different one as his wife.

Barry, with his naïve misconceptions about marriage, tried to control her, to stop her—like a father would control his daughter. She didn't need a father. She already had one, and he had never tried to control her.

Madeleine marched against the war in Vietnam around the ROTC building while Barry was inside. She marched with five thousand students through the streets of Athens, Georgia. She went to rock concerts, smoked pot, read *MS* magazine from cover to cover, and tried to persuade Barry to loosen up, be more of a free spirit like her. She was expected to be home in time to cook dinner for Barry and to study so she could get her BA a year early.

Barry was perplexed by Madeleine's behavior. He loved the fact she was a free spirit, but he wasn't ready for the full-blown feminist she'd become. Her natural desire to question authority exploded into rebellion at everything including values and behaviors Barry held dear. It wasn't that she didn't love Barry. She loved Barry very much and wanted him to come along with her as she explored all the new options available to her. He could have that freedom too, if he wanted to explore with her. She begged him to try to be more flexible, risk more, and be like her.

Madeleine and Barry loved each other but weren't equipped to deal with the realities of marriage. Madeleine tried talking to Barry about her feelings. She attempted to create an emotional connection to her husband but couldn't. She'd blame him, saying he was emotionally handicapped. She'd become volatile, and yell, and cry; only making it worse.

Madeleine believed she could have her marriage to Barry and have her freedom. They discussed it and agreed to it. Madeleine could have the freedom to do what she wanted within reason as long as she was honest with Barry. With the comfort of knowing that Barry supported her freedom, she discovered books and people like herself not like her husband, his family, or hers.

It shocked her when she found herself attracted to other men. Madeleine believed that once you married, you'd never be attracted to another man. That somehow being married put a protective shield around you. That you were immune to other men.

No one had ever talked to her about marriage and what to expect. She had created her own fantasy of what marriage was. She didn't act on her attractions to other men. She felt guilty for having the desires. Sex with Barry was satisfying. She and he enjoyed it. *So, why were other men attractive?* She wondered.

***

The first crack in Madeleine's marriage began when she met a man, Dan, who was in her graduate program and part of her study group. He had long curly hair and a reddish brown beard. A poster of Che Guevara hung on the wall behind his bed. One night when they had not finished studying until ten o'clock, he walked her to her car. They looked at each other and didn't speak.

Finally, Madeleine said, "I just had the most amazing feeling as I looked at you."

"I did too. Like electricity?" He replied.

"Yes. I think I am a little bit in love with you," she said, terrified of what he'd say next.

"I've been attracted to you since the moment I met you. But you're married, so I didn't say anything," Dan said, and he moved closer to Madeleine and kissed her.

From that moment on, Dan and Madeleine saw each other every moment they could. Barry was studying all the time and noticed nothing different about his relationship with Madeleine. In fact, he thought they got along better than they had for the past year.

Dan gave Madeleine the emotional connection she craved. He had some of the same revolutionary ideas she had, but his were more extreme. They talked about everything, shared everything, and lived in their own world. A world full of working together, smoking pot, rebelling against the establishment, having sex when ever possible, and piercing passion. The other members of their small study group knew about Madeleine and Dan's affair, but they didn't care.

Dan wanted more from Madeleine and pushed her to leave Barry.

"I can't," she told him. "I know he will some day make a great father. My parents would kill me if I left him. I love you, but I won't leave Barry."

"Yeah, you say you love me, but you won't leave your husband," Dan said. "You aren't happy with Barry. Why stay?"

"Because I just have to," she cried. "I can't explain it, but I have to try and make it work. I want a stable life. You talk about revolution, traveling, and not settling down. Please stop asking me to leave him."

As the time to graduate came closer and closer, Madeleine decided she couldn't lie to Barry anymore. She felt guilty and ashamed of herself. She hated lying. Madeleine told Barry about the affair, and he was devastated. He hadn't even noticed any difference in their relationship while the affair was going on. Silently, Madeleine thought, *That's part of what is wrong with us. You didn't even notice.*

Barry said he'd try to forgive Madeleine, and Madeleine promised it would never happen again. In spite of her love for Dan, her betrayal of Barry, and her smoldering drive to be part of the feminist revolution, Madeleine thought she could make her marriage work. They were going to start a new life in Atlanta. Everything would be better once they moved and found jobs. Then, Madeleine could get pregnant, and they'd start a family like everyone wanted her to do. At least Madeleine hoped this was true.

Although Madeleine told Barry the affair with Dan was over, she continued to have sex with Dan whenever Barry was studying late at the law library. Dan still hoped she'd leave Barry and be with him. Dan couldn't comprehend Madeleine's diametrically opposed ideas. Her need for security and her desire to be the good wife and mother alongside her ideas of freedom and exploration. *Why, if Madeleine told Dan she didn't want a conventional marriage, did she stay in one?* Dan wondered. Madeleine wondered too.

Shortly before graduation, Madeleine's fear that Barry would find out she'd lied once again drove her to end the relationship with Dan. The idea that she could lose Barry, her parents' approval, and her reputation kept her awake at night. She had panic attacks and couldn't concentrate. She thought she was going crazy. There was no one she could talk to about it. Not her friends or her family. Not Barry and not Dan. No one.

In her most dark despair, she realized there was one person who would forgive her: her father. He would eventually understand and love and support her. Definitely, not her mother. *It's okay.* She thought. *If Barry and I get divorced, Daddy will take care of me.* Her father was her safety net, to catch her if she fell.

Madeleine counted on Leo to rescue her. She didn't consider the fact that he might not be there when she needed him.

Chapter Eighty-Nine

1971 - 1972

Leo committed suicide on January 2, 1971 by running his car full speed into a telephone pole. The medical examiner found an excessive amount of Darvon in his system, which enabled the police report to say "accidental overdose resulting in fatal car crash." He had been diagnosed with pancreatic cancer in December 1970 and told there was little hope of his living more than six months.

Sophie, while shocked, was not surprised. She believed Leo saw his cancer diagnosis as a reason to quit living. He had been in pain, physically and mentally, for such a long time that he had given up on ever feeling better. When the police called and told her about the accident, she suspected that he had planned it. He'd increased his daily intake of pain pills dramatically since his diagnosis. Sophie suspected that Leo made sure he took a high enough level of Darvon that day to make it look like an accidental overdose.

Sophie was now responsible for the family and the businesses. She had to keep all of it going. She had to finish paying for Madeleine's last few months of college and save enough for Jeff to go to college.

She told her friends how angry she was at Leo. "Damn him. Killing himself? As if he wasn't going to die anyway?"

"Aren't you being a little harsh?" one friend replied. "Don't you miss him?"

"Of course I miss him. Leo made so many of my dreams come true. But the last two years have been hard, very hard," Sophie said, silently crying. "Right now, I'm more concerned about what people will say about the accident. Will they believe it was an accident? How will my children feel if it comes out it might have been a suicide?"

Sophie believed it was good that three of the four children were married. They would have someone to lean on during the mourning process. Jeff was the only unmarried child. Jeff and Sophie supported each other.

Once the children were home for the funeral, they sat in their parents' house and grieved. The boys, although sad, didn't appear devastated like Madeleine. She was beyond comfort. Her body and soul ached. Barry was not emotionally equipped to handle her. He'd never experienced the death of a close family member and was unable to provide emotional support. When she turned to Barry, he turned away feeling helpless and inadequate. He walled her out in silence.

Her only comfort was that on her first night back in her old bed in Florida her father came to her in a dream. It felt so real that Madeleine believed her father's spirit was absolutely present. He said, "It's going to be all right, Butterfly. I'm here."

As if losing Leo wasn't enough for Sophie, shortly after Leo died, Hannah began showing signs of senile dementia. She pestered Sophie and the children, when they were at home, "Where is Leo? I haven't seen Leo."

Hannah's questions disturbed everyone, but particular, Sophie. "I feel like she's doing this to torment me," she told Ruby on the phone. "She's also started leaving the house and wandering all over town. The police called me yesterday to come get her. She'd made it to the train station and was trying to get on a train to New Jersey without a ticket."

"Oh, Sophie, that's got to be hard. I know how Hannah can be difficult. Maybe you should find a place that will take care of her," Ruby suggested.

Sophie did just that. Within four months, Hannah was settled into a Jewish facility in Jacksonville, FL for seniors with dementia. She complained constantly. No one visited her enough.

She was too far away from the family. Where was her friend Marie? Sophie regularly got phone calls from the nurses, asking if she objected to upping her mother's medication.

"Yes, please up it. I know how difficult she can be in her right mind, so I can only imagine how she is now," Sophie told the nurse.

The next year, in late December, after Hannah had been diagnosed with inoperable colon cancer, Sophie received the call that she dreaded and hoped for. Her mother was dead. No more Hannah to orchestrate her life. No one to yell at her. No one who knew about Sophie's secret child.

Chapter Ninety

1971 - 1978

Madeleine and Barry moved to Atlanta almost immediately after Leo died. Madeleine was as fragile as she had been since the year her father was in the hospital for his depression. She began working with disturbed children and adolescents at a mental health center. After long stressful days at work, she would cry as soon as she got home and spend the rest of the day grieving, in a fog. Barry was unable to say or do anything that helped. Her strong emotions scared him. He responded to the situation by pulling away from her, watching sports on TV, and joining a men's baseball team that practiced one day a week and had games on Saturdays.

Madeleine, more afraid than ever to leave Barry, suffered because she didn't feel the love or emotional connection she wanted with her husband. She lied, acted out, partied without her husband, and developed a group of friends comprised of cavers, actors, whitewater paddlers, and longhaired hippies. Barry's friends were his former fraternity brothers and their wives, his cousins, and men from his various sports teams.

On weekends, Barry and Madeleine lead completely separate lives. She'd go rock climbing and caving with her friends, and he'd play sports with his.

Madeleine unexpectedly met Pat one weekend on a trip to Beyer's Cave. The two Volkswagen buses full of spelunkers stopped at Pat's apartment to pick him and his gear up for the trip. Madeleine stood near the front door while everyone talked. A blonde-haired fifteen-month-old baby ran around the room. He stopped in front of Madeleine and said, "up," while he held his arms in the air. She bent over to pick him up and said, "Sure, cutie. What is your name?"

His mother, Gretchen, responded, "His name is Ricky. You better give him to me," she continued, "his diaper really needs changing. I'll take him." She grabbed him from Madeleine and went to the baby's room to change him.

Madeleine was taken aback by the roughness in Gretchen's voice and actions, as if Madeleine had done something wrong.

Immediately after Gretchen took the baby from Madeleine, the most incredibly handsome, bearded man walked over and held out his hand. "I'm Pat. I am amazed how quickly Ricky took to you. He's generally not good with strangers."

Madeleine laughed and said, "I've always had a soft spot for blonde boys."

The group's unofficial leader, Tom, interrupted the conversation. "Everyone back in the vans. We have to get going if we want to get there before dark," he said.

"Dark?" Madeleine said, a quiver in her voice. "We aren't going caving in the dark? Are we? I know caves are dark, but I like getting out of them while the sun is still out."

"No," replied Dave, another man in the group, "You just might get out of the cave at midnight if you go with Tom."

The rest of the group laughed because it was true. Tom wasn't always on time, and there were multiple trips that ended in the dark with people struggling to find and pack their gear, even with headlamps on their helmets.

"Madeleine, why don't you ride with me," Pat said. "I can teach you more about rock climbing which is more fun than caving."

"I'd like that," Madeleine said. They talked non-stop during the ride to the cave, telling each other intimate details of their lives. He was eight years older than she and was a professor at Georgia Tech. She didn't quite understand what he taught even after he tried to explain it. She told him about her job, her marriage, and her affair with Dan. Not sure why she felt she could trust Pat. By the time they met up with the rest of the group, she knew that she would have an affair with this man.

Very quickly, she fell in love with Pat, and he with her. Life became very complicated. Madeleine and Pat saw each other twice a week on their lunch breaks and got to spend a few nights together when they were on climbing or caving trips. After eight months, Madeleine said she'd leave Barry. But Pat wouldn't leave Gretchen. It was his second marriage, so he was reluctant to leave his wife and baby. He had three additional children from his first wife, and he felt guilty about not seeing them often enough. He told Madeleine, "I just can't leave Ricky."

Their affair continued, and Madeleine felt like the woman her grandmother accused her of being. *A whore. A slut.* And worse, Madeleine was a liar. It ate her up, her feelings of guilt. She loved Barry and Pat, and she didn't know what to do.

Eventually, Barry found out. Gretchen followed Pat and Madeleine one day to Madeleine's house and confronted them. Pat never acknowledged the affair to Gretchen. He said he and Madeleine were just friends, but she knew differently. She wanted to make Madeleine's life miserable too, so she called Barry.

"Barry, this is Gretchen. Remember we met at a party. Your wife goes caving with my husband, Pat."

"Sure," Barry said, puzzled why this woman was calling him.

Gretchen blurted, "Do you know your wife is having an affair with my husband?"

Barry trusted Madeleine because she had promised she'd never have an affair again after Dan. She had kept her promise, he thought. "I don't believe you. They just go caving together. I trust Madeleine."

Gretchen was furious. She couldn't even ruin Madeleine's marriage. She didn't trust her husband, though. She knew she had cornered Pat into marrying her by having a baby. She suspected Pat resented her for that. What kept him with her was Ricky. Pat adored his son and would stay married to her because he didn't want to leave another child with a former wife.

Madeleine and Pat still saw each other, but it was a challenge. Madeleine continued to believe Pat would leave Gretchen one day. But, it didn't happen. She began seeing him less and less because all they did was fight about why he wouldn't leave his wife.

Chapter Ninety-One

Sophie, not knowing about her daughter's infidelity, hounded Madeleine, "When will you have a baby? Adam and Joey have children and Jeff's wife is pregnant. All are married to Christian girls. I love them dearly. But you're my only hope for a Jewish grandchild. Judaism is passed on through the mother, not the father, you know."

Madeleine's mother-in-law drove Madeleine crazy, too, with her questions. Barry's mother tried very hard to control Madeleine like she had always done with her only son. Phone calls with his mother usually ended with the question, "When will you have children? It is passed time to have your first child."

One evening after dinner, Barry asked Madeleine, "When will you be ready to have children? I don't understand why you won't agree to have a baby now."

"I want a career. I want to take art classes and photography classes. I want to go camping on weekends; go rock climbing and caving. I can't do that with a child. You would expect me to be a mother full-time," she tried to explain.

"No, I'd help you out. I can baby sit. I know there are many things I can do to help you with the baby," he declared. He desperately wanted children, to have a family like his sisters and all his cousins did at his age.

"That's just it. *You'd help me with the baby*. Like its 100% my responsibility. I'll be the one stuck at home," she cried. "Then, you'll want another child. Please, can't we wait a few more years? I'm only twenty-four. Women can have babies until they are thirty." Madeleine sobbed.

"Madeleine, don't be ridiculous. I can't stay at home. I have my career and can't build my practice if I have to take care of the baby during the day," he said. "Are you crazy? What can I do to convince you to agree to get pregnant?"

"You can sign a document that says you are responsible for the child fifty percent of the time," she said. "You don't have to actually take care of the baby, you can hire a baby sitter. It's just that fifty percent of the time it's your responsibility to make sure he or she is taken care of."

Barry scrunched up his face in bewilderment. "What do you mean? Sign a document?" he yelled. "Where do you get these ideas? From your friend Jessica? She's divorced and she wants you to be too." He turned bright red. "What about the contract you signed with me?"

"What contract?" she asked, truly puzzled about what he meant.

"Our marriage contract? To have a Jewish home and have children? To be my wife, foremost, above all the rest of this crap you want to do. I thought that is why we got married," he said as his eyes filled with tears.

Madeleine didn't know what to say. She stood motionless. Her eyes darted from side to side as if she was watching a movie. She slowly approached Barry and hugged him tightly. "I am so sorry that I'm not ready to be just a mother and wife with Friday night dinner on the table. I don't know what is wrong with me. I'm afraid I am going crazy." She struggled to take a deep breath. "Barry, I can't breathe."

"Then get your inhaler," Barry said sounding annoyed. "So, what do you want to do about us?"

"I love you. Please give me some time. I'm so confused." She was crying when she added, "I do want children one day, and I'll try to be a better wife. Let me have a profession first." She finally took a deep breath. "Anyway, we need the money now."

Barry pulled away from Madeleine and added, "I love you too. Please don't wait too long. I want a family soon. I'll figure out a way to support us. I promise."

***

Shortly after their heated discussion, Madeleine was diagnosed with severe endometriosis. Madeleine's periods had been painful ever since she first started having them at age twelve. The first time she had her period, the pain was so bad that Leo had to pick her up from school and take her home. She was mortified that her father knew she was having her period, but her mother was at a meeting and couldn't be disturbed.

Her OB/GYN told her that with endometriosis as severe as hers, the chances of getting pregnant decreased with every year she waited. In spite of this, she knew she wasn't ready to be a mother. How could she bring a child into her marriage to Barry when they couldn't agree on her role? How could she have a baby when she loved Pat and Barry?

Madeleine knew she couldn't turn to her mother for support. Sophie could not be counted on to be supportive when Madeleine needed her. Sophie only criticized Madeleine and condemned her behavior. Madeleine couldn't remember a time that Sophie held her and said, "I love you."

Luckily, Madeleine had women friends who also struggled with the changing roles of mother and wife. Friends who weren't part of Barry's circle of friends. All his friends were people they knew from college or were part of his vast group of cousins. Her friends understood her mental anguish. Feeling guilty about what she did. Hating herself. Conflicted about wanting to be free and to be married. Wanting to have children and a profession.

She believed what she read in MS magazine and what she saw on the news. She wanted it all: freedom from traditional roles, a profession, children, and a loving husband who had access to his inner emotional life. It was incredibly difficult for Madeleine to balance what she wanted and what she had. The tension was unbearable. She couldn't sleep, and the stress was affecting her work. She had to take some action to survive.

Chapter Ninety-Two

Barry, too, was under pressure at home and work. He was an associate at a small law office in downtown Atlanta and was having difficulty building a client base. His monthly income was less than Madeleine's, and she made very little. The firm's two partners were not generous in how they dealt with their junior associates. Barry had been led to believe that the two partners would give him clients, ones they didn't have time to handle. So far, they hadn't kept to their agreement.

Barry met a paralegal, Kathleen, who worked in an office down the hall from his office. They had lunch together a few times a month to commiserate about their jobs. Once a month they met for drinks after work in the bar on the first floor of their building and talked about their personal lives. Kathleen was the daughter of a wealthy Jewish family and wasn't married. She'd been engaged once, but her fiancé ended the relationship because he didn't want children yet, and she did. Barry confided to her about Madeleine and their marital problems.

"So, where is Madeleine tonight," Kathleen asked one night as she sipped her gin and tonic. She knew Madeleine usually left on Friday nights to go on one of her climbing or caving trips. Kathleen and Barry disapproved of this practice because they thought it was important to have Friday night, Shabbat, dinner at home with your family either before or after temple services. This Friday night was an exception for Kathleen. For Barry, it was the norm because Madeleine didn't want to commit to a rigid Friday night schedule or to going to temple.

"On one of her caving trips. I think to North Carolina," he answered. He'd found Kathleen attractive since he met her. She was pretty with long black hair and deep-green eyes, and they had similar viewpoints about marriage, religion, and family. She could tell Barry found her attractive by the way he blushed when she caught him staring at her tonight at the bar.

"So, you're a free man this weekend?" she asked. Kathleen liked Barry and couldn't understand why his wife was gone so much. She'd like to be married to a Jewish lawyer, someone like Barry. She was ready to have children but hadn't found the right man yet.

"Yes, until late Sunday night. I am available," he laughed.

"Want to come over to my house and have dinner? I have a lasagna I made last night, and it's great warmed up," she asked as she placed her hand on his thigh, moving it slowly upward.

"Why not?" he said. He felt the warmth of her hand and was afraid his growing erection would be obvious if she moved her hand half an inch further up his thigh. He was horny much of the time because Madeleine seemed to have lost interest in having sex as much as they used to have.

***

Barry and Kathleen drove separate cars to Kathleen's apartment on Peachtree Street not far from the house Madeleine and Barry rented off Piedmont Road. While he drove, Barry thought about Kathleen and the potential situation. By the time they met at her front door he'd decided to act on the attraction he felt to her. *Why not?* He thought. Madeleine had been urging him to have an affair so she wouldn't feel guilty about hers. Until now, he had said he couldn't do that. He hadn't wanted to condone Madeleine's behavior by his having an affair.

Once Kathleen closed and locked the door, Barry reached out and pulled her to him. He kissed her with all the pent-up passion he'd wanted with Madeleine. He sucked on her bottom lip while gently holding the back of her neck so she couldn't move away from him.

"Wow," Kathleen said when Barry let her go. She was overcome with desire. "I think we can skip dinner."

She led him to her bedroom with its fancy linens and layers of pillows. The light from the living room illuminated the expensively decorated room. They continued kissing. His hand found her breast. His fingers circled her nipples that stood erect under her thin blouse. She placed her hand on his penis over his pants and moved her open hand up and down the length of his erection. He almost came in his pants, but stopped himself by moving back from her hand.

"Wow," she said. "You are really well endowed. I think I am going to enjoy this."

They barely got their shoes, slacks, and underpants off. "Hurry," she'd said. "Skip the foreplay. Just do it. Oh, please. Do it." She hadn't made love to anyone in almost a year since her broken engagement and was shaking with desire.

Barry came quickly, but ground his pelvis into Kathleen's like he did with Madeleine to see if Kathleen would come. She did with a quiet moan.

Not bad for a first time. She thought as she untangled herself from him.

Minutes later, they stood and took off the rest of their clothes. Her inner thighs were sticky with semen.

"I'm sorry," Barry said. "We made a wet spot on your bedspread." He pointed to a dark stain on the blue bedspread.

"It's okay," she shrugged. "It can be cleaned."

Barry had learned a great deal about sex since he met and married Madeleine. They had explored *The Joy of Sex* together and tried many of the positions. The next time he and Kathleen made love, Barry tried his new techniques on her. At first, Kathleen was uncomfortable with the ways Barry explored her body with his fingers and mouth, but she gave in to the pleasure she felt.

They spent the rest of the weekend together, other than when Barry went home to get more clothes and a toothbrush. Kathleen cooked food she had in the refrigerator, and they ordered pizza. They made love and talked. For the first time, he understood how appealing it was to have a secret lover. How wonderful it must have felt for Madeleine to have an affair. To be with another person besides your spouse. He felt it too, but he was wracked with guilt.

Sunday morning after breakfast, Barry and Kathleen sat side by side on her living room sofa holding hands. "Kathleen," he started.

"Don't say it," she interrupted. "I know. You don't want to see me any more."

"It's not that. Really. I want to see you, but I can't," he said and he squeezed her hand. "My marriage is already not working, and I don't want to add sneaking around to the list of problems we have. It's been a wonderful, no, spectacular, weekend. I'll never forget it."

Kathleen nodded and cried softly, "So, no more lunches and drinks after work?"

"No. I think it's best if we don't see each other," Barry said.

He packed his few belongings, hugged Kathleen, and left, wanting to be home before Madeleine returned. Time to take a shower, watch a game on TV, and try to forget about his illicit weekend. He wanted to maintain the moral high ground with Madeleine, so it was best to not think of the weekend again.

Chapter Ninety-Three

Madeleine truly thought she was going crazy. She loved and hated Barry. Wanted to be with him. Didn't want to be with him. Wanted Pat to leave his wife. Hated herself. Missed her father. She knew she had to find a good therapist. One of her friends at work recommended Dr. Tenant, a highly regarded Atlanta therapist who worked with couples and families.

She poured out her emotional pain and despair. About her marriage, her lovers, and her family. About how Sophie and Hannah treated her and called her terrible names. After several sessions, out of the blue, he asked, "Did your mother have a child out of wedlock?"

Stunned and confused, she said, "No. Why would you ask me that?" She was truly puzzled why her therapist would ask her such a question, seemingly out of left field.

He answered, "Because what you describe to me about your family, your mother, and your marriage sounds like women whose mothers had children out of wedlock. Women who have had illegitimate children live in fear that their daughters will do the same."

"I think you're not listening to me," Madeleine said. "That has nothing to do me. I just miss my father so much. He would be there for me. I know it. Even if I left Barry, my father would still love me. I wouldn't be so afraid to leave Barry. My mother hates me. She never says anything nice to me. Why is she so angry at me?"

The therapist said, "A woman gets affirmation about her mothering from how her daughter is as a mother. You refuse to have children. She sees that as an indictment of her. Maybe this is why she is so upset about your refusing to have children."

***

After several years of individual and couples therapy with Dr. Tenant, Madeleine wasn't any happier with her marriage. She and Barry weren't any closer. In fact, they were further apart. They separated several times, and then reconciled. Each time putting another rip in the fabric of their marriage.

It was the day she thought, "I will either kill him or me," that she knew it was time to end it. Finally, after years of both loving and hating her husband, Madeleine asked for a final separation and divorce. It was a sad and painful process for Barry and Madeleine. They had lived through so much together and admitted they still loved each other, but it was time to end it.

Six months after the divorce was final, Madeleine still grieved the death of her marriage. It surprised her. No one had prepared her for the sadness that accompanies the end of a marriage, especially one that was not a bad one. Madeleine called her mother for comfort and reassurance. Sophie responded, "How could you leave the only good thing you have ever done in your life?"

"Mom, it's not that I don't love Barry. He just didn't love me in the way I wanted. He and I want different things out of life," Madeleine tried to explain to Sophie. She desperately wanted her mother to understand why she left Barry. Madeleine added, "Just look at him now, Mother. I am the one who wanted the divorce, and he's the one getting remarried less than a year after we separated. To someone he knew. Someone who worked in his building."

Sophie said, "Well, what did you expect? He was good to you. He didn't hurt you. So, don't be upset another woman wants him."

"Never mind, Mother. I don't know why I tried to talk to you about it," Madeleine replied. "You have never accepted me as I am. You have always wanted a different daughter. If you can't be accepting of me, I don't want to hear from you again." Madeleine said as she hung up the phone.

Madeleine wrote as a way to understand her previous marriage and her mixed feelings about their divorce. Besides talking

279

to her women friends in the "women's support groups" that were so popular, Madeleine wrote in a diary, on scraps of paper, and in notebooks. She only showed one poem to Barry years later when both of them were remarried and had reconnected as friends.

To Barry, My Former Husband

I've been crying all day
Since the door was locked behind me.
I've been crying
For the times you accepted me
Even when I didn't understand
What I was doing.
And you didn't either.

I've been crying
For the times
I felt so distant,
Yet didn't know
How to reach out to you.

I've been crying
For all the little hurts
We inflicted on each other.
Over our growing up together.
For all the things we didn't do right.
For our stubbornness
And our perseverance.

I've been crying over
The potential that was there.
And the dreams we both had.

There are tears
For all the memories
Good and bad
And the realization there is nothing else to do.

I've shared so much of myself with you
And yet so little.
My father gave me away
To you
Now I give myself away to
Uncertainty.

I cry for
All the things that
Will never be.
I cry for our unborn children
Our unfulfilled dreams.
And I wonder where
Why and how it all went wrong

Chapter Ninety-Four

1980

At age thirty, after being a psychologist for almost ten years, Madeleine decided to go back to school to get a PhD, something she gave up years ago so she could move with Barry to Atlanta once he finished his law degree. Her clinical clients had asked her to speak at their businesses and do workshops for their employees. Madeleine enjoyed the work and it paid better than being a psychologist. She'd originally decided to be a psychologist to save her father, but she hadn't been able to do that. Getting a degree in psychology and business would allow her to finally make enough money to live the way her father and mother raised her.

Madeleine called her mother one Sunday, the day they usually talked. "Mom, do you think you might be able to help out with me going back to school?" She paused and caught her breath. "I know there is money left from when Daddy died. Maybe I could borrow some of that to help pay for graduate school. I know you lent Adam $10,000 as a down payment for the house he bought for his family. My two jobs working as a therapist and teaching at night don't pay enough for me to get by. Maybe a little each month?" She prayed silently that her mother would say" yes.".

Sophie was silent for a minute as she gathered her thoughts. "Madeleine, I'll think about it." Sophie twisted in her seat on the couch. "I may be able to give you a little each month. What's left of your daddy's money plus the little I make managing the business is what I have to live on." It sounded like she felt bad that she couldn't give Madeleine an absolute yes. "Maybe I'll leave my condo to you in my Will so you'll have a home here in West Palm when I die."

"Okay, I appreciate your thinking about it and the offer of the condo. You're not going to die soon, so don't worry." Madeleine remained optimistic.

Madeleine went back to college, worked two jobs, and partied hard. She dated and fell in and out of love with a series of men. At one point, she lived, platonically, in a house with two men.

Sophie went crazy when she heard about her daughter's living arrangement. "How can you live in a house with two men? Are you sleeping with both of them?" she accused Madeleine.

"No, Mother, I am not sleeping with either of them." Madeleine took another toke of the joint she had rolled before she called her mother. It helped calm her before these conversations. "Why must you always think the worst of me? What did I ever do to make you feel that way?" she cried softly. "When Joey got a girl pregnant, didn't you tell me that you always thought it would be me who needed an abortion one day? Why did you always favor the boys over me? I am your only daughter."

"Madeleine, you are exaggerating. I never said that," her mother asserted. Sophie's heart sunk at Madeleine's comment about being the "only daughter."

"You did say it." Madeleine controlled her voice. "I am sick and tired of your criticism. You never say anything nice to me. You call me names." She stood up. "I don't think you ever loved me. Either you stop verbally abusing me, or I'll never see you or speak to you again. Do you understand?" She tried not to sob into the phone.

"Madeleine, I am sorry you feel that way. Of course I love you. I love you more than you'll ever know. I'll try to be better about showing it." Sophie was in tears now too. She wished she could grab Madeleine's hands and hold them as she spoke "I never wanted to be like my mother, but I guess I was to you. I'm sorry. Please come visit for a few days. I'll try to be better."

Several weeks after the phone call, Madeleine flew to Florida for a long weekend. Sophie and Madeleine went to Nando's in Palm Beach for dinner one night when the Shah of Iran was at the next table. There was a bomb scare, so they were asked to leave and never had to pay for the meal. Another night, Madeleine invited several of her high school friends over for dinner. Sophie laughed with the younger women and shared stories about her high school years. For Sophie and Madeleine, the healing process had begun.

Madeleine called her brother Jeff before she left and told him that she thought their mother didn't look good. She was very overweight, had high blood pressure, and her complexion was very gray.

One month later, Sophie dropped dead of a massive heart attack at the Tallahassee Airport in front of her grandchildren. She was visiting Adam's and Joey's families—both brothers lived in Tallahassee. Her grandchildren adored her. Sophie was an incredible grandmother: empathetic, demonstrative, and loving. Something she found difficult to do with her own children.

Sophie had always shown more favor to her sons than to Madeleine, so her passing away was harder on the boys than on Madeleine. She was the strong one this time as opposed to when Leo died. Her brothers were angry at her that she didn't cry or talk about how much she would miss her mother.

"I won't miss her," Madeleine announced when her brothers were talking about how kind and generous Sophie had been to them.

"How can you be such a bitch?" Adam asked her.

"I learned it from her. She was a bitch to me until the last few weeks of her life. It's hard to grieve for something you never had. She may have been a great mother to you guys, just not to me. Let's just drop it," Madeleine replied.

Madeleine's peace with her mother didn't last long. Although Sophie might have meant well when she told Madeleine she would help her with college tuition and leave her the condo, none of the promises Sophie made to Madeleine were in her Will. Everything was split between the four children including the condo. Madeleine ended up getting one-fourth of her mother's estate, which she used to pay a portion of her tuition and to put a down payment on a house in a transitional part of Atlanta near the Zoo.

Even though it was difficult to finish school on the money she made working and the money from her mother's estate, Madeleine knew she needed the PhD to do what she wanted to be: an industrial and organizational psychologist. She had great people skills from her experience as an individual, couple, and group therapist. She had received positive feedback on her training and facilitation skills. People she met through her work in mental health encouraged her to use her skills in the business arena. She would get her degree no matter what obstacles stood in her way.

Chapter Ninety-Five

1985

Four years after her mother's death, Madeleine finished her PhD. Her mother's desire for Madeleine to have a child was never going to be fulfilled. As it would happen, Madeleine's endometriosis reached a point where a full hysterectomy was the only option.

"I guess I'll never have a baby of my own," she told her best friend Jessica. "Maybe this was the plan all along. Maybe this is my punishment for how I was with Barry and refusing to have a child with him."

"That is nonsense. It's not a punishment. Don't give up yet," Jessica said. "You could adopt. Or one day, you might marry a man with children. You never know what will happen in the future." She always knew what to say to Madeleine to comfort her. She was her best friend, sister, and good mother figure. Madeleine felt fortunate to have met her.

The day after Madeleine graduated, she had her surgery. She was only thirty-seven years old. The cycle of women in her family having babies out of wedlock was broken. Madeleine had no idea how her never having children changed the pattern set by her mother and grandmother. She had no idea each of them had a child and gave it away.

Although Madeleine lost the option to give birth to a child, she had achieved other goals she had set for herself years ago with the promise of "feminism." She was hired by a nationally famous consulting firm that allowed her to fulfill her professional dreams. She loved her job. She traveled all over the United States, often in first class, to work with business clients. She gained a positive reputation in her field, wrote papers that were published in journals, and gave speeches at conferences. Best of all, she supported herself financially and was able to save and invest money for her future.

Madeleine had a circle of great friends whom she considered her family in Atlanta, and old friends scattered all over Florida. Her brothers' families became her family, and she doted on her nieces and nephews.

She might not have a husband, but she had a series of men in her life. Several of them, who she thought were her soul mates, broke her heart. Others, inappropriate because of age or values, she broke up with after a short period of time. By the time Madeleine was in her mid-forties, she was tired of dating.

"I swear," Madeleine told her friend, Jessica. "I think I have dated all the men in Atlanta. None of them interest me for long, or they decide I am not the woman of their dreams. I wouldn't mind finding the 'right' one."

Jessica told her, "Madeleine, your problem is that you always date down. Men who are not right for you in too many ways."

"I know, but they are the cute ones. They are fun to be with. And great sex partners," Madeleine agreed.

Another friend, Cathy, told her, "Set your expectations lower. Then you won't be disappointed!"

Madeleine let everyone know she wanted to meet a man who was respectable and possibly marriage material. No more handymen, carpenters, country musicians and the like. Or men who were separated from their wives and not divorced "I will go on a date with anyone that meets this criteria," she told her friends and acquaintances. "You never know who I might meet."

Chapter Ninety-Six

One of Madeleine's clients told her about a good restaurant down the street from the hotel where she usually stayed. This hotel in Raleigh, NC was home for four nights every week when she came to consult with her two biggest clients in the Research Triangle Park. Usually, she went straight to her room after work so she could check her e-mails and be on conference calls with her team until 10:30 p.m. Dinner was usually a burger with fries that room service delivered.

This particular night, she wanted a drink before heading to her room. It had been an especially long day due to the firm's CEO and his leadership team. The meeting that was supposed to end at 4:00 ran until 6:30. Part of her job was to give feedback to the CEO after the meeting and he kept her in his office for another hour. She decided to try out the recommended restaurant before going back to her hotel.

She found the restaurant and took a seat at the bar. She ordered a glass of the good cabernet, not the house red. The bar and restaurant were crowded with people dressed in their professional work clothes. She was lucky to find a seat.

Near to her barstool was a table with eight people drinking and talking loudly. They drowned out the piano player's music. One of them backed into her, causing her to drop her glass of wine. It broke on the corner of the bar and red wine spilled onto the top of the counter, dripping onto her new tan pantsuit. Madeleine jumped from her chair and accidentally stepped on a man's foot.

"I am so sorry," the man said as he pulled out a white handkerchief from his pocket. "Here, let me help you wipe that up." He placed his handkerchief over the spreading puddle of wine as the bartender came over with wet rags to sop up the mess.

"That's okay," Madeleine said with a shrug of her shoulders. "The suit can go to the cleaners." She turned back to the bar.

"Wait, I can at least buy you a new drink," he said. "What were you having?"

"You'll have to ask the bartender. I don't remember its name." Madeleine responded. She quickly assessed the man. "You don't have to buy me a drink."

"Yes, I do," he said. "I am a Southern gentleman." He laughed and sat down on the surprisingly empty barstool next to her. "My name is Jim. What's yours?"

"I'm Madeleine," she answered.

Jim had thinning blonde hair and startling blue eyes. He looked like he could be any age between forty-five and fifty-five—Madeleine couldn't tell. He was tall, at least 6'2", and, like her, could stand to lose fifteen pounds.

Madeleine and Jim sat at the bar and talked late into the night. They talked easily about themselves, their work, what they wanted out of life, and why they were single. Jim had been married twice and had been divorced a year since his last marriage.

"I'm tired of dating," he told Madeleine as they ate the dinner they ordered at 9:00 P.M.

"Me, too," Madeleine said. "It's been fifteen years since I got divorced and I feel like I've dated most of the men in Atlanta."

"I know the feeling. I can't tell you the number of women I've met at this bar or brought here." He glanced around the room. "I met my second wife here. She was barely old enough to drink. We drank too much when we were together and got married too quickly. She was really too young for me," he explained.

It was 12:00 a.m. and the bar was closing in an hour. Jim and Madeleine looked at each other, and both said almost simultaneously, "I want to see you again."

"I have a question I need to ask you now though," said Madeleine. "Not after we start dating, if we do," she said.

"Okay," Jim said as he sipped his wine.

"Do you think you'll ever get married again? Not to me, just to anyone," she asked.

Jim laughed at her question. "Yes, one day I would. Why?" he asked with a bemused grin on his face.

"Because if we date, I want to know if it's a possibility. I want to get married again and don't want to just date people," Madeleine explained.

Jim didn't answer immediately. Instead of panicking and making excuses for her bluntness, Madeleine waited. She watched him close his eyes for a moment and opened them. He appeared to be looking at a spot off in the distance.

"I have tried marriage twice and failed both times, although the second time wasn't entirely my fault," he said very seriously. "But I'd like to think it is possible to have a good marriage. I'd have to be very sure, but yes, I'd get married again."

"Thanks. I appreciate your honesty." Madeleine picked up her purse and briefcase as Jim stood up to leave with her.

As they walked to the restaurant's front door, he said, "When will you be back? Can we set a date for then?"

"Yes. Thank God you didn't say, 'I'll call you.' I would have screamed."

After that evening, neither Madeleine nor Jim dated anyone else. They spent as much time together as any long-distance relationship would allow. Madeleine wanted her friends to meet Jim. It was important to her that they liked him. Likewise, Jim wanted Madeleine to meet his friends, to see if they got along.

Jim had a three-year old son, Preston, with whom Jim and his second ex-wife shared custody. The first time Madeleine met Preston, she was very nervous. She wanted him to like her. Jim had prepared Preston for meeting her. "You will like her, kiddo," Jim told his son.

"Why, Daddy?" Preston asked.

"Because I like her. I love her and hope you will, too, one day," Jim said.

"Okay, Daddy." Preston said as he returned to playing with his Legos on the floor.

It all worked and a year later, Madeleine and Jim got married. She agreed to move to Raleigh.

One day, six months after Jim and Madeleine were married, Madeleine sat in the rocking chair in Preston's room, rocking him to sleep. She put her nose close to the top of his head and smelled his baby shampoo and baby powder. She had once read a study that showed that mothers could recognize their own child just by the baby's smell. She wanted to do that with Preston.

In spite of the stumbling blocks along the way, Madeleine thought that her life had turned out okay. She had a career like she'd hoped, but thought she'd never have a child. She had come to terms with this hard, cold truth. Yet, here she sat, rocking "her" baby to sleep, quietly telling him, "I love you. You have a second mommy now. Me. I couldn't love you more if I'd given birth to you myself."

Part IV

Secrets Revealed

"Do you want to know a secret?

Do you promise not to tell?"

The Beatles, 1963

Chapter Ninety-Seven

2005

Sophie, whether she ever knew it or not, was right about the prediction she made when her illegitimate daughter was born. Her cousins Edwin and Martha did keep Sophie's baby girl. They named her Ellen. Ellen was the first of three little girls Edwin and Martha adopted. For some reason, Edwin and Martha never told Ellen she was adopted. Maybe it was because she was Sophie's baby, and they never wanted Ellen to know that her parents' own cousin was her real mother.

Martha, Edwin, and Hannah had decided that when Sophie left the baby with the Blums it would be better if everyone thought Ellen was Martha's birth child. When Sophie stayed with them, she thought Martha was gaining weight. Sophie brushed it off as Martha's eating more due to the stress of Sophie's condition. She never gave a thought to the idea that Martha did this purposefully so neighbors would think she was pregnant.

When Ellen was born, they bribed the doctor to write Martha's name down as the mother and Edwin as the father. Her birth certificate showed that Ellen was born to the Blums. There were moments when Martha felt bad about the lie, but it was the price they paid for their first child. Ellen never needed to know she was adopted.

Ellen, like Sophie, was a bright child. When she started school, the principal suggested to her parents that she skip first grade and go directly from kindergarten to second grade. Her parents worried about the effect this would have on Ellen's social development, but it turned out that Ellen adapted very well to children a year older than she.

When Ellen was four, the first of her sisters was adopted. Ellen adored her sister and was a constant help to her mother. Two years later, a second baby girl was adopted.

"Mommy, what does it mean to be adopted?" Ellen asked Martha one day after her second sister came home.

"It means you are a very special baby who Mommy and Daddy got to pick out. But you are also special because Daddy and I had you the way most people have children," Martha explained, starting the pattern of lying early in Ellen's life.

Ellen grew up feeling superior to her sisters because she thought she was her parents' only real daughter. They might have picked her two sisters, but God gave Ellen to her parents.

Ellen was a natural leader always organizing her sisters. If they played a game, she explained the rules, even if she made them up as they played. If someone had to take the blame for something bad that happened, she told her parents which child had done it.

As Ellen grew up, she became a beauty with curly black hair, large breasts, and a tiny waist. She noticed that neither her mother nor her father looked like her, but she knew there could be recessive genes to account for the familial differences. She accepted it that her sisters wouldn't look like their parents or her, so her sisters' appearances didn't bother her.

The three sisters were physically and emotionally different, but Martha and Edwin tried to raise the girls as equally as possible. All three girls were given the same love and opportunities. After a while, Martha and Edwin forgot Ellen was adopted. Many years later, when Jeff called to ask if Sophie was Ellen's mother, Edwin swore Ellen was not adopted, and he meant it. Edwin was so incensed by Jeff's question that he never spoke to him again.

Chapter Ninety-Eight

2005

Several days before she died, Sophie's best friend, Ruby Fox, sat straight up in her bed in the Good Samaritan Hospital. Formerly a size fourteen, she was so gaunt that her skin thinly covered her skeletal frame. She commanded Ben, her husband of sixty years, to call Jeff Rosen and ask him to come to the hospital as soon as possible. "I'll die this week," she said, matter-of-factly. Her tone changed, becoming more forceful. "I must talk to Jeff Rosen now. Tell him to come immediately. I don't have much time." Sitting up had physically drained her. She lay back on her pillows, closed her eyes, and began to softly snore.

Ruby's two children had been born at this hospital, in the maternity ward that was the first home for eighty percent of the children in West Palm Beach born from 1944 – 1955, the post-World War II children. In those days, the rooms had been powder pink and sky blue, with bright red balloons and pastel-colored clowns painted on the walls. Fathers and grandparents with gleaming eyes and smiles that stretched from one ear to the other paraded the halls between the new mothers' rooms and the nursery.

Now, Ruby's current room smelled of Lysol, urine, and decaying flesh. Visitors came and went from the fourth floor with grim expressions and tears running down their faces. The fourth floor was home to the terminally ill. Those who chose not to die at home in their own beds with colorful sheets and blankets familiar from years of use, but in a room with white sheets, gray walls, beeping monitors, and no happy pictures painted on the walls.

When Ben reached Jeff on his cell phone, Jeff had spent the day driving from West Palm Beach to Boynton Beach and then to Fort Lauderdale to fix computers and networks for three small businesses. His right arm was numb, and his neck ached from driving and crawling under desks. All he wanted to do was to go home, change into his favorite pair of khaki shorts, and sit on his screened porch drinking a glass of red wine. Good Sam, the name the natives used to refer to the hospital, was situated on Flagler Drive and provided a clear view of the Lake Worth Intercoastal Waterway and of the ornate houses and stately hotels in Palm Beach.

Frustrated, Jeff thought, *the trip adds forty minutes of extra driving. I am not in the mood to visit sick people.*

Jeff parked in the sweltering, three-story parking deck behind the hospital and walked in the front entrance. His shirt's back and armpits were wet with perspiration. His balding head was tomato red from his exertion in Florida's ninety-five degree August climate. The twenty extra pounds he carried and his lack of regular exercise exacerbated his physical reaction to heat, particularly in the summer months. Passing through the sliding door, he was assaulted by cold air that smelled slightly of recently washed floors and floral air fresheners. He stopped at the information desk, situated in the middle of the rotunda, and asked the blue-haired, wrinkled-faced receptionist for Ruby's room number.

Ruby's room, 404, three doors down from the central nurses' station, was silent. No television blared. No conversations could be heard in the hallway. He took a deep breath, opened the door, and tried not to show his shock at how Ruby looked. Jeff had seen Ruby two or three times since she retired from the bookstore where she had worked for over thirty years. The store on Clematis Street had closed ten years ago, when the rest of downtown had fallen into disrepair and the suburban malls drew the customers who used to go downtown.

Ruby's skin was the color of old parchment. Her hair, which she had worn in a 1960's bouffant cut, was sparse and matted to her head in greasy clumps. A heart monitor, an IV morphine drip, an oxygen hose, a blood pressure cuff, and a bag to catch her urine were attached to her frail body.

He swallowed, took a deep breath, and announced, "Ruby, this is Jeff Rosen. You asked to see me." He waited for what seemed like five minutes, and then said again, "Ruby, it's Jeff. I'm here."

Ruby slowly opened her eyes and tried to focus in spite of her mental fog from the heavy pain medication being administered to her every four hours. "Jeff. It's good to see you." She paused to take a deep breath. She coughed and rasped, "Please come closer, it's hard to talk." Ruby, having smoked for over forty-five years, was dying of lung cancer. "How are you? How are the children?" She paused again, and her eyes closed.

"Ruby, everyone is fine. Ben said you had to see me. Please tell me what you want me to do." At this point, Jeff imagined several scenarios: Ruby wanted him to handle some business? Ruby had some object she wanted to give him? Ruby had a story to tell him?

Ruby opened her eyes, appearing to be more alert than when Jeff first arrived. Her eyes focused on Jeff's, and in a drugged but coherent voice said, "There is something I must tell you about your mother. I am one of the last people alive who knows, and I can't die without telling you." She paused before continuing. "Your mother had a baby out of wedlock. It was before she married your father. No one knew. I only found out for sure in the last few years."

Jeff was stunned. A child out of wedlock? "Who was the father? When did it happen? Was it a boy or a girl? Did my mother tell anyone about the baby? Who else knows?"

Ruby continued. "Information is very sketchy because no one was supposed to know. We pieced the information together by talking to my daughter."

"Your daughter? Why your daughter?" Jeff asked, puzzled by what Ruby's daughter, Bess, had to do with his mother.

"She got pregnant while in high school, senior year. She had a baby shortly after that. Your mother was so kind to Bess. She told her there was nothing wrong with what she did. That it didn't mean she was a bad person. Sophie encouraged Bess to keep the child and not give the baby away like Sophie was made to do. After your mother talked with Bess, she and her boyfriend, Judd, decided to get married and keep their baby" Ruby explained. "Sophie then confided in her about her illegitimate child."

"When did Bess tell you this?" Jeff was suspicious.

"After your mother passed away, Bess called me and told me what Sophie had told her. Your mother told Bess that her baby had gone to relatives in New Jersey. Do you know any relatives in New Jersey?" Ruby, although showing signs of fatigue, continued.

"I do. The Blums. They had three daughters. Two or three of them were adopted." Jeff paused and was quiet for a few seconds. "I'll call Edwin and ask what he knows. Come to think of it, I met one of the daughters a few years ago when she moved to Boca part-time. I remember being struck by the fact that she reminded me of Mom." He paced the hospital room. "But I blew it off, thinking it was natural to have some family resemblance. But now, in retrospect, it is hard to believe this woman could have my mother's characteristics and never have spent time with her. It had to be her. Her name was Ellen." He waited for a reply while Ruby closed her eyes. "Do you know if it was a boy or a girl?" he rushed to ask her before she went back into a drug-induced sleep. "Did my father know?"

"I don't know for sure, but I think it was a girl. I don't think your father ever knew." Ruby slurred her words.

"And she never talked to you about it? You two were close for over forty years. You talked on the phone every day, and she never told you anything about it?" Jeff still found it hard to believe what Ruby told him.

"No, she never told me about it or anyone else, except Bess. I think the father could have been my cousin Richard, whom she dated before she met your dad." Ruby adjusted her position in bed.

"You know, your mother was so young compared to the rest of us. And so smart. One spring, we thought she was moody because of her grades or something. I remember she went away one summer during college and didn't come back until school started. She and your grandmother told everyone she was babysitting her cousin's children to earn extra money to finish school." She paused and wheezed. "I tried to talk to her about that summer, but she refused to discuss it."

"Why didn't she tell my father?" Jeff asked.

"Knowing Aunt Hannah, I bet she told Sophie to never tell Leo the truth. Hannah must have convinced your mother that no one could ever know. You remember how your grandmother was about being proper and doing things a certain way," Ruby said as her eyes turned glassy. "I need to sleep…"

As Jeff left the hospital, he knew the first person he had to call was his sister Madeleine. Madeleine always wondered why her mother and grandmother said mean and hurtful things to her. He knew that shortly before their mother died, Madeleine told her mother how fed up she was with how she had been treated all of her life.

Luckily, Sophie realized she was losing her daughter by being like her own mother—so mean and judgmental. At least Madeleine and Sophie had made up before Sophie died.

Jeff called Madeleine as soon as he got in his car and turned on the air conditioning. He told Madeleine what Ruby had just told him—she believed it immediately.

"Of course I believe you and her," Madeleine said, trying to control the emotions that were careening throughout her body. "It explains so much. The names Mom and Nana called me. The reason why Nana lived with us her whole life. She probably blackmailed our mother."

As her words sunk into her consciousness, Madeleine put more pieces of the puzzle together. How her mother was afraid Madeleine would get pregnant. She remembered what she had said to her on her wedding day: "Now if you get pregnant, it won't be out of wedlock." Madeleine always thought that was a strange thing to say.

"I want to find her. I want to find my sister," Madeleine announced. "I know she is out there, and I want to find her. A client is waiting for me right now. I have to go. Let's talk again later."

Madeleine called Jeff back that evening when she returned home.

"Have you talked to anyone else since calling me?" she asked her brother.

"Yes. At least you believe me. Adam dismissed it as a dying woman's hallucinations. He doesn't even want to know about it," Jeff said.

Madeleine replied immediately, "He's threatened by knowing he wasn't the firstborn. I am sure this rocks his whole world. The idea that he may have been the first boy, but he wasn't the first baby born. So, do you want to find her or not?"

"Let's do some other research before we start looking for her. Will you call Lois, Ruby's sister, and see if she knows anything else? I'll call Edwin and see if he knows anything," Jeff proposed. "And I'll call Joey when I get home."

"Okay, I'll call Lois, and I'll check birth records from 1941. Let's talk tomorrow," Madeleine agreed. "Okay. Love you. One last piece of information: twenty years ago, I had a therapist who asked me if I knew if my mother had a child out of wedlock. I laughed and said, 'Absolutely not.' I wonder what he picked up. I wonder what he saw to ask that question."

Madeleine got off the phone and kept saying over and over, "I have a sister. My mother had a baby before she married my father. I have a sister..."

Chapter Ninety-Nine

Jeff sat in a cushioned lawn chair on his lanai. The sun was going down and the humid south Florida air felt less suffocating than earlier in the day. He called Joey to tell him what he found out about their mother and about Adam and Madeleine's responses to the news.

Joey was out of the country on an assignment for the magazine he worked for since his baseball career ended. His wife, Angela, answered the phone, so Jeff told her the unimaginable story.

"Wow!" Angela said in her strong Southern accent. She was originally from Alabama and hadn't lost her accent in the years since she married Joey. "That's quite a story. I promise to tell Joe when he calls. Or would you rather tell him?"

"No, it's okay for you to tell him. I bet he would love to write a story about this." Jeff took a gulp of the beer he had in his hand as he sat by the covered pool he and his wife had added to their house last year. "Life is stranger than fiction." He got up, went outside the lanai, and began to water the bushes as he talked. "Tell him to call me when he can. I'd like to know his thoughts on finding our supposed sister."

He paused and then continued. "Madeleine thinks we should look for her. Jim thinks it is a bad idea...that if our other sister wanted to know us, she would have looked for us." He paused, waiting for his sister-in-law to say anything, but she didn't. "You know how my wife Bonnie is. She thinks we should leave well enough alone. She thinks we might disrupt someone's life that doesn't want to know about this. Who knows? Maybe this person doesn't know she is adopted. Then, we are really opening a can of worms." He laughed. "Just tell Joe to give me a call some time. Love to the kids, too. Bye." And he hung up.

Chapter One Hundred

Adam never lost the desire to be the center of attention. Over time it became evident to those closest to him that it was built into his personality. He showed little regard for others unless that person contributed value or benefit. He had once gone to a therapist because his wife made him. The therapist thought he was a narcissist with mild manic/depressive and sociopathic tendencies. He, of course, rejected this diagnosis and never went back to that therapist. His narcissism served him well as a politician. *What politician wasn't narcissistic to some degree?* He had thought.

The public didn't see his worse behavior, but his family did. Especially, his siblings. He tolerated his brothers and sister, but they served no useful function in his life. They had unfairly accused him of hurting them at various points in their childhood. They couldn't provide anything additional for him than what he provided himself. Mainly, they had reduced the love, attention, and money that should have been his growing up.

Adam was going through a rough period. He and his wife of thirty years just finalized their divorce. His children, who didn't want to see him, were grown and had children of their own. His bid for state senator failed. What else could go wrong to hurt his ego?

Finding out about a sister born before him? *Outrageous*, he thought. *I was my mother's first and most loved child. I was. I am the most important child. I am important!*

Although he told Jeff he didn't believe the story about their mother having a child out of wedlock, he couldn't dismiss it outright. He was very curious about this possible sister. Through his legal practice, he knew several reputable private investigators. He decided to call a few of them. Hear what they have to say. Then he would decide what to do.

Chapter One-Hundred One

Adam told his brothers and sister that he didn't believe the story about another sibling. The idea was preposterous; he was the firstborn child. But, being a politician, he knew it was important to make sure there were no skeletons in his closet when he ran for his next office. Just in case, he hired one of the private investigators he had heard about to search for any possible other children his mother might have had. He used an assumed name, Mark Johnson, and he gave the PI a phone number linked to a burner phone that he purchased at a 7-11 store.

Much to his surprise, the investigator found a sister. Her name was Ellen Berger, and she was a famous author and lecturer on the Holocaust. Upon hearing the news, all the jealousy and rage he felt toward his parents and siblings for how his life turned out flooded his mind. Losing his wife, his position and status, and his identity left him simultaneously furious and depressed. He felt like everyone was out to get him now. He couldn't eat or sleep. He drank wine and popped prescription drugs to quiet his racing mind.

I know what I have to do. I know the root of all my problems. It's her! No one can know about her. It is her fault that that I feel so depressed. If I get rid of her, it will all be right again. I must get rid of her. His mind raced with thoughts of murder, a foolproof murder. No one would know it was he. How could they? No one knew he even had another sister. Not even her.

Once Adam had his plan, he called Ellen and said, "Is this Ellen Berger? My name is Mark Johnson, and I believe your grandfather was my grandfather's first cousin," he said in a voice tone slower and softer than his own. "Some information has come to light about a possible inheritance. I am going to be in Boca later today and would like to bring documents for you to see this evening. If you are the right person, you stand to inherit a great deal of money." He paused but didn't wait for an answer. "I am aware it is unusual for me to come to your house, but I will only be in Boca for the day. I'd like to get the process rolling for you."

"Yes. I'm Ellen Berger. Can you tell me more about what you want to know?" She asked

"Yes, I can. Do you mind a few questions now?" He continued.

"Well, I have a couple of minutes to talk now," she said, curious about their possible family connection.

"Were you born in 1941?" he asked.

"Yes," she answered.

"Did you live outside of Newark, New Jersey, when you were growing up?" Adam continued down his list of questions.

"Yes, the same house most of my life," she said again.

"Were your parents Edwin and Martha Blum?"

"Yes. They were wonderful parents."

"Were you adopted?" he asked nonchalantly, as if the answer to this question wasn't important.

"My parents always said I wasn't, but my two younger sisters were. I began to doubt that. I always wondered why they didn't tell me the truth and if I was adopted or not," Ellen elaborated.

"Did you ever meet Hannah Horowitz or Sophie Rosen?" He tried to control his excitement at finding the right person.

"Yes. She stopped to see us in New Jersey several times with her family when they were on summer vacations. Why do you want to know this?" She looked puzzled.

"You meet all the criteria set out in the inheritance documents. These were questions I was required to ask, and your answers were a 100% fit." Adam was delighted with her answers. She was the woman he was looking for, his older sister. He had a plan in mind. "Could we meet later this evening? I could drop by your house."

"I have plans tonight and won't be home until after 7:00 P.M." She hesitated. "Anyway, I don't know you, and I feel uncomfortable having you come to the house. " She sounded skeptical and suspicious.

"I can understand that. Why don't we meet for breakfast then? Tomorrow? At a convenient restaurant." he asked. "I'll call you later this afternoon after I am finished with my other business in town. We can arrange a place to meet tomorrow. I really look forward to meeting you and sharing the documents I found."

Ellen hesitated. *I think it will be safe to meet him in a public place. I am curious about the family connection.* She thought and then said, "There is a Toojays near my house. Let's say 9:00 AM."

"That's a good suggestion," Adam said, knowing he wouldn't be there in the morning. She gave him directions to the restaurant, and they hung up.

He rented a car at the Orlando Airport under an assumed name with a fake ID he bought from the private investigator, and drove to Boca Raton. On a new burner phone, Adam called Ellen. "Hi, it's Mark. I just finished up my business. Are we still on for tomorrow?"

"Sure," Ellen said. "I'll have on a tan suit. See you at nine tomorrow."

Earlier in the day, after receiving the strange phone call, Ellen had called one of her sisters and asked if she knew of a distant cousin Mark Johnson. Her sister thought they might have a cousin by this name. They decided meeting him in a public place would be safe.

"I'll see you then. Good bye," Adam responded and hung up.

Adam didn't plan to meet Ellen in the morning. Instead, around 6:30 PM he drove to her neighborhood and parked his car a few doors down from her house. The house sat on a golf course in a new development near the turnpike. Empty lots were on all sides of her house and across the street. The front light was on. He sat in his rental car in his disguise, a blonde wig, blue contact lenses, and dark-framed glasses, and waited for her to come home.

At 7:00 PM a blue BMW drove into the garage at Ellen's house. Adam waited five minutes and walked to her front door. He rang the bell and a short, slightly overweight version of Sophie opened the door.

Before she could speak, he shoved her into the hallway and kicked the front door shut. The syringe filled with potassium chloride was in his gloved hand. He jabbed it into her neck and held her struggling body until it stilled. He gently lowered her to the floor. Adam put the syringe back in his coat pocket. He planned to throw the syringe and cell phone into one of the many canals he would pass on his way back to the airport.

He quickly found her purse on the kitchen counter and removed her cell phone and erased any records of their calls. He knew ultimately the Police would find the phone number on her cell, but it didn't matter. It was a burner phone that he planned to destroy.

He breathed a sigh of relief as he got into his rental car. No one was outside. No one noticed him. It would have been okay if someone had seen him in the disguise. No one would recognize him.

As he drove away, he said, "I am still the firstborn. The most special. The child my parents wanted and loved most."

Epilogue

In 1945, a Nazi war criminal, Heinrich Werner, was put to death for his role in the atrocities carried out on the prisoners held in concentration camps throughout Germany. His wife and son survived the war. With Heinrich's death, there was no one left who knew that his boy was Hannah's son, adopted by Heinrich and his barren wife, Brigitte. After Hannah left the baby boy at the hospital, a German woman picked up the infant and took him home. This woman was Heinrich's wife. Neither she, the hospital, nor the agency that managed adoptions like this during the war kept any documents showing who the mother or father was.

Acknowledgements

This novel has been almost sixty years in the making. Without the following people, it would not have happened. First, to my deceased best friend Michele McNichols' daughter, Clea Callaway, who introduced me to the Tom Bird organization, and whose writing a novel before me propelled me to write this novel.

To my wonderful and supportive husband, Asa Shield, who encouraged me throughout the entire process and who helped fund the birth of the book. He continually told me how proud he was of me for undertaking this endeavor and never criticized me when I took inordinate amounts of time away from other parts of our lives. He's also a great editor.

To my early readers who, before they said anything else first, told me they loved the book. They edited and made suggestions and improvements to my early versions. Thank you to Jai Essenmacher, Frankey Jones, Miffie Hollyday, and Asa Shield.

To Greg Keesey at Silver Knight Solutions, who built and manages my website and my blog, thank you for sharing all your knowledge in such an understandable way and answering the same questions over and over again.

To Denise Cassino, who has taught me about Internet marketing, Amazon's functions and how to use Twitter, thanks for your patience and knowledge. You are the best. The book would not have a front cover without you and your many talents.

To Tom Bird for his tools, methodology, and for expertise.

To Ramajon for his patience, coaching, and guidance to complete the arduous process of publishing this novel.

Back cover portrait: Glen McClure, Norfolk VA